For Kodi Benjamin and India Roberts.
And for my dear old dad.

A special thanks to Anna Dingley for her knowledge of Japanese culture and the Kyumeikan dojo for their expertise in kendo. And to all the lovely people at Quercus for their help and support.

1

I woke on my fourteenth birthday feeling as brilliant as the sunshine that came through my window, but I never got up. I just lay there thinking about last night. I'd won my fiftieth kendo contest for my dojo and now I could apply for my sixth dan. My father would have been so proud. He was a champion himself, at one time, and he'd brought me to the dojo when I was only four years old. There's a photograph on my wall of that very day. Me holding a wooden sword and wearing a headband with the Rising Sun. Him dressed in his body armour and holding his headset. He looked so tall and distinguished.

My father didn't speak much. He was a quiet man. But he'd talk passionately about kendo for as long as you'd listen. And he knew all the stories of the great samurai swordsmen, like Musashi, who killed his first man when he was no more than a boy. And Bokuden, who beheaded over two hundred of his opponents. And he knew much about the castles of our country and the generals who lay siege to them. In fact the next photograph is of me and my beautiful mother at Hemiji, the greatest castle ever built.

We went there when I was ten, the last vacation we'd ever take together. Dad died soon after. The truck he was driving slid off an icy road not far from Sapporo and he drowned in a lake. I've often imagined him struggling to climb through the cabin window. Then losing consciousness and floating in the water like a Japanese ghost. Grandmother often said he was a cold fish, but he wasn't. He was just a little quiet like I said.

My mother, who used to work as an air stewardess, now lives in Vancouver with her pilot boyfriend. She always sounds guilty in her letters, but she needn't be. I don't miss her so much and I'm glad she's happy. Anyway, I have the twins. They're in the next photograph over. Miko's on one side of me and Hiroshi, her brother, is on the other. I have my arms around them and our smiling faces are pushed together. We're ten at the time but I've known them since I was six. And every time the kids from school see us they say, 'Oh, look, it's the triplets.' Because we're always together and we always will be. Even now we're planning to get an apartment when we leave school.

I got up and put my bedroll and duvet in the built-in wardrobe and then I did a forward roll on the tatami floor. It's just something I do and I have the space. My bedroom's bigger than most people's living rooms.

'Yukio, are you up?'

'Yes, Grandmother.'

I sort of live with my grandmother. She has the ground floor of the house and I have the top. And I say sort of, because I only see her once a week, which is more than enough for both of us. I trotted downstairs and went into her room, which smelled of cat food and smoke. 'Grandmother.'

She was in the back and so I switched on a lamp and looked at her photographs. They were of the Royal Family and not a descendant was missing. Grandmother worships the Royal Family, and I mean worships. You see, our emperors are said to be descended from the Shinto sun goddess, Amaterasu.

That's how they got their divine status. But when we surrendered to the Americans General MacArthur said they couldn't be divine any more. It must have been hard for Emperor Hirohito having to give up his divine status, and having to surrender. He did it for the good of his country, of course, and while Grandmother curses the day that he did, she still admires him. But her real hero is her husband, who died defending Iwo Jima with less than a dozen men. They'd run out of bullets and so they fixed bayonets and charged the Americans with empty rifles. They were cut to pieces, of course, but as Grandmother says, 'It's better to die with honour than to live with shame.' Then I heard her come in behind me.

'Morning, Grandmother.'

She sat with some dignity in her high-backed chair, like an empress taking a throne. And then putting a cigarette in a long thin holder she lit it. Grandmother likes to smoke. She smokes like a dragon and she drinks green tea by the ton. But I've never seen her eat, not so much as a rice cake.

'I went out this morning and a Chinaman spat right in front of me! Why they spit so much I don't know. Their whole country must be as slippery as an ice-skating rink.'

Grandmother doesn't like the Chinese, or the Koreans. And she hates Americans. The only people she does like are well-dressed Japanese people. And even if you were well-dressed and Japanese, the chances are she still wouldn't like you.

'And those peasants in the park should be beaten with sticks.'

I always found it funny that Grandmother thought Tokyo's homeless people were peasants. She kind of lives in the past.

'And have you read the paper? Three politicians caught in a massage parlour with prostitutes. Their heads should be cut off.'

Grandmother's kind of bitter because she used to be rich, or her father did. And she was brought up like a princess with servants, and ponies, and people waiting on her hand and foot. But they lost everything after the war, or so she says. She owns this house, and a few more, and she's never short of money.

'How is your sword training coming along?'

'I was lucky enough to win last night's competition, Grandmother.'

'Well,' she said begrudgingly, 'you've never brought shame on the family. And you never will,' she said in a threatening tone. 'Now, what are you up to today?'

'I'm going to hang out with the twins, Grandmother.'

She scoffed. 'Why you associate with those children I don't know.'

'We're the same age, Grandmother. I'm only a day older.'

'But you are a man, Yukio, descended from a warrior clan! And they are just children!'

Grandmother could trace our ancestry back to the Takeda, a powerful samurai clan who reigned during the fourteenth century. She could even name names and quote dates. Grandmother might have been as ancient as a tomb, but her mind was as sharp as a machete. She pointed to some envelopes. 'Money and cards from your mother. Take them and go.'

'Thank you, Grandmother,' I bowed and left, and sprinted up the stairs to my room. I couldn't wait for the twins to come, and then I heard them outside.

'Yukio, it's us.'

I went out on my balcony and looked down at their smiling faces. 'Door's open,' I said.

I quickly looked at the cards and the cash and then I sat there pretending to read my manga.

I could hear the twins take off their shoes and shuffle upstairs. Then they came in smiling and knelt on the tatami floor in front of me. They were small, even for Japanese kids, and with me being tall I kind of towered over them. But they were good-looking kids, with bronze skin and almond eyes, and their hair was more brown than black. I joke around with them sometimes and call them cartoon kids, but they don't mind. There isn't a kid as happy as Hiroshi, and his sister Miko is as pretty as they come. And she's getting prettier every day. She took a present from her rucksack and bowing she put it in front of me.

'Happy birthday, Yukio.'

I couldn't help but smile as I ripped the package apart, but I froze when I saw what it was. It was a pair of kendo gloves, which we call *kote*, and they were the best money could buy. She must have spent all her babysitting money on them.

'Do you like them?' she asked.

'We didn't want your hands to get hurt,' said Hiroshi.

They didn't want my hands to get hurt. That killed me! 'Yes, I like them.'

They could tell I was touched and so nothing more needed to be said.

'Let's go swimming!' said Hiroshi.

'OK,' I said, and put my stuff in my rucksack.

We stepped out into the brilliant sunshine and headed over to the Olympic Centre, just five minutes away. That's the great thing about where we live – everything's so close. We can walk to Shinjuku and Shibuya, and to Harajuku as well. And if we wanted to go to Ginza or Ueno we can take the train from Sangubashi station. And there's always things to do in Tokyo. The whole city's like a theme park. And if we had nothing better to do we just hung out in Yoyogi Park.

We walked behind each other, because the streets are so narrow, but then we made a dash for the crossing. But the beating gong sounded and the barrier came down and so we had to wait for the train. Miko put her hand on my shoulder. She's been doing that a lot lately. Then she looked up at me. 'Congratulations on winning your competition.'

'Who told you I won?'

'You always win,' said Hiroshi.

I don't always win. But I've been winning a lot lately and people were starting to notice.

When the train passed the barrier raised and we walked across the tracks. Then running across the road we headed into the Olympic Centre.

'I'll pay,' said Miko.

Me and Hiroshi hurried into the changing rooms and rushed to get changed. Then we ran out and dived into the empty pool. I swam submerged in the cool silent water with the sunbeams flickering above me. Reaching the other end I swam back. As I did I saw Miko's silhouette swimming above me. She could swim like a tuna and she never got tired. It was one of her many skills. But she couldn't swim as well as she could sing. Miko could sing like a superstar. Me and Hiroshi wanted her to enter one of the talent contests on the TV. But she wouldn't because she was shy.

I broke the surface and sat at the side of the pool. I laughed at Hiroshi, who was splashing about in the water. That's all he did. He didn't like swimming and he hated contact sports. And I'm not just talking about judo or karate. He hated football and basketball or any sport where he could be bumped. It's because he was sick when he was a kid and he had to stay in hospital. He's not sick any more, but he still gets upset if he gets knocked over.

Miko climbed out and sat next to me with her hair dripping. I watched her as she pushed it away from her pretty face, and then my eyes roamed. Not too much, but she raised her eyebrows and gave me a look. Hiroshi swam over to us and treaded water. 'You two will be kissing next.'

He always said that and we always laughed. But now we sort of blushed and looked away.

'Come on, Miko, finish your laps. I wanna go see the nun.'

'She's not home yet,' I said.

'Yes, she is. Grandad saw her.'

I swam lengths with Miko until she'd finished and then we got dressed and went to see Hiroshi's nun. We found her one day on our travels around Tokyo and she invited us to tea, and we've been going to see her ever since. She's a Buddhist nun, but she lives in the grounds of a Shinto shrine. Shinto's our other religion. It has a lot to do with being in harmony with nature. It's even said that there are Shinto spirits called kami who dwell in rivers, mountains, and trees. And people can become kami after they die. I wouldn't mind coming back as a tree, as long as the twins could be trees as well.

The shrine's at the top of a hill, just up from

where we live. It's like a little sanctuary nestled between our neighbourhood and the horrible dual carriageway that's always under construction, and it's really nice. There're exotic plants and stone paths with Shinto gates above them. And the temple is carved from cedar and built on granite, and it has large lion dogs standing guard either side. And no matter how hot it gets, it's always cool here because the tall trees bathe the place in shade.

We rang the bell in front of the temple and we clapped to summon the gods. Then we bowed to show them respect before running to the house where the nun lives. Her name's Natsuko, which means child of summer. And it suits her in a way because warmth comes from her. I'm not kidding. Every time you're with her you feel warm inside. But even if you don't, she's still nice. She has big eyes, and a perfect bald head, and skin the colour of cream. And she always manages to make you feel special. We all liked the nun, but she was Hiroshi's nun because he liked her the most.

When we knocked on the door the old nun answered.

'We want to see Natsuko,' said Hiroshi.

The nun grimaced a little. You're not supposed

to use their first names. 'I'll let her know that you're here.'

She closed the door and we sat in the wicker chairs and waited. Hiroshi kept looking at the entrance. He was dying to see the nun. I think he looked at her as a sort of mother. The twins' real mother had run away when they were first born and she hadn't been seen since. And he always talked to Natsuko like a boy talking to his mum, but that wasn't it. There was a bond between them, but I could never work out what it was.

When she appeared in the doorway we stood up and bowed. She smiled as she came towards us and putting a tray on the table she bowed back. And so we bowed lower. You always bow low to a nun, or someone more important. And as we're still kids we bow low to just about everyone.

'How are you, children?'

'Very well!' said Hiroshi.

We took a seat and watched her preparing the tea. She even brought a single flower and some cakes to add to the occasion. It was like our own little tea ceremony. In Zen tradition the tea ceremony is to purify the spirit and make you feel peaceful. And we always felt peaceful when we watched her. But as she offered us the cakes we could see she was ready to cry.

Hiroshi's face clouded over. 'You didn't like Cambodia? The people were mean to you?'

'No, the people were kind,' said Natsuko. 'But the children sleep in the streets and they're hungry and afraid. Some have lost limbs to landmines and many are sick. And there's no medicine to make them better! In the end I became sick myself and I had to come home.'

She covered her mouth to stop herself from crying. Miko turned to me for help but I couldn't think of anything to say, and I felt so bad for her. But Hiroshi stood up and put his hand on her shoulder. You should never touch a Buddhist nun; it's a big insult.

Miko's eyes widened. 'Hiroshi!'

But he ignored her and putting his small hand on her face he smoothed away her tears. Miko looked down at the ground, while I sat there feeling embarrassed. But suddenly Natsuko seemed calm. She even smiled. Then I saw what it was between them – they were both sensitive. They felt each other's pain and they got upset by things like landmines and poverty and kids without limbs.

'You have to meditate to make yourself better,' said Hiroshi.

'I will,' said Natsuko.

'Yukio meditates. Don't you, Yukio?'

'Sometimes,' I said, wishing he'd sit down.

'Anyway, I've made you a picture,' said Hiroshi, and taking a roll from his rucksack he showed it to her.

Natsuko looked amazed. 'Oh, Hiroshi!'

'He's been working on it for weeks,' said Miko.

Natsuko showed it to us. It was a portrait of her looking as beautiful as she could. You see, Hiroshi, while he was just a kid, was as talented as an artist twenty years older. He could put a flower arrangement together and paint it to perfection. It was like someone had taken a photograph. And lately he'd taken to drawing the girls at school. They were lining up to be his models.

All the sadness left Natsuko's face then and she was happy again. And that being the case she and Hiroshi talked excitedly about art and things, and me and Miko were left out. It was always like that. But we didn't mind and it was fun to watch them. Besides, we held hands as they talked and they didn't even notice.

After tea we said goodbye to the nun and headed off to Harajuku.

'Come again soon, children,' she said.

'We will,' said Hiroshi. 'We're off school.'

We walked back down the hill, and crossing the train tracks we passed the small park where we used to play as kids. Then we crossed the road and ran up the concrete ramp that led into Yoyogi Park. There're nicer parks in Tokyo, but Yoyogi is our park. It's close to where we live and we've been coming here since I can remember.

As we made our way through the trees Miko put her hand on Hiroshi's shoulder. 'I don't think you're supposed to touch the nuns, Hiroshi.'

'I know, but she was upset. I think it's OK if they're upset. Isn't that right, Yukio?'

'Maybe,' I said, but I didn't think it was. But I knew that Hiroshi would never offend Natsuko, or anyone else for that matter, so I suppose it wasn't too bad. Besides, I couldn't have been happier. I was with Miko and the sun was shining and we had the whole of the summer holidays ahead of us!

We headed across the wide common, passing the courting couple and the families picnicking on the grass. And everywhere we went there was music.

We passed Brazilians beating drums, a guy playing a guitar and a girl blasting away on a trombone. And as we neared the exit we saw some of the Harajuku Girls. They were the costume-play crowd who dressed up as Gothic Lolita. They had strange clothes, mad make-up and wacky hairstyles, but they were fun to look at. And so were the rockabillies who dressed in black and danced as cool as they could.

We came out of the park and headed down the beautiful Omotesando Boulevard, where the tall trees act like a canopy to keep off the sun. Grandmother said that artists and painters lived here at one time. But today it's lined with designer stores as far as you can see. It's all Armani and Gucci, and girls shopping for the latest fashion, or just parading up and down in it. The whole street's like a catwalk.

We lost Hiroshi in the crowd, and turning we saw him with a salesgirl outside Omotesando Hills, a designer building built to hold high fashion. Hiroshi likes girls and he's not shy about talking to them. He talks to shop assistants, and the girls at school, and their mothers if they come to collect them. He even talks to the cleaning women. And whenever we lose sight of him he's always talking to some girl or another. I talk to girls as well, besides Miko, but it doesn't come so naturally.

When he'd finished we walked all the way down to the Prada Building, which is a glass structure with sticky-out windows. It looks like an apartment block wrapped in bubble wrap.

'Let's look inside,' said Hiroshi. 'We've never been inside.'

'I don't know,' said Miko, intimidated by the posh look of the place.

'We can look inside if we want. Can't we, Yukio?'

'Sure,' I said. And so that's what we did.

It smelled nice inside and it looked nice, and the clothes were nice as well. I looked at the shoes while Miko went to where the bags were. I don't know what it is with Tokyo girls and Prada bags, but they go wild for them. But Miko doesn't, not usually, but then she looked at one bag like she was in love.

'You'll turn into a Harajuku Girl if you're not careful,' said Hiroshi, and wandered off to talk to the saleswomen.

Miko smiled at the bag, but she cringed when she saw the price. A smartly dressed salesman appeared, and seeing she couldn't afford it he very politely took it away. She looked embarrassed and so I pretended not to have noticed.

'What shall we do now?' I asked.

'Let's have a picnic at the Imperial Palace,' she said.

'Yes,' said Hiroshi. 'And we'll pay because it's Yukio's birthday.'

I didn't like the twins spending their money on me because they didn't have much. Their grandad was too old to work and so they had to get by on his pension. My mother's always sending me cheques and Grandmother gives me more than I need. But I didn't say anything because I didn't want to hurt their feelings.

We bought packed lunches from the Anniversary Café and then we took the subway to Tokyo station. When we came up to street level we cut through the skyscrapers and headed down to the Imperial Palace.

We like to hang out there because it's free to get into and it looks like a castle. It has huge walls and wide moats, and ramparts with towers above them. And we like the bridge, which we call Spectacles Bridge, because of the arches that look like eyes. As a small boy I'd often imagine armies battling on that bridge, but I don't think it had ever seen action.

We passed through the powerful East Gate and wandered around until we found a bench where we could have our picnic. Then we ate and drank while looking at the gardens, and the short trees, and the perfectly groomed lawns. Not far in the distance was another wall, with tall trees at the top, and beyond that was the Imperial Palace and the emperor. Hiroshi drank some Coke from the bottle and then he turned to us. 'You think Emperor Akihito's at home?'

'I don't know,' I said.

'Sing for him, Miko, and he might come out.'

'I can't.'

'Come on, Miko, it's my birthday. You have to sing.'

She looked around to make sure that no one was watching and then she sang a song called 'Summertime'. Her voice rebounded off the stone walls, twirled around the towers and echoed under the bridge. She had such a soothing voice that it made me lie back. But what was more amazing was that she didn't seem to make much effort. There wasn't the slightest strain on her face, even for the high notes, and yet her voice carried so far. I was sure that if the emperor was home he could hear Miko. I imagined him having tea on his balcony and wondering where the singing was coming from. I felt proud then that she was my friend. And for the first time I thought about asking her to be my girlfriend.

We stayed there until the sun started to set and then we took the subway back to Yoyogi Park. The Harajuku Girls had gone by then and so had the Rockabillies. But there were still plenty of joggers and cyclists and people walking dogs. And it was nicer now because it was cool and the grounds were bathed in a pink tint. We went to our usual spot, on the common, and Hiroshi pulled the orange frisbee from his rucksack. It was the first present I ever bought the twins and we still got a real kick out of throwing it. It's strange how the little things can make you happy. And it had been such a great day I found myself wishing we could throw it in the park for the rest of our lives. But then the wind picked up and the sun set and the sky turned as red as blood. I'd never seen it so red. And there was something frightening about it. I had the strangest feeling that something bad was going to happen to us. The frisbee flew past me.

'You're not concentrating, Yukio,' said Hiroshi.

'What's wrong?' asked Miko.

As soon as I saw her face the bad feeling faded away. 'Nothing. I was just . . .' But I couldn't explain what had come over me. I threw her the frisbee and she laughed as she ran to catch it.

'It's just a red sky,' I said. 'There's nothing to be scared of. Nothing at all.'

2

I ran up the subway steps and down Omotesando Boulevard. It was already eight and I had to pick up the twins by nine. Their grandad had taken them to Tokyo's Disneyland for the day, but tonight I was taking them to a nightclub, a real club as well. I'm not kidding. I'd seen the advertisement in Shibuya and bought the tickets. One of the clubs – Paradise, it was called – was opening its doors to kids aged fourteen to seventeen. It closed at midnight and there was no alcohol, of course, but I knew that Hiroshi would love it.

But now I was late! I'd been at kendo practice all morning and in the afternoon I decided to go for a run. Then I'd taken a nap. Now I was running for real because I'd overslept. What's more I had to go to the Meiji Shrine to have a prayer said for my father. He died four years ago today, or close to, and I knew that Grandmother would ask me if I had done it. I didn't mind doing it. In fact I wanted to. But I had to get home and get ready to go out.

I ran down to the Prada Building to buy the bag. I didn't care how much it cost. I wanted Miko to have it, and I wanted to be the one to buy it for her. And so I ran all the way to the store, and moving straight to the bags I looked for the one that she'd liked. But I couldn't remember which one it was. And I didn't want to buy the wrong bag. The smartly dressed salesman came towards me. He was tall and about twenty and he had stylish hair like a footballer. He picked up a bag and smiling he handed it to me. Straight away I knew it was the one.

I paid for the bag and left as quick as I'd come. The Prada people bowed to me as I was leaving. And following me outside they bowed some more. But I was already running up Omotesando Boulevard, weaving my way in and out of the many shoppers. But it wasn't long before I had to stop and walk with the crowd. I swear, Tokyo's the worst city in the world when you're in a rush. I was on the verge of getting pavement rage, but then I got a break and I made the most of it. I ran past Ralph Lauren, Louis Vuitton and Versace, and crossing the road at Harajuku station I headed towards the Meiji Shrine.

I passed under the huge Shinto gate, which was shaped like soccer posts and built from tree trunks, and ran down the wide gravel path. The path was lined with tall trees that blocked out the noise of the city and all of a sudden it was like being in a forest. I kept going until I saw the Meiji Shrine, which was dedicated to Emperor Meiji and his wife, Shoken. They used to come here when they wanted to get away from things, and so when they died a shrine was built in their honour.

I came to a sink and washed my mouth and hands. It's important to wash before entering a shrine because cleanliness shows respect for the gods. I went to the shrine shop and bought a wooden plaque from one of the maidens, whose name was Tomoko. She was as cold as the nun was warm and I'd never so much as seen her smile. All the maidens were straight-faced, if you ask me, but she was more so because she was the head priest's daughter.

I wrote a prayer on the plaque and hung it

around the divine tree, which was just outside the main courtyard. The plaques would be collected that night and the prayers would be read out at the morning ceremony. I didn't need to have the prayer said here, but this was where my father's birth was registered, and so it fitted in with tradition. And we're kind of traditional in Japan.

Before I left I faced the building where our old emperor was enshrined and bowed before running back down the path. I ran around the corner and sprinted into Yoyogi Park. Then I turned around and ran back. I'd left the bag at the shrine shop! I ran as fast as I could and headed through the gate. As I did one of the security guards tried to stop me. 'We're closed,' he shouted. But I ignored him and carried on running. There's no way Miko wasn't getting her bag on her birthday.

When I got back to the shop three of the maidens were looking at it.

'Here he is,' said Tomoko. It was the first time I'd seen her smile. I didn't think she knew how. 'Who's it for?' she asked, handing me the bag.

'My girlfriend,' I said. I don't know why I lied. But it wasn't such a big lie. And maybe it wasn't a lie at all.

'She's a lucky girl,' said Tomoko. 'Getting a bag like that.' Then the three of them started to giggle. What they were giggling at I don't know. Girls giggle for no reason.

I took the bag and ran all the way to the house, where I showered and changed. And then I ran downstairs with my damp shirt sticking to my back. Then I ran up them again because I'd forgotten the bag. And then I jogged over to the twins' place just five doors down. They live in a one-bedroomed apartment and it's pretty small at that. Their grandad sleeps in the living room on a bedroll and rolls it up in the morning. But they've got the place as nice as it can be and it's pretty cosy at night.

I ran up the steps and knocked on the door. And there they were, looking as smart as I'd ever seen them. Hiroshi was wearing black pants and a white shirt, like me. But Miko was wearing the black dress that she'd made herself, and boy did she look good. What's more she was wearing make-up. I'd never seen her in make-up before. It made her look older, and prettier.

'Happy birthday, Hiroshi. Happy birthday, Miko,' I said, and I handed her the bag. But she never smiled like I thought she would. For a second

I thought she was going to cry. Suddenly she threw her arms around me.

Hiroshi rolled his eyes. 'You two are going to be kissing next.'

We laughed then and she let go. Then their grandad shuffled to the door. 'Are you all ready?'

'We're all ready,' said Hiroshi.

Their grandad, who was older than my grandmother, looked kind of concerned. 'Well, look after them, Yukio. And have them back by midnight.'

'I will,' I said.

'Come on then. Let's go!' said Hiroshi.

I bowed to their grandfather and we trotted down the steps.

'I can't believe I'm going to a real nightclub!' said Hiroshi. 'Miko showed me how to dance. I'm going to dance all night!'

We laughed, but we were quiet as we made our way down to Shibuya. I was a little nervous. I suppose I was worried because I wanted the twins to have a good time. And it must have rubbed off on them. Hiroshi looked like he was trying to think of something to say, and Miko looked a little awkward in her high-heeled shoes.

'Shall we get a taxi?' I asked.

'Don't be silly,' she said, and put her arm through mine.

I was happy then and all the nervousness went.

There weren't many people on the streets on our way to Shibuya, but as we neared the centre they started to fill up. First there were tens of people and then hundreds and then, when we reached the Shibuya Crossing, there were thousands of people swarming back and forth. The sun had set by then but it was still hot and Shibuya was ablaze with lights. The streets buzzed with music and excited talk, and shouts from the touts as they enticed people to various restaurants. Happy businessmen came from the bars while groups of people came from the karaoke clubs, filling up the already crowded streets.

I held on to Miko's hand, and following Hiroshi we weaved our way through the crowds. We turned up a backstreet and headed towards the club. As soon as we did we saw a long line of kids waiting outside. They were our age or older and they were all talking excitedly or swaying to the music that was coming from inside.

Hiroshi stood on his tiptoes. 'Are they letting us in yet, Yukio? Can you see?'

'Not yet,' I said. 'But soon.'

And then the line started to move and we headed for the door.

It seemed to take forever to get there but we were soon inside. We passed a doorman, and handing a woman the tickets we scurried downstairs. The place smelled of stale beer and smoke, and the carpet was sticky to walk on, but boy was it buzzing! The music was blasting, the spotlights were beaming, and then the dance floor lit up like a rainbow. Everyone scurried to get a seat, but we grabbed a booth by the bar. More kids poured down the stairs and within no time the place was packed. But when the girls took to the dance floor the club began to rock.

'This is great!' shouted Hiroshi.

I got three Cokes from the hard-faced barmaid, and by the time I got back Hiroshi was on the dance floor. I'd never seen him happier. He was dancing with two girls at once and he was dancing well. And then I felt obliged to ask Miko.

'Do you want to dance?'

'Do you?'

'I don't know how,' I said.

'Come on. I'll show you.' And taking my hand she led me on to the dance floor. Miko danced an easy dance and I tried to do what she did. But I ended up looking like a robot that needed oil. I saw some girls laughing at me. I felt embarrassed at first, but then Miko laughed and I didn't care. She was having a good time and that's all that mattered.

We danced to half a dozen tunes and then we took a seat, but Hiroshi didn't. He kept on going, and when there were no girls to dance with he danced by himself.

Miko cradled her bag. 'It's the best present anyone's ever bought me.' She looked right in my eyes. 'I just love it!'

I felt kind of shy and I had to look away. And that's when I saw them.

It was the Tanaka girls, Riko and her psychotic sister, Louise. They paraded in with their entourage and their yakuza bodyguards. The yakuza are the Japanese mafia, and the girls were princesses in a criminal empire, known nieces to gangster godfather Uncle Benni. Why they called him Uncle Benni I don't know. But there was a big stink in the paper, not so long back, when he was photographed at a banquet with the Mitsubishi board of directors.

The girls were his brother's kids, but the brother was in prison. And from what I heard he was never getting out. And so Uncle Benni looked after them, or he tried to. They were as wild as they come and they were famous in Tokyo because they were the only teenage girls to have committed *yubitsume*. You see, when a yakuza fails in their duty they're expected to take a sharp knife, cut off a section of their pinky finger and hand the amputated part to the person they've offended. Not even Uncle Benni could protect them from that ritual. Louise had lost a section of one pinky, but Riko had lost a bit of them both.

But now there's an operation you can have. They amputate your little toe and sow it on to your pinky, so no one would ever know you were yakuza. But the girls didn't care. They had steel claws made and put them over their missing digits. They were yakuza to the bone and they always would be. They even had tattoos. Tattoos are taboo in Japan. Even yakuza men keep them covered up. But the girls had them all over their arms and backs, and Louise, who was younger, had serpents curling up around her neck. She looked scary, but she was nowhere near as scary as Riko. Riko was blind in one eye because of a beating she received from her gangland boyfriend. But then her boyfriend had to answer to her stepmother, Matsu. And she wasn't an eye-for-an-eye sort of person. Whatever you'd done to her she'd do double to you.

You see, there used to be two rival yakuza clans who were always at odds. The Tanaka, led by Uncle Benni, and the Yamamoto, led by Tomi Yamamoto, who now rules Osaka and everything south of it. But when Uncle Benni met Tomi's sister, Matsu, it was love at first sight. They were married and an alliance was formed with Uncle Benni at the head. Matsu couldn't have kids and so she doted on the girls. And when she found out what had happened she went ballistic. She scoured Tokyo, with a crew, until she found Riko's boyfriend, and then she put things right. He ratted her out, of course, and she was given ten years. When the judge asked her if she had anything to say about the awful thing she'd done, she quoted a samurai saying: 'If you're going to stab, stab to the eyes.'

There was nothing fuzzy about the Tanaka, and the Yamamoto were just as life-threatening. You see, I knew all about the yakuza because of this kid at school called Kane. His father was a cop in the Organized Crime Division. He'd tell his son stories, and his son would tell them to me. He even gave me books on the yakuza to read. But I didn't need a book to know who the Tanaka girls were. They were like celebrities in Tokyo and everyone knew them, or knew of them. And everyone knew to keep away.

They took a booth opposite us and bottles of sake were brought to their table. And boy could they drink. They knocked back one shot after another and kept it up like it was a competition. And if it was, Riko was winning. You could tell the girls apart because Louise had dyed blonde hair. But even if she hadn't, Riko's right eye gave her away. It was like a cat's eye caught in the dark and it blazed in the lights like a blue gem. Then her face hardened like a mask carved for the Noh theatre. She'd noticed us looking and she didn't like it. Without taking her eyes from us she said something to Louise. And then Louise said something to a guy next to her. That's when I recognized Kako.

He used to go to my school, but he was expelled over an incident that happened between him and a woman teacher. I never heard much about it because it was hushed up. But he was always making himself out to be yakuza, which he wasn't. And he told everyone that he was a Tanaka. But that wasn't quite true either. His name was Kakomo and he was the illigitimate son of one of Uncle Benni's distant relatives, but he'd been killed in a car accident. And so the only real connection he had to the Tanakas was that he dated his cousin Louise.

Louise went to the DJ stand and the music changed. Then she got on the dance floor and danced like a drug-crazed zombie to a song called 'Psycho Killer'. And didn't she look like death on the dance floor. Then a drumbeat played over the song and Riko got up. Talk about psychopathic, she looked like a loon trying to get out of a straitjacket. Everyone started to move away and I didn't blame them. Then their whole crew took to the floor and danced like they were possessed.

Hiroshi came running over to us. 'The Tanaka girls are here! They're so cool! I love this place!' He went off to dance near them.

'Hiroshi!' I shouted, but he never heard me.

I was going to get up, but the girls paid him no attention and so I sat back.

Then I saw Kako ogling Miko. And then he started dancing next to Hiroshi. They were laughing and joking and then Kako introduced him to the Tanaka girls and they all danced together.

For obvious reasons I didn't like it. And when the song ended they came over to us, which I liked even less.

'This is my twin sister, Miko,' said Hiroshi.

Kako gave her a sickly smile and taking her hand he kissed it. 'Very pleased to meet you.'

Miko wasn't pleased. She just looked embarrassed.

'And this is our friend Yukio Takeda.'

'You don't have to introduce me to the best kendo swordsman in our school,' said Kako. 'How are you, Yukio?'

'OK,' I said. I was kind of cold towards him, but I have to admit I felt boosted that he knew my name. We'd never spoken at school, not once.

Riko sat down next to Miko. 'A kendo swordsman – how quaint.' Then she stared at me with her good eye. 'He's very good-looking.'

Louise almost sat in my lap. 'He is, isn't he?' she said, her breath stinking of sake.

'Would you like some?' she asked, putting the glass near my face.

'No, thanks.'

She smiled at me and I felt her hand on my knee. Then I felt a sting, and looking down I saw the steel-tipped silver claw on her little finger.

Riko tapped her fingers, and claws, on the table in an agitated way. Then she turned to Miko. 'What a great bag.'

'I want it!' said Louise.

'You want everything!' snarled Riko.

Miko looked a little nervous. 'It was a birthday present from Yukio.'

Riko looked sick. 'Pretty girls get everything.' Then she glared at me like I'd done something wrong.

Louise whispered in my ear. 'I'll do for you what she did. If you buy me a bag like that.'

'Are you talking about me, Louise?' screamed Riko.

'Relax, bitch! I was only asking the boy to dance! You wanna dance, boy?'

'I don't mind,' I said. But I did mind. I wished they'd go away.

'Hey, if you're dancing with my girlfriend,' said Kako with a sickly smile. 'I'm dancing with yours.'

'And I'll dance with Riko!' said Hiroshi.

'He's like a little wind-up toy!' said Riko. But then she smiled. 'Come on then, toy, let's dance.'

So we all got up and moved on to the dance floor.

'I didn't know you knew yakuza!' said Hiroshi.

I'd never seen him so impressed. 'Some,' I said. And then I felt proud that I did.

We got on the dance floor and danced to the screaming techno music. Riko danced in a frenzy, like she hated life itself. But Louise tried to dance sexy. She came close to me and rubbed her hands all over. She was trying to turn me on, but I was too busy watching Kako. He kept pulling Miko towards him and shouting in her ear. She kept trying to step back, but he kept hold of her. And he kept touching her! My heart was pounding with the drumbeat. I swear, I was ready to go over there! But then one of the Tanakas' bodyguards came on the dance floor and said something to Riko. She didn't look happy. She shouted something to Louise and left. Louise shouted something to Kako and walked away, but he didn't follow. So she came back and snarled in his face. He looked sick at having to leave Miko, but he followed her like a dog and their whole crew left the club. Just like that they were gone.

Me and Miko took a seat but Hiroshi danced on. I don't think he realized they'd left.

'They're so strange!' said Miko.

I was still angry over Kako. 'I don't think they come any stranger!'

But she took my hand and smiled. 'They're gone now.'

As soon as she said it I felt soothed. I put my arm around her and we snuggled up. It was nice then. Sometimes even nasty things like the Tanakas coming along can make things nicer. And I felt like things were starting to happen between me and Miko. And that was the nicest thing of all.

We watched Hiroshi dance with different girls and as the night went on his dancing got better. We even saw some of the girls trying to copy his moves. And he was having such a good time we could have watched him all night. But when it neared midnight we had to make a move. 'Hiroshi, we have to go.' I said.

'Just five more minutes!' he pleaded.

When ten minutes had passed he asked for one last dance, which we gave him. But then he danced on and so me and Miko took him by the arms and pulled him away. And he was still dancing as he came. But just as we reached the top of the stairs Kako came running through the door. He stopped dead when he saw us. 'Surely you're not leaving!'

'We have to get home,' said Miko.

'I'll give you a ride,' said Kako.

'She has to be home by twelve,' I said.

'Who are you – her dad?'

He was three years older than me and just as tall but he didn't frighten me. And I gave him a look that let him know it.

'Just kidding, Yukio. I'm glad she has someone to look after her.' He turned to Hiroshi. 'And as for you, my little Hiroshi, you're welcome here any time.'

'Is this your club?' asked Hiroshi.

'No, it's Riko's. But I work on the door and, well . . . I can let some people in for free.' He turned to me. 'The same applies to you, Yukio. Come any time you like.'

But as we left the club I saw him in a mirror. The smile had gone and his face had soured with spite. I knew he was scum. I was just about to warn Hiroshi to stay away from him, but Miko took my hand.

'I had a great time, Yukio,' she said, and she kissed my cheek.

I felt humbled and happy and I flagged down a taxi without even realizing it. But it was worth it. Because driving through Shibuya, cocooned in the cab, was the icing on the cake of a great evening. It was nice looking out at the swarms of people with the lights shining in on us. And knowing we would soon be home. When I looked at Miko she was smiling, and when I put my arm around her she smiled even more.

When we pulled up Hiroshi scurried up the steps to their apartment. We could hear him talking excitedly to his grandad. Then the cab drove away, leaving me and Miko alone. We laughed as we listened to Hiroshi raving about the club. Then Miko came closer.

'So you're going on vacation with your grand-mother.'

'Don't remind me,' I said.

'It won't be that bad. But I won't see you for a whole week.'

'I suppose not.'

'Well, this won't wait,' she said, and standing on her tiptoes she kissed me. It was a long lovely kiss, our first, and it felt so good my eyes closed. Then I realized I wasn't doing anything and so I kissed her back. I heard their grandad shuffling on the landing. He appeared above us, but his eyesight wasn't that good. 'Are you there, Miko?'

'Yes, Grandad.'

She smiled and kissed me, quickly this time, and then she trotted up the steps.

'Did you have a good time?' he asked.

'We had a great time, Grandad.'

Miko waited patiently as he made his way into the apartment, and then she looked over the landing. 'I'm missing you already,' she said. And then she went inside and the door closed.

I was smiling as I walked back to the house and I couldn't seem to stop. I slipped off my shoes in the doorway and ran up the stairs to my room. It was warm and my head felt woozy and so I went out on the balcony. There were a few stars and a sickle-shaped moon above the twins' apartment. And there was that summertime smell that made the night seem sweet. And then it dawned on me. Me and Miko had always been childhood sweethearts. It wasn't something that had happened lately; it was something that had always been. Then I laughed when I thought about Hiroshi's words: 'You two will be kissing next.' After all these years he was finally right.

The lights went out in the twins' apartment and I turned to go to bed. But just then I saw something. It was the tips of a pair of shoes in the street light. There was a man standing in the shadows. He started to urinate against the side of the twins' block. I tried to see who it was but it was too dark. I was just going to shout something but he turned and walked away. I leaned out as far as I could and looked into the street. But all I could see was his shadow shrinking in the street light, and the sound of his footsteps fading away.

3

Five days of boredom. It could have been worse. It could have been six. Six would have driven me crazy. Don't get me wrong – Nikko's a nice place. The countryside's beautiful, the people are pleasant, and there are some great temples. But five days with Grandmother was as much as I could take. She complained about everything, and I mean everything. There were too many tourists at the temples, she didn't like the weather, and she didn't like the hotel that we were staying at. She even complained about the trees. Who complains about trees?

I was glad she kept to her usual habit of going to bed at ten, but then I'd end up wandering around the town by myself. And while Nikko was nice, it wasn't exactly exciting. There were no game shops or pachinko parlours, and there's no nightlife to speak of, not even for a fourteen-year-old boy. I mean, I don't play pachinko and I don't like computer games that much. But it would have been nice if they'd been there.

I did have a conversation, in English, with a black American woman staying in the same hotel, but even that was boring. How old are you? What do you want to do when you leave school? How do you like living in Japan? How do I like living in Japan! How would I know? I've never been anywhere else. I think she only talked to me because she was unhappy. It must have been something to do with her husband. At breakfast they rarely spoke, and when they did it looked like it pained them.

'She should never have married him,' said Grandmother, who never misses a thing.

I had another conversation with a monk one night when I was out walking. He was sweeping up the leaves in a temple courtyard and I sort of gave him a hand. He was old and funny and he kept talking about baseball. He was baseball mad. And he knew everything there was to know about the New York Yankees. That's the thing about monks. You think they're all about Buddhism and meditation, but they like normal things as well.

One night I was really missing the twins. And Nikko was only a couple of hours from Tokyo. I was thinking of jumping on a train and going home, and coming back in the morning. But if Grandmother found out, there'd be hell to pay. But on the fifth day it didn't matter. 'Pack your bags,' she said. 'We're going home.' I pretended to be disappointed and I thanked her for the nice vacation. But I couldn't pack my things fast enough.

We took the fast train back to Tokyo and then we took a cab to the house. Yoshe came out to greet us and I gave her a hand with the bags, but I didn't have to. She's a well-built woman who's done judo since she was a girl because her father wanted a boy, and she was as strong as an ox. She's been with us for years. How she could put up with Grandmother for so long I don't know, but I was glad that she did. I like Yoshe a lot. She has a good heart and a kind face and she's a great cook too. Sometimes she brings her baby boy with her and he crawls around the house. I find him in the strangest places: like sitting in a basket in the bathroom, or hiding in my cupboard. I picked him up one time. He weighed a ton and he stunk of pee, but he laughed and so I liked him.

'You have a good time?' asked Yoshe, rubbing my shoulder. I gave her a look that told her I didn't. 'Never mind,' she said. 'You're home now.'

I took Grandmother's bags to her room and put them by her bed. That's it, safe for another year, I thought. But when I came back I saw how tired she was. She sat in her high-backed chair with her eyes closed tight. I felt sorry for her then, and I was sorry she never enjoyed her vacation. And then I felt guilty because Grandmother, mean as she was, did a lot for me. I was never short of money, and if I wanted something I only had to ask. And so in that way I suppose she was kind.

She noticed me watching her. 'Do you know, Yukio, there was a time when I was a beautiful young woman. Men came from all over Kyoto to admire me. And I was invited to parties and banquets where I would meet movie stars and heads of state.' She seemed distant then, as though remembering those times. 'How fast it all goes.'

I felt more sorry for her then. And she had been beautiful in her day – I'd seen black-and-white photographs. In one of them she's surrounded by men. You can tell that they're smitten by her. And in another she's dressed up for a ball. She looks tall and proud, like a princess, and her dark eyes are shining like coal. It's hard to believe it's the same person. She looked at me and sighed. 'Go and look in the garden. Your belated birthday present should be there.'

I couldn't understand why it would be in the garden, but when I saw it I stopped dead. It was a motorbike! It was only a scooter with a small engine, but it was a motorbike! I rushed back inside and ran into Grandmother's room. But I was so excited I didn't say anything. She looked at me sideways. It was the first time, since I can remember, that she seemed happy. She never smiled or anything, but the bitterness left her face.

'Well, be careful on it,' she said.

'I'm only fourteen, Grandmother. I don't think I can ride it until I'm sixteen.' As soon as I said it I was sorry. Now I'd have to wait two years!

But the bitterness returned to her face. 'Rules are made for stupid people! You're not stupid, are you?'

'No, Grandmother.'

'Then you'll ride it now. But I warn you, Yukio, I'll never have a television in this house!'

Grandmother hated technical things like televisions. She even hated cellphones and computers and so I wasn't allowed to have them. I think it was the noise she didn't like. But who wants a television or a cell when they've got a motorbike!

'Now go and tell Yoshe to bring me my tea.'

I went to leave but I stopped and said, 'You're still beautiful, Grandmother.' Then I bowed and left.

She probably thought I was lying. But she does have a beautiful face, in a wrinkly sort of way. And she's still distinguished-looking, despite her age.

I rushed past Yoshe, who was coming in with her cats. 'She wants tea.'

'It's boiling,' said Yoshe. 'And listen! You be careful on that – do you hear me?'

'Yes, Mother.'

'If I was your mother, Yukio, I wouldn't let you have it!'

I think that 'mother' comment stung her, and so I stopped. 'I'll be careful,' I said. 'How's the baby?'

She smiled. 'He's fine. I think he missed you.'

'I missed him too!' I shouted, and rushed out to my new Honda Zoomer. It was beautiful and black with a single seat and a sparse frame, and its tyres were fat and chunky. There was even a helmet with it. I didn't want to ride it at first, because it looked so new, but then I put on the helmet and pushed the bike outside. I sat on it. It was as comfortable as a couch. I kicked the kick-start and the engine came to life. I was buzzing like a beehive but I was intimidated as well. I'll just ride it to the station, I thought, until I get used to it.

I pulled back on the throttle and it crawled forward. I pulled back some more and it moved away. I navigated my way around the narrow roads until they straightened out, and then, passing Sangubashi station, I headed out on to the dual carriageway. Then I let loose! I pulled back on the throttle and blasted alongside Yoyogi Park. The wind thundered in my ears and my eyes watered, but I felt like I was flying.

I stayed back from the police car which I could see up ahead, and then taking a left I headed over the hill to Harajuku. I rode up by the station and then I blasted down Omotesando Boulevard with everything whizzing past me in a blur. But then some fool in a Mercedes threw his door open. I braked hard and blasted my horn. What an idiot! I can't stand people who do things like that. Especially when I'm out on my new bike. He threw his hands in the air, as sort of an apology, but I sounded it again as I rode away.

I cut through Aoyama Cemetery and headed over to Roppongi, which I could see in the distance. And as I rode pink petals fell from the plum trees like a fanfare parade just for me. It was a beautiful day at the height of the summer and everything was in bloom. And I couldn't believe how green Tokyo looked. It was like being on a tropical island. 'My beautiful Tokyo!' I shouted, and rode as fast as I could.

Within no time I was rounding Tokyo Tower, which is like our version of the Eiffel Tower, and then cutting through Roppongi I headed towards Ginza. I whizzed past the House of Representatives, where the politicians hang out, and then heading down to the Imperial Palace I came to the moat. I rode alongside the water, and the high walls, and following them around I rode into Ginza. I couldn't believe how fast I'd got there. The bike had opened up a whole new world for me. Leastways the world had got a lot smaller, and Tokyo had become tiny. Then I thought about Miko and I had to see her. I took a cheeky turn by the East Gate and went back the way I'd come.

Now everything was about speed. The chunky tyres gripped the road like glue and rolled over the potholes like they were pimples. I was confident enough now to look around as I rode. And at one stage I took my hands off the handlebars, just to see if I could. I overtook a taxi that was going too slow, and gave way to a lorry that wanted to back out. I felt like a real motorist then.

I blasted back up Omotesando and shot around Yoyogi Park. Then taking a shortcut I cut across the railway tracks and screeched to a halt below the twins' apartment. I sounded my horn and sat there like a big show-off and waited for them to run out. But they didn't, and so I parked and ran up the steps. I knocked a little too loud and I heard their grandad grumbling. Then he opened the door.

'Are they here?' I asked, forgetting to apologize.

'Hiroshi's in bed with a cold.' He looked puzzled. 'I thought Miko was with you.'

'No, I've been on vacation with Grandmother.'

He looked more puzzled. 'I'm sure she said she was going out with you.'

'Can you ask Hiroshi to come to the door. He doesn't have to come out.'

He shuffled down the hall and I heard him knock on the bedroom door. Then he came back.

'Sorry, Yukio. He must be asleep.'

I was disappointed then. I was dying to show off the bike and I really wanted to see Miko. But it wasn't to be, and so I thanked him and said goodbye.

I rode around for the rest of the afternoon. I swear I couldn't get off the bike. I rode all the way to my dojo so I could show it to my sensei. Then I rode all over Roppongi and Akasaka and went down as far as the port. After that I rode all the way up to Ueno and cruised around the university looking at the girls. I would have kept going until it was dark, but when I got hungry I headed for home.

I parked the bike outside the house and took off my helmet. And then I saw Miko outside her apartment building. 'Miko!' I shouted. But she ran up the steps . . . That's strange. Maybe she hadn't heard me. I walked over to her place like I was walking in slow motion. That's what happens when you've been riding at speed – everything seems slow. I ran up the steps and knocked on the door, but not too loud this time.

Their grandad answered. He turned straight away

when he saw it was me and wandered down the hall. 'Miko, Yukio's here.'

I heard Miko mumble something and then he came back. 'She said she's taking a shower and she'll see you tomorrow.'

'Oh. OK.' I was kind of taken aback. 'Well, what about Hiroshi? Is he awake yet?'

Their grandad went down the hall and came back again. 'Sorry, Yukio, he's still asleep.'

'OK, I'll call tomorrow. Tell him to get well soon.'

I was really disappointed. But I was hungry as well and I wanted to get back on the bike. So I ran back to the house and went in the kitchen.

Yoshe had made a pork broth with vegetables and there were fresh ramen noodles in the pan. I put them both on full heat and wolfed them down while they were warm. Then I put the bowl in the sink and went outside. I was surprised to see that the sun had set. I'd never known a day to go so fast. But I kick-started the engine and headed up to Shinjuku. I was dying to ride through the city with the bright lights blazing. I was even thinking of heading back to Ueno. But then I got a bad feeling and pulled over. Miko said she would see me tomorrow. She's never brushed me off before, and she never even came to the door. And when I think about it, she must have heard me. There's something wrong!

As I pulled out I heard a screeching sound and a lorry braked hard. The driver blasted his horn and roared out the window. I was so shaken my heart was pounding, but I was just as shaken about Miko. I took all the backstreets I could and raced back to her place. Pulling up outside, I ran up the steps.

Their grandad answered – again. He was a nice man but he looked irritated, like he was tired of seeing me. I gave him a deep bow. 'Sorry, but I have to see Miko.'

He looked at me a little more sympathetically. 'Dying to show her that new bike of yours, hey? I saw you riding around on it. OK, let me get her.' He shuffled away and went down the hall. Then I heard him coming back. 'The lights are off and they're both asleep.'

'But it's only ten fifteen.'

'What can I tell you, Yukio? She must have had a hard day. And I have to get to bed myself.'

He said it like he didn't want to be disturbed again, and so I said goodnight and left it at that. I was about to ride to Shinjuku, but it started to rain, and so I put the bike in the garden and called it a day.

I ran upstairs to change my damp T-shirt and then I went out on the balcony. I was just in time to see their living room light go off. The wind picked up and the rain blew in on me, and so I went downstairs to make tea. The manual that came with the bike was lying on the kitchen table and so I flicked through its pages. I felt better then because I was sure I knew what the problem was. It was because we kissed, that's all. And now she's feeling strange about it. I suppose I'll be a bit embarrassed too when I see her. But I'd reassure her in some way. Girls always need reassuring, I think. Leastways they do in the movies.

I took some more tea and went to my room. I put on a sweatshirt and went out on the balcony. Lightning flashed and the rain rattled on the roof. I like the rain, especially when I'm dry and indoors. I went to the right corner and looked over at their place. What I was expecting to see I don't know. It wasn't like they were going to wake up and come out. But just then I saw two figures sneaking down the steps. It was the twins! What are they doing? They never go out when their grandad's in bed!

I rushed downstairs and putting on my shoes I ran outside. But I couldn't see them and the rain was coming down really hard. I ran down as far as the railway tracks, but they were nowhere in sight. But as I ran back I heard crying. I saw them in a gap between the houses. Hiroshi had his head in his hands and Miko had her face pushed against a wall. I'd never seen them so distressed. They were so hurt they couldn't even comfort each other.

I went to them. 'What's wrong? What's happened?' I tried to turn Miko towards me but she pushed her face to the wall. She even banged her head. 'Miko!' I turned to Hiroshi. 'Hiroshi, what is it?' I took his hands away from his face. 'What's happened?' They were so upset I almost started crying myself.

'We're in a lot of trouble, Yukio!'

'Don't tell him, Hiroshi!' pleaded Miko.

'Tell me!' I said.

He tried to stop crying. 'When you went away I started hanging out with Kako. Remember that old florist in Shibuya? Well his son owed the yakuza a gambling debt. They wanted the florist to pay, but he wouldn't. We were only supposed to smash his window.' He started crying again.

'It's OK. Come on – you can tell me.'

'Kako threw his brick and it smashed the glass. Then I threw mine . . . It hit the old man on the head and he fell to the floor . . . He was bleeding so badly!'

He started sobbing like a child and so I held him. 'It's OK. It's OK because you didn't mean it!'

'Are you going to help us, Yukio?'

'Of course!'

He turned to Miko. 'You have to tell him, Miko.'

'No!'

'If Yukio's going to help us, he has to know . . . Louise said that if Miko didn't go with Kako she'd go to the police and tell. And I'd be taken away from Grandad and Miko. And they wouldn't be allowed to see me again!'

I turned to her. 'Miko, tell me you didn't!' Her eyes closed tight and I knew that she did!

'It's worse,' said Hiroshi. 'Tell him, Miko, you have to!'

Miko took a deep breath. 'When it happened with Kako there must have been a camera in the room. Louise has the video. I begged her to give it to me! I offered her all the money I have. I even gave her my Prada bag, but she just laughed. Riko said that if I didn't go to work for her in one of her massage parlours that she'd show the video to Grandad . . . I couldn't have him see me like that! I'd sooner be dead!'

I felt as if I was going to be sick.

Miko looked up at me. 'I had to do it, Yukio! She would have told the police. And you know what me and Hiroshi are. They don't like us. They'd have taken him away!'

My head was spinning.

Hiroshi came to me. 'Do you still want to be our friend, Yukio?'

I was so confused I couldn't speak.

'Do you, Yukio?'

Miko took a step towards me. Her face was desperate and pleading. She wanted me to understand. She wanted help. But all I could think was, how could she have done that with him?

She saw the disgust on my face and bursting into tears she ran away.

'Miko!' shouted Hiroshi, and he ran after her.

I just stood there with the rain running down my face. I couldn't move for a minute. Then I went back to the house and climbed the stairs to my room. I never dried my head or changed my clothes. I never even put the light on. I just slid down the wall and stayed there with the rain dripping from my hair.

An hour passed, maybe two. I heard a commotion in the street and a man crying. Then sirens wailed and my room lit up in red lights. I got up and went to the balcony. There were people by the twins' apartment. And an ambulance and a police car were pulling up outside. As I flew downstairs I was filled with a sickening fear. But I ran towards the people and pushed my way through. I saw the twins' grandad screaming in the street. His face was filled with so much pain it was like he was on fire. Two neighbours had hold of him and the woman from the swimming pool was trying to calm him down. But she couldn't and so she threw her arms around him. I saw reflective jackets coming out of the twins' apartment. It was the paramedics. They started to carry a stretcher down the steps.

Their grandad tried to break free. 'Miko!'

I almost staggered. 'She's going to be OK!' I shouted. But I felt myself starting to sob. 'Please let her be OK!' But as they neared me I saw there was a sheet over her face. And there was a rope hanging down! 'No!' I pushed towards the stretcher, but a big cop blocked my way. I looked for Hiroshi, but I couldn't see him. Then I caught sight of him running. 'Hiroshi!' I'd never seen him run so fast. He sprinted down the street and turned the corner.

He was heading to the train tracks!

I ran after him as fast as I could. I heard the beating gong and bolting around the corner I saw the barrier come down. 'Hiroshi!'

Hiroshi slipped under the barrier and turned towards me. Then, like he'd done a thousand times before, he calmly raised his hand in farewell.

'No!'

He turned to face the oncoming train. There was a sickening smack and his obliterated body flew through the air.

It was a beautiful morning with a clear blue sky. The green trees swayed in the warm breeze and the summer flowers were flourishing in all the colours they could. I watched a bee bounce between them, and then it flew past the hem of Natsuko's orange robe. Normally she wore white but today she wore saffron orange. I never knew that nuns wore orange. It's such a beautiful colour. But I found all this beauty offensive. Even the sunshine was an insult. It should have at least rained. It could have rained blood for all I cared.

The older nun took Natsuko's arm and escorted her away. She never looked at me as she passed. I don't think she noticed I was there. Then I realized that the monk had finished praying and people were moving away. There weren't many of them. A few girls from school, a couple of neighbours, and a kid from Hiroshi's art class who came with his dad. We were so close we never made many other friends. Besides, suicide's another taboo in Japan. Nobody talks about it, but thirty thousand people a year do it. I just never imagined . . .

I heard the girls ride away on their bikes, and when I looked up the twins' grandad was leaving. His face was deathly pale. A ghost from one of the graves would have had more life. He gave me a look as he passed and I wondered what it meant. He was devastated, of course, and so there was lots of sorrow, but there was disappointment as well. Yes, that was it. It was a look of disappointment. It was as though he was saying, 'I trusted you to look after them, Yukio. What happened?'

The monk who performed the ceremony had a robe the same colour as Natsuko's. He held his hands in front of him in a dignified way and waited. Then I realized that I was the only one left and he was waiting for me to leave, and so I did. I left the Aoyama Cemetery and headed up Omotesando without seeing a thing. I don't remember if I walked through the park or not. And I don't remember walking back to the house. All I remember is coming into my room, drawing the blinds to block out the light and laying down.

In four days I've only got up once. And that was when the men came to clear out the twins' apartment. The bigger stuff they carried down the steps, but the smaller things they threw off the landing. They threw down Miko's dolls, which she'd kept from when she was a kid. Then Hiroshi's easel cracked on the pavement, followed by his paintings. A guy on the ground looked at them and then scrunching them up he tossed them into the garbage. Then the guy on the landing threw down Miko's rucksack.

'I'll keep this for my kid,' said the guy on the ground. 'Is there anything else?'

The guy on the landing glanced in the apartment. 'No, it's all junk. They were Buraku, you know.'

That's what the headlines said: 'Two Buraku-min Kids Commit Suicide'. The Buraku are Japan's untouchables and they've been persecuted in our country for centuries. They're associated with slaughterhouses, and killing cattle, and other such dirty work. And so they themselves are looked upon as dirty. The twins had never so much as been near a butcher's, but they were Buraku by birth and so, to certain people, they were known as '*eta*' – extreme filth.

There was a Buraku kid who went to my school this one time. When the other boys found out what he was they bullied him until he left. The thing was, everyone liked him before they found out, even the teachers. And those same teachers must have known what was going on. I mean, I knew the twins were Buraku, but I told no one. How the papers found out I'll never know. But as soon as I saw those headlines I knew there'd be no investigation. Our police would sooner bow down to the yakuza than defend the Buraku. That's just the way it is. But who was I to talk? They might have been loathed by most people, but they were loved by me! And wasn't I just as disgusted when I found out what she'd done? When I close my eyes I can still see her face, pleading and looking to me for help. And so I close them tighter and force myself to sleep.

In my dreams I'm back in the club. I can see Kako with Miko and he won't let her go. 'Let her go!' I try to shout. But the words come out jumbled and he laughs in my face. I see Hiroshi leaving. I push through the people and run after him. But I end up crawling up the stairs in slow motion. I see him heading for the tracks. I run towards him but it's like I'm wading through water. I hear the beating gong and the barrier comes down. 'Hiroshi!' He waves farewell and the train slams into his small body.

Hiroshi, who hated contact sports, standing in front of a train. He could never have done that, not in a million years. Not unless he saw Miko. I lay there half awake and half asleep, rewinding things in my mind. If only I hadn't taken them to the club. If only the Tanakas had gone somewhere else. If only we had sat where they couldn't see us.

Then I see Hiroshi in the club. He's looking up at me. 'I didn't know you knew yakuza, Yukio!'

I should have told him to stay away, but I decided to show off instead. 'Some,' I said.

I see him moving towards the Tanakas. 'No, Hiroshi! They're animals!' But the music's blasting and he doesn't hear me. I try to fight my way through the crowd but I fall on my face. Suddenly the club's empty. Miko's ghost comes from the dark. She still has the rope around her neck! 'You shouldn't have said that, Yukio. That's what got us killed!'

I woke up to see Yoshe's baby boy looking down

at me. He looked puzzled, as though wondering why I was in bed in the daytime.

'Come out of there!' whispered Yoshe.

The baby waddled out of the room and Yoshe came in with a tray. She knelt down and spoke softly. 'Try to eat something. If you don't, you'll get sick.'

I closed my eyes and slept. When I opened them again it was night and I was hot and sweating. Then I saw someone sitting in the shadows. For a second I thought it was a real ghost. The face turned towards me and I saw it was Grandmother. I'd never seen her upstairs, let alone in my room.

'You were crying in your sleep,' she said. She stood up and raised the blinds and the room lit up in moonlight. 'When I was a girl there was a boy. A beautiful boy. He used to look after the horses in our stables. He loved those horses, but there was a pale stallion he loved more than anything. He was never allowed to ride it, not in daylight. But on nights like tonight, when the moon was full, he'd ride it for hours. Some nights I'd sneak out of bed to watch him, to be with him. His pale skin would glow in the moonlight as he rode. Such a beautiful boy. But my father found out. One night I went to sneak out but the doors were locked. The next day they found him dead. They said that the horse had thrown him and he'd hit his head on a rock. But I saw him and that horse together; they moved as one. My mother told me that if it was meant to be, we would be together when I died, and so that's what I'm telling you.' She closed the blinds and opened the door. 'I'm sorry about her, Yukio, and the other one. You know me – I wouldn't say it if I didn't mean it.'

When she'd gone I thought about that terrible sky that had hovered over the park. We'd played so happily beneath it, but we were like the children of Hiroshima oblivious to the falling bomb. I'd often imagined them holding hands and singing on their way to school. Then they were screaming and on fire and death couldn't come quick enough. Because as sure as that bomb brought hell to Hiroshima, the Tanakas had brought hell to us.

I slept deeply and woke in a field. There were black clouds and a blood-red sun and Louise, who was dancing like a demon. 'You! It was all your doing!' I ran at her and struck her with a sword. But it turned into a snake and wriggling from my hands it crawled up around her neck. Louise looked at me and laughed out loud. Then I heard screaming, like the falling of a bomb, and there was Riko riding a pale horse. Behind her came a roaring army of yakuza, their bare bodies displaying their demonic tattoos. 'Get him!' she screamed.

I saw a temple and running inside I barred the doors with a bolt. But then I turned to see Miko hanging by her neck. It was such a horrible sight. She tried to speak but her eyes bulged. I put my face in the corner so I couldn't see her. 'Please, no!' Something touched my head.

'You have a fever, Yukio.'

I woke in the daylight to see Natsuko kneeling next to me. I went to get up but my head started pounding and I felt so hot. She put her hands on my shoulders. 'Lie back.' She poured some purple-coloured tea into a cup and brought it to my lips. 'Drink this. It will help you get better.' She held my head and I drank. We'd never been so close. If I hadn't been so dazed I would have been embarrassed. She took the cup away and rinsing a cloth in a bowl of water she placed it over my forehead. It felt cool and soothing.

'I couldn't bear to be here,' she said. 'And so I went to stay with my sister in Kyoto. She's a geisha – did I tell you? Probably not. I don't really tell people.

They judge, you see. They think I was the good daughter and she was the bad, but it's not like that. My sister's lovely and she gets such joy out of life. And when you're with her the joy rubs off. I told her about the twins. She never said anything silly or offered any kind words, she just listened. She's a good listener. But when she asked me why they did it, I didn't know.' She took the cloth from my head and rinsed it in the water. As she did her face filled with the pain. 'And that's when I knew I had to see you. To try to understand why they did it. Why they never came to me. I would have laid down my life for them if I had to!' She stopped for a second, as though trying not to cry. Then she placed the cloth back on my forehead. 'But when I saw you in such pain I knew that you were just as puzzled. I know you're sad. But know this: they were beautiful people and they've gone to a better life. Sleep now, and when you're better we'll talk.'

My eyes closed like I was hypnotized. When I opened them again it was dark and I was alone. I felt like my fever had broken and my head had stopped banging. But then I thought about the twins and that pain was worse. I remembered the man urinating outside their apartment and realized that it must have been that dog Kako marking his territory. But how could he have found them so fast? He must have followed us home. The anger got me to my feet, but I stood up too quick and my head spun. I held the wall to steady myself. All of a sudden I needed air.

I got dressed and grabbing my keys I went out on the balcony. I put on my sneakers and slid down the drainpipe. I hadn't done that since I was a boy, and why I was doing it now I don't know, but I had to get out of there. Then I was in the dark. It was quiet and still and I stood there for a minute not knowing what I was doing. I opened the steel door and headed to the twins' place. I crept up the steps, like a cat burglar, and looked through the living-room window. It was bare inside and there was a sign on the sill: 'Apartment for Rent.' I wasn't surprised. I knew their grandad would never come back here. How could he?

I opened the door with my spare key and went inside. My footsteps sounded loud as I headed to their room. And opening the door I saw that their bunk beds had gone, and so had their dresser. But there were still some remnants lying around. A shoe here, a T-shirt there. And there was the mic that

Miko used to sing into when she was a kid. I picked up the tin box where Hiroshi kept his crayons. It was empty, but there was a Polaroid on the floor. It was of me and the twins on the Ferris wheel at Yokohama. We must have been about nine at the time. Me and Miko were laughing, but Hiroshi had his arms folded. He didn't care for heights. He didn't care for heights or contact sports, but he still stood in front of that train. And Miko, where had she . . . ? I looked around and then I went in the bathroom. It was the only room without a window and so I had to switch on a light. There was a pipe running across the ceiling. Not a thick pipe, but Miko never weighed much. I could just see her standing on the tiny bathtub and tying the rope. I saw her hanging in my mind. And then I swear I saw her for real! I staggered backwards and went down the hall. I tried not to run as I left the apartment but I did, and I couldn't stop. All I knew was that I wanted to get away. And I wanted the pain to end.

I heard the beating gong and saw the barrier come down. I slipped under it and stood by the tracks. The train moved fast. It'd be here in seconds. 'All you have to do is take one step forward and you'll be with them.' Once I said it, it was settled. I was just about to take that step when I heard Miko's voice. 'Don't be silly,' she said. And I could almost feel her pulling me back.

There was a loud swish, and the wind from the train buffeted my face. Then it was gone. The gong stopped and the barrier came up. It was quiet then and I stood there for a second feeling strange. I crossed the road and headed up the ramp that led into Yoyogi Park. I made my way through the dark trees, passing the homeless people who were sleeping and snoring on the benches. And then I made my way out on to the common, which was floodlit by the full moon. I found myself at the place where we used to throw the frisbee. I'd never felt so alone. I was never going to see them again and it was my fault. I never warned them about the Tanakas and I turned my back on them when they needed me! I felt the pain rise up inside me. It ached my heart and hurt my chest. Then it became a real pain. I was in agony. I dropped to my knees and screamed like an animal. Then my face hit the dirt and I cried for my best friends, who I loved so much. My tears ran into the dirt and I breathed dirt into my mouth, but I couldn't get up. The pain of their deaths, and the shame I felt at not helping, were weighing me down. 'I'll kill them all!' I cried.

As soon as I said it I saw it. The vision froze in my mind and dried my tears. I was calm then, and quiet. The samurai have a saying – 'Fall into the pit of hell and find the true self within.' Well, I was in that hell and I had found myself. And I saw the path I was going to take. It was caked with yakuza blood.

I wiped my face and got to my feet. There were a dozen homeless people staring at me.

They huddled in fear as if some strange creature had crept into the park.

'I'm going to kill them all,' I said.

They cowered and stepped back. And as I walked through them they stepped aside. I went back to the house, where I rinsed my face and drank some tea. Then I drank some more tea and felt better. 'I'm going to kill them all,' I said. It was such a soothing thing to say.

5

It was early morning when I climbed up into the loft. I opened the large chest, that looks like it belongs at sea, and started to take out Grandfather's things: his military uniforms, his medals and the stacks of letters wrapped in red ribbons. But I wasn't interested in them. I was interested in the swords that lay at the bottom of the chest. Because they were what I was going to use to kill Kako and the Tanaka girls, and as many of those yakuza scumbags as I could.

I removed the Rising Sun, and holding it up I saw it was torn and soiled, as if it had been bloodied on a battlefield. I folded it neatly and put it to one side, and then I saw my little black book. I hadn't seen it for years and I had wondered where it had got to. My father made me copy out famous samurai sayings, and the ninety-nine precepts of the Takeda clan, who Grandmother reckons we're descended from. The ink was still strong in the book, and opening the first page I saw my neat childhood handwriting: 'Yukio Takeda's Bushido Code'. 'Bushido' means 'Way of the Warrior' and the code evolved throughout Japan's history. It involves seven virtues, which I'd written on the second page: 'Justice, Courage, Benevolence, Politeness, Honesty, Truthfulness and Honour.' But I was only concerned with justice. Justice for the twins. I read some of the sayings. 'Never be a coward in battle . . . Caution is your castle and negligence is your enemy . . . While you rest your enemy practises.' Then I saw Hiroshi's favourite: 'You do not have to outrun the bear. You only have to outrun your friend.' I felt sad then, but it brought a smile to my face too. He was such a great kid. Then I saw the one I could never get out of my head: 'The way of darkness always brings great power. The way of darkness always brings a great price.' I never understood what the way of darkness was, but it used to scare me as a boy.

The swords were wrapped in a red kimono, and pulling it out I took it to my room. After the war the Americans said that all samurai swords had to be handed over because they were lethal weapons. But Grandmother would sooner melt them down than give them to her enemy and so she hid them away. And there they would have stayed had the twins not died.

I slid the long sword from its mounting. It was a typical machine-made katana, curved and slender with a single-edged blade. But it was shorter than its mounting by at least a couple of inches. You could tell when you put them together. The blade was blunt and the steel was dull, but when I took it in both hands I knew it could do damage. Then I took up the short sword. It was used by the samurai to commit 'seppuku', what the Westerners call 'hara-kiri'. I held it in both hands like a dagger and imagined what it would be like to thrust it into my stomach. I have to admit I found it scary.

I put the long sword in the black nylon bag that my father had used for his fishing rods. And I put the short sword in my sports bag. Then leaving the house I cut through the backstreets and headed up to the Sword Museum, which was only ten minutes from where I lived. I entered the main building, which looked like a big white apartment block, and running up a flight of steps I bought a ticket from a woman.

'You have to leave your bags outside,' said the old security guard, indicating some shelves.

I put my bags on a shelf and took out the swords.

He shook his head. 'You can't bring them in here.'

'I can't bring swords into the Sword Museum?'

He had a think. 'No.'

'Why do you want to bring them in?' asked the woman who took the money.

'I want Mr Sato to look at them.'

'Is he expecting you?' she asked.

'No, but he was a friend of my father's.'

'What's your name?' asked the security guard.

'Yukio Takeda.'

'Wait here,' he said, and went into the museum. A minute later he came back. 'Follow me.'

I followed him into a large dimly lit room where we passed dozens of cabinets lit up by spotlights. The lower cabinets held only parts of swords that looked like they'd been dug up from the ground. But the wall cabinets contained full swords, some of which were hundreds of years old. Some belonged to famous samurai warriors. Others had been used to behead captives, defend castles and slaughter

Mongols. I'll bet there wasn't a sword in the collection that hadn't drawn blood.

The guard opened a door at the back of the building and I was shown into a room where Mr Sato was working. 'Yukio Takeda,' said the security guard, and closing the door he left. But Mr Sato never even looked up. He was surveying a sword on a glass table, lit up by its own light, and he was lost in his own little world. He was a balding man in his eighties and he had liver spots on his hands and forehead, which smoothed out or wrinkled with the curves of the sword. But his eyes were still sharp and he was almost smiling as he went about his work. A minute passed and then another. I thought he was never going to speak, but then he did. 'You know, when I see craftsmanship like this it makes my heart sing. People think that sword making is a thing of the past, but this sword was made at the Nittoho Forge just one month ago. It's reminiscent of the Rai school and yet there is something of the old Shinto masterpiece about it. Would you like to hold it?'

I put my swords on the table and held his in both hands. It was heavier than my sword and a lot longer. The double-handed grip was bound in leather cord and the circular guard had the design of a sea monster. And when I turned it to the light it gleamed like a laser.

'Look at the mounting,' said Mr Sato.

I put down the sword and picked up the mounting. It was black lacquered wood, beautifully decorated with golden dragons.

'They're real gold, Yukio,' said Mr Sato. 'They brought a smith down from Sapporo to design them. He did an excellent job. You know, every year we have a competition for a newly made sword, and such is the level of the craftsmanship that this may not even be the winner.' He slid the sword into its mounting and locked it in a steel cabinet. 'Now, what have we here?' He took the long sword from its mounting and scrutinized it without speaking. I was glad he was quiet then, because I knew my sword was getting the same intense treatment. He held it out, and putting it close to his face he looked along its back. He looked at the grip and the guard before concentrating on the blade. Then he laid it down. 'Yes, well, it's seen better days. It needs a good polish, the binding on the grip needs replacing and it's rather blunt. But that said, the blade is still in good condition.'

'I was hoping to get it sharpened. I'll be willing to pay.'

He sighed in a disappointed way. 'We are a museum, Yukio, not a business. Besides, it will be a joy to work on such a piece. But if you ever decide to sell it, please remember us.'

'But it's machine-made.'

'No,' he said, giving it another look. 'Lots of katanas were, around the time of the war, but this one is handmade . . .'

I felt so uplifted then. I don't know why.

'. . . although it has suffered some damage. The end has been broken and the sword has been shortened to compensate. But even that was done by a craftsman. Some expert smith long dead no doubt.

'How could it have happened?'

He looked exasperated. 'In battle, of course! How else does a sword get broken?'

I was amazed. For some reason I'd never imagined that the sword had seen action.

'Come back this evening and I'll have them ready.'

'Thank you, Mr Sato.' I bowed deeply and headed to the door.

'You look more like your father every time I see you. He was a good man, Yukio. Honour his name.'

'I will,' I said. And bowing again I left.

I ran up the main road, and making my way

into the massive Shinjuku station I weaved my way through the crowd. I took the escalator down to the packed platform and waited in line for the train. A handmade sword broken in battle! It filled me with such fire I couldn't wait to get in the dojo. And then the train came and we crammed on board like cattle. There wasn't enough room to raise a hand, but I didn't care. I only cared about kendo. I could already see myself warming up and doing the katas. Then, when I changed trains at Ikebukuro, I watched myself block my opponent's blows. And on the final leg of the journey I was striking my opponent's head and throat. When I reached my stop I sprinted from the subway to the Kyumeikan dojo in a matter of minutes.

I slipped off my shoes and bowed to the flag and the shrine. I bowed to the photograph of my father. And then to Sensei Kubo who I'd only just seen, and who was giving me a look that told me I was late. I scurried up the stairs and into the changing rooms, and looked for a place to change. I put my bag between the big-bellied American, who we call G.I. Joe, and Akeno, who was the star pupil of the dojo. He was slim and muscular and as cool as ice. He was the opposite of the American, who was always sweating as if someone had poured a watering can over his head. But the Yank was no fool when it came to kendo. He might have looked like he ate all the burgers, and he must have been about forty, but he was highly skilled and he could move like lightening when he had to. He gave me a tough look and pushed past me. He was always kidding around, but I wasn't in the mood.

'You were not here for your birthday,' said Akeno. 'Many happy returns.'

'Thank you, Akeno.'

I was happy then, if only for a second. You see, Akeno was like my hero. Him and Dad used to train together, or rather my dad used to train him. And he always remembered my birthday and Dad's death. And I felt like we were really good friends, even though we rarely spoke.

I saw a ponytail pass by the changing rooms. It belonged to Anna. She was not only the best kendo girl in the dojo, but she was also the prettiest. But she's leaving next month to learn English in London, and we're all going to miss her. Especially Akeno, because from what I heard they've just started dating.

I changed into my body armour as quick as I

could, and then trotted downstairs to the dojo. It mightn't have been the largest dojo in Japan, but it was one of the oldest, and there are some great swordsmen here. And everybody tries to help everyone else. I swear, we're like a family, and as soon as I was in there I started to feel better.

I was just in time to bow to the Japanese flag with the others. Then we warmed up by doing katas, which is going through the motions of striking an opponent with a shinai. But let me explain something about the shinai. Kendo came about because the heavy wooden swords used by the samurai in training could cause severe injury. And no shogun wanted his soldiers injured. And so the shinai was developed. It's just four bamboo sticks joined together with a rubber tip and a handle. But with it the swordsman could train without fear of being injured and so he could concentrate on his skill.

I moved across the wooden floor in my bare feet, taking firm strides and striking with the shinai like I was striking an opponent's head. I scream as I strike because it releases energy, what the Chinese call chi. Chi comes from the cosmos and flows through your body. The kendo scream is supposed to be this chi energy being expelled. I know it sounds silly, and I'm not saying I believe it myself, but sometimes I think I can feel it.

'Make ready,' said Sensei Kubo.

Sensei Kubo was in his fifties, but he was as fit as a man half his age. His black hair had no grey and his face was as smooth as stone. They say that kendo practitioners live a long time, and seeing him I could believe it. And he had such a great knowledge of kendo. When he talked about it he was calm and wise and his words carried weight.

We knelt on the floor and put on our head towels, which keep the headsets secure. Then we put on our headsets, which we call *men*, and tied them tight. But when I picked up the *kote* my heart sank. They were the gloves the twins had bought me for a birthday present. And once again I heard Hiroshi's words: 'We didn't want your hands to get hurt.' I could feel tears coming into my eyes.

'You OK, Yukio?'

I looked up to see G.I. Joe.

'Sure,' I said. When he wandered away I tried to straighten up. If I was going to avenge the twins I'd have to put them out of my mind, at least for now, and so that's what I did. I pulled on the *kote* and picked up my shinai, which is just under four foot long. Then I faced my opponent, Alex the Austrian. He was ten years older than me and twice as broad and so I forced myself to focus. But then a train went past the dojo and hearing it I saw Hiroshi. This seething hatred flowed through me and my mind set like metal.

We lined up in two rows, facing our opponents, and we bowed to each other to show respect. It's important to show respect to your opponent, because it's through them that you will become a better swordsman. But the true purpose of kendo is to become a better person. You see, kendo is based on the bushido code because that's what the samurai lived by. They never used their skill as swordsmen for personal gain. It was used unselfishly to defend the community and protect the weak. And following this code, which revolves around the seven virtues, gives your life guidance. It helps you become a stronger person, and in some cases a warrior.

'Begin.'

The dojo became noisy with screams and shouts and the crack of the shinai as it struck armour. Alex never made any unnecessary moves. But when he did move he was fast and accurate.

What was worse was that it was never a single strike. It was always a strike to the *do*, the piece of body armour that protects the torso, followed by a strike to the *men*, or head. And the speed of these double strikes showed how skilled he'd become. But he had two weaknesses. One was that he was slow on his feet, and the other was that he'd always look at the first place he was going to strike. And if I saw him doing it, which I often did, I'd block the blow and counter. I was having a lot of success hitting his right *kote*, which mightn't seem like much. But it scores points in competitions because a swordsman without a hand is done for.

I stepped up a gear. I snapped the shinai to his *men* in quick flicking movements. You see, it's better to flick the shinai than to strike with a heavy blow. A heavy blow allows you only one strike and it leaves you open to attack. It's always better to use less force and flick the shinai with a snap of the wrists. And with this strategy I struck Alex three times on the *men*. He was beaten and I bowed to him before switching opponents.

Then I got the muscle-bound Miyamoto, who we call the mammoth. He was a big guy, but kendo requires thought rather than physical strength and so his size was no advantage. Besides, he was slow and I was the more experienced. Through the bars of my *men* I could see him readying himself like a rhino. Then raising his shinai he charged. I blocked his blow with ease and moved to a defensive stance.

There are three basic stances in kendo: *jodan*, an attacking stance where the shinai is held above the head; *chudan*, a middle stance where the shinai is held level, ready to attack or defend; and *gedan*, a defensive stance where the shinai is held down, making it difficult for the opponent to leap forward. But this meant nothing to the mammoth who kept wielding his shinai like a barbarian with a baseball bat. A dozen times I sidestepped him and struck him in the throat. I kept doing it over and over in the hope that he would do something different, but he didn't. The best he'd do was dodge my shinai, which would then strike his shoulder. And he seemed happy with this. But kendo is based on sword fighting! If you get hit on the shoulder with a samurai sword you're as good as dead. I was training for battle and they gave me this buffoon. I heard another train pass and I saw Hiroshi in my mind. Suddenly I sidestepped Miyamoto and struck him on the back of the *men*. He fell to his knees and I raised the shinai . . . !

'Yukio!' Sensei Kubo came towards us. 'Miyamoto, Anna is looking for an opponent.' Miyamoto bowed and walked away and the sensei turned to me. 'A clear mind can topple even the strongest will. How many times have you heard me say this?'

'Many,' I said.

'But your mind is not clear, Yukio. Why don't you sit to one side and watch. You can learn much by observation.'

I sat on a bench and took off my *men* and head towel. The sensei was right. I'd need a clear mind for tonight. Otherwise I was done for.

It was dark when I got up. I hadn't slept, but I'd had a rest and it's important to rest before battle. I switched on the lamp and took the long sword from its mounting. I was amazed at how new it looked, and when I felt the blade it was so sharp it cut my finger. Mr Sato had stripped both swords of their handles and cord wraps and left them to soak in a cleansing solution. He'd fitted new handles and wrapped new cord around them. He'd even replaced the mounting for the long sword with one that fitted. He'd expected little thanks for his hard work and so I told him that, upon Grandmother's death, the swords would go to the museum. And he seemed happy with this.

I went to the bathroom to rinse my finger and then I did some katas. My room's quite large and so there's plenty of space to thrust and slash from the *gedan* and *chudan* stances. But the ceiling's too low to raise the sword in the *jodan*. But it made no difference. I was just getting used to the feel of the sword. And there wasn't much difference between the sword and the shinai.

I put the sword in the black nylon bag and fixed it so it was resting on my back. Then I turned to the photograph of the twins, and kissing my fingertips I put it on their smiling faces. I bowed to both them and the statue of the Buddha before going out on to the balcony. I slid down the drainpipe and put the sword under the seat of the bike. I put on my helmet and pushed the bike out into the street. Then kick-starting the engine I rode down to Paradise to kill Kako.

There wasn't much of a plan. I'd put on my hooded top so most of my face would be covered.

That way I couldn't be identified by witnesses or CCTV. I'd park the bike where I could run to it but not too close. Then I'd head up the backstreet and wait outside the club. My biggest problem would be if the Tanaka girls were there with their bodyguards, because I wouldn't like to take on too many at once. But if they were, so be it.

It was around midnight as I rode through the Shibuya Crossing. It was a Saturday night and as hot as hell and the crossing was really busy. I turned away from the bright lights and took a quick tour of the backstreets. Then I parked the bike in a side road just behind the Tokyu Department Store. It would only be a short run from the club, and the road was fairly dark. But as I locked my helmet to the bike the butterflies came. I couldn't help but worry about being caught, or killed, and the thought of prison was never far off. But quite often a samurai had to choose between breaking the law and the bushido code. I knew that what I was about to do was criminal, but it was also justice.

I held the bag with the sword to my side, and pushing the handle up into my armpit I headed up to the main road. I pulled my hood up when I saw two security guards at the back entrance of the

Tokyu building, but they were only concerned with their conversation. But when I got to the corner there were punk rockers hanging around outside the FamilyMart. I even noticed a leather-clad girl glaring at me, as though wondering what I was concealing. Or maybe she was wondering why I had my hood up in the heat. I must have looked so shady. I kept the sword close to my side and crossing the road I headed up to Paradise. The backstreet was more brightly lit than I remembered and it was just as busy as the main road. The music was blasting from the clubs and the reggae bars and there were partygoers parading up and down. I passed the couples waiting to enter Club Asia and the younger crowd outside Club Atom. And as I passed them I could feel them watching me. It was as if everyone knew what I was about to do. The butterflies turned septic in my stomach then, and the street, which stank of pizza and perfume, made me feel sick.

But then, as I neared Paradise I saw a man outside. He had his back to me but it looked like Kako! My legs began to quiver and my hands shook as the adrenalin pumped through my body. I looked back down the street to see how far I'd have to run. It wasn't too far but it was packed with people. I was dying to kill him, but I was just as desperate to get away. Then, in my mind, I saw Miko smiling up at me. I saw Kako ogling her. Then I saw her hanging by her neck. 'Do it, Yukio!' I took the sword by the handle and headed towards him. I was so close I could hear him speaking on his cell. I got ready to draw the sword, but suddenly he turned and came towards me. It wasn't Kako. It didn't even look like him!

I waited for the guy to pass and then I moved towards the entrance of the club. If Kako's in the doorway, I'll kill him where he stands! But the door was closed and there was a padlock on it. I couldn't understand it. It was Saturday night. A girl in long boots came by.

'What happened to the club?' I asked.

'I think the cops closed it,' she said without stopping.

I pulled the hood from my head. He wasn't here and he wasn't going to be here. And I didn't know where to find him. I felt so drained when I thought about it. But for now there was nothing I could do. And so putting the sword under my arm I headed back down the street.

6

I ran on the road that went around the inside of
Yoyogi Park. It was a nice morning with a fresh
breeze and the sun was flickering through the trees.
But inside my head there was rage and pain. I kept
seeing Kako with Miko, and Louise laughing, and
Riko dancing like a demon. And then I started to
run faster, and as I ran I killed them in my mind.
I kept going until my lungs were screaming, and
they were dead, and sweat was pouring from my
head. I put my hands on my hips and sucked up
deep breaths. I couldn't think where Kako could be!
The club was the only place I ever saw him outside
school. And I don't think anyone there knew him
besides Kane. But I couldn't ask Kane, because if
Kako turned up dead . . .

I stretched for a bit and then I jogged back to the house. I'd left the sword on the bike the night before, and I wanted to put it in my room. It made no difference – the bike was in the garden and the sword was in the nylon fishing bag. No one could see it, but it was best to keep it out of the way. Then it came to me – fishing! I'd seen Kako fishing! My mind started racing before I'd put all the pieces together, and as it raced I ran. I got the bike from the garden, and kick-starting the engine I rode away.

There was this kid at school not so long back who couldn't make his baseball game. And so he'd asked me to go in his place. I couldn't say no because he helped me with my geometry. But I didn't want to turn up and bat for a team I didn't know, not by myself, and so I asked Hiroshi to come with me. The game was being played down by Tokyo Bay, just below the Rainbow Bridge. But when we got there we found out it had been cancelled. We'd gone all that way for nothing. But as it was still early, and as we had nothing better to do, we decided to explore the docks. There were lots of quays with boats and tugs with tyres attached to them. We even climbed on a few because we wanted to see how far we could go without having to walk on the road. We managed to make it for a mile or so, but we were stopped in our tracks when we came to a container base. It was surrounded by a mesh fence and there was barbed wire on top. If we wanted to keep going we'd have to edge our way around the dock wall. But if we fell, we'd fall into the water. I would have done it but Hiroshi hesitated, and then some guy in a crane told us to get lost. And when he did I saw this kid sit up in a fold-up chair. He had a long fishing rod in front of him and he looked half asleep. And that kid was Kako. I couldn't understand why the guy hadn't told him to get lost. I figured it must have been an uncle, or a friend, or some fool who was frightened of him. But it brought back something I'd heard about Kako. Every Sunday night, without fail, he went fishing. And if that was the case, then he'd be there tonight.

I followed the signs for the port and then for the Rainbow Bridge. And then I saw the sea and the row of red cranes that ran along the waterfront. I knew that the container base was below the cranes and so I cut off before I came to the bridge. Then I spiralled down a concrete causeway and rode on to the dock road. I passed the seagulls and the ships, and the machinery waiting to be loaded on to them. Then

I came to the container base, where the different coloured containers were piled high.

As I slowed I saw two guards at the gate and so I rode around to see if there was another entrance, but there wasn't. And so I stopped to survey the fence. It was ten-foot high and there was plenty of barbed wire running along the top. It would be difficult to climb over with the sword, and it'd be a real hazard to a quick getaway. But that was where he'd be and so that was where I'd have to go.

I took a quick tour of the backstreets opposite the base, to see where I'd stash the bike. And then I rode home. And as I did I thought about the fence. It wasn't just a question of getting over it; it was getting away when the time came. I could throw a blanket over the barbed wire and climb over, but somebody might see me, a passing car maybe. And if someone saw me kill Kako and gave chase . . . I imagined them grabbing my legs as I tried to climb over. And I imagined me kicking at them, desperate to escape.

Then it came to me. I'd cut a hole in it with the wire cutters in my father's old toolbox. And the container base wasn't that large. It shouldn't be a problem finding him once I was inside. And when

I thought about it, it was easier than killing him in Shibuya. A lot easier.

By the time I got back to the house I thought I had everything covered. I put the bike in the garden and walked around to the front feeling fairly satisfied. All I needed was for him to be there tonight and then I'd kill him. And nothing would stop me! But then I opened the door and saw the Lump, and somehow I knew she'd cause trouble.

The Lump was a sort of cousin and she looks like a lump as well. She's not that fat, but she has a chubby face and she's short and as round as a beach ball. So there's definitely something of the sumo about her. And she always has her hair tied up in a palm tree because she's too lazy to do anything else with it. And she dresses bad. And if that isn't enough, she gets on my nerves!

She bowed to me as I took off my shoes, but I ignored her. It didn't matter because you can't hurt her feelings; she's kind of backward. She's not mental or anything, so there's no need to feel sorry for her. She's just hard of thinking.

'What the hell are you doing here?'

She didn't say anything, but her mouth curved into an unhappy face and she looked at the floor.

She rarely speaks anyway, and when she does it's only one or two words. And she always looks a little glum. It's like she's expecting something bad to happen to her at any moment. And who knows, with a face like that it probably will. The only thing she does with any real relish is eat. You could put nuts and bolts in front of that kid and she'd eat them. She ate more than any nine-year-old alive.

'Yukio, can you come in here for a moment?'

I went into Grandmother's room, where she sat smoking with a cat in her lap. 'As you can see, your cousin is here on a visit.'

I love the way Grandmother puts things. 'On a visit.' What that meant was that the Lump had been dumped on us and we had to put up with her. You see, Grandmother used to have a sister called Mai. And she had a daughter named Sashi who lives in Sapporo, which is where the Lump is from. Sashi was married to some failed opera singer and the Lump was their daughter. But they never had much time for her because she's a little slow, like I say. But they had an older daughter, Hatsu, who was a gifted pianist. They treated her like a princess and she acted like one too. And every time they took her on tour we got the Lump.

'So we'll have the pleasure of her company for a while,' said Grandmother.

That's rich, coming from her. She's never spent ten seconds with the kid.

'And while she's here I'll expect you to look after her.'

'Can't Yoshe take care of her?'

'She could, but I'd like you to do it. She'll be company for you now that your friends are gone.'

I swear, right there and then I could have put Grandmother on my to-kill list! 'But she's only nine. She doesn't even speak.'

'Of course she speaks!'

'But—'

'But nothing!' said Grandmother, getting mean. 'I never ask you to do anything for me. Do I ever ask you to clean your room or go to bed early? No! So this one thing I ask, you'll do!'

I could see that all sympathy for the twins' death had gone. Not that there was much of it!

'Yes, Grandmother,' I said, and went to leave.

'Oh, and Yukio – if you're not nice to her, I'll know.'

I don't know who was more frightening, Grandmother or the yakuza. Grandmother probably!

I went to my room and stood there seething. All this hassle and I had to kill Kako tonight.

I saw the Lump through the gap in the door. 'Go downstairs! You're not supposed to be up here!'

Yoshe popped her head out of the spare room. 'She has to stay up here. You remember what happened last time.'

'How could I forget?'

If there weren't enough annoying things about the Lump, she was a sleepwalker as well. And not just your average sleepwalker. She was the queen of it! One night they found her planting flowers in the garden. Another night they found her on a train to Osaka. And the last time she stayed here the cops found her wandering around Shinjuku at four in the morning. Her and that scary doll of hers. She has this decaying head that looks like it's been shrunk by an African witch doctor. It looks like the skull of monkey and it has this greasy black hair that never seems to stop growing. The thing gives me the creeps and she never goes to bed without it. Come to think of it, the Lump gives me the creeps and now she's invading my space. She was a little fat space invader!

The last time she was here I dumped her on the twins. She even stayed over there a few nights. Miko loved her and Hiroshi never got tired of trying to teach her how to draw. What they saw in her I don't know. But they were the sort of kids who liked everyone. It was a shortcoming they had. And it's probably what got them killed . . . Kako better be there tonight!

'Hey, dummy. You see this room? That's my room. You stay out of it!' The Lump looked a little scared and she scurried down the stairs. And I was glad. She shouldn't have been here in the first place.

Yoshe came out of the spare room and followed her. 'Lunch is ready.'

I watched her go and then I climbed up into the loft and got the wire cutters. I tried them out on some copper and they cut OK, and so I went to the bathroom and washed my hands.

By the time I got to the kitchen the Lump had finished one bowl of noodles and Yoshe was serving her another. I've never seen a kid as happy as the Lump when she ate. You'd think she'd never been fed. I gave her a dirty look as I sat down, but Yoshe was smiling like a Buddha. 'She's got a good appetite!'

The Lump looked happy like it was something to be proud of.

'She's a greedy pig is what she is!'

The Lump sort of froze and her face soured.

'Ignore him,' said Yoshe. 'He's just in a bad mood.'

But the Lump slid down from her seat.

'It's OK, really,' said Yoshe, trying to console her.

But the Lump left the kitchen without looking back. I just picked up my chopsticks and started to eat. What did I care? But Yoshe wasn't happy. She gave me a look as she cleared her bowl away.

'Well, she is greedy.'

'Do you know they had to take her out of school because she was being bullied?'

'What's that got to do with anything?'

'If people weren't so mean to her, she mightn't eat so much.'

'People are mean to her because she's a retard.'

'What a nasty thing to say!' said Yoshe. 'She's not a . . . There's nothing wrong with her! She just has speech problems, that's all.' She put the dishes in the sink and started to wash them. But then she leaned on it like my words had really hurt her. 'What happened to that nice little boy who wanted to help me with my housework?'

'He's dead,' I said.

She dried her hands and took a seat in front of me. She had her hair pulled back tight from her face and it made her look tough, which she was in a way. She was one of those hardworking Japanese women who was nice to everyone but who took crap from no one. Not even from Grandmother, and definitely none from me.

'The twins' death was a terrible thing, but you can't take it out on your cousin. All she wants is to be loved. And if you gave her a chance you'd see what a great kid she is. I can't make you be nice to her, Yukio, but don't be mean. Enough people are mean to her already. OK?'

I felt a little bad then. 'OK.'

When I'd finished eating I went out into the garden. I knew the Lump was out there and I thought I'd say something that wasn't mean. But she wasn't there and the steel door was open. I went out into the street but I couldn't see her, and so I walked down for a bit. And then I saw her knocking on the twins' door. She tried to see through the window, but she was too short and so she went back to knocking. She couldn't have known they were dead. But there was something about it that made me so angry. 'Come down from there!'

She looked scared when she saw me and she trotted down the steps as quick as she could. 'Twins,' she said.

'They're not there!' I said, and walked back to the house.

'Twins,' said the Lump.

'They're gone!'

'Twins!'

I turned on her. 'They're dead, you dummy! Now shut up!'

She looked shocked. I don't know if it was because I shouted at her or because she understood. But either way I didn't care. I only cared about killing the people responsible.

It was around midnight. The rain was washing the windows and the wind was howling. I stood, fully dressed, in the dark, but I never moved. I don't know what I was waiting for. I'd put on my dad's rain gear, the wire cutters were in my pocket and the sword was on the bike. All I had to do was ride there, kill him, and get back to this room without being seen. It was the perfect night for it. I bowed to the twins and the Buddha, and leaving the room I went downstairs. I didn't use the drainpipe because

I knew it'd be slippery. There was no need anyway. Grandmother slept like the dead – nothing woke her. She even folded her arms across her chest like a corpse in a coffin.

As soon as I opened the back door the rain hit me. And so I put on my helmet before pushing the bike out of the garden. I closed the steel door and pushed the bike down the hill before kick-starting the engine. Pulling back on the throttle I rode around the park with a powerful wind pushing me back. I could see it tearing at the trees and rippling the puddles that had formed like lakes. It was no surprise that Omotesando Boulevard was deserted and that the roads through Roppongi were dead, but I felt like I was riding through a ghost town. And when I got down to the docks it was even more dead. There wasn't a soul, or a single car, or even a light coming from a window. Not until I neared the container base, that is. It was lit up with spotlights, and there were vehicles moving around inside. The only place I didn't want to see people, and they were there.

I turned into a side street opposite the base and parked in the darkest spot. The street was lined with lifeless warehouses and lit by a single light. I could see the heavy rain pouring through its beam. And at the end of the street I could see the fence and the containers that were piled up behind it. I put my helmet on the seat and took the sword from underneath. Then I pulled my hood up and headed down to the dock road. There were no cars coming, but inside the compound I could hear the vehicles moving around. I walked in the opposite direction to the noise, but I stopped when I saw a broken street light above the fence. It was dark below it, a good place to cut the hole. The wind howled and so I put my back to a wall and waited. A rat ran across the road and then it ran back. But nothing else happened and no one came.

I gripped the wire cutters and running across the road I knelt by the fence. I put a line of wire mesh into the jaws and squeezed, but nothing happened. I tightened my grip but it still didn't snap. And so I knelt on both knees and squeezed with all my strength. I was relieved when it cracked and I moved on to the next piece. It was hard work and the rain made the handles slippery, but I soon had a gap big enough to squeeze through. I made my way through the maze of containers with my damp sneakers squeaking as I walked. But then I found myself back at the fence. It was difficult to get my bearings because the containers walled me in. But then I saw the sea, and heading towards it I peeked around a corner. I saw a ship being loaded at the far end of the dock. And I saw the dockers in reflective jackets, driving forklift trucks. But the rest of the waterfront was deserted.

All I could do now was wait, and so I sheltered from the rain as best I could. I was shivering, even though it wasn't cold, and the sight of the sea made me shiver more. My sneakers were soaked and so were my socks, and my feet felt wrinkly. I wished I'd worn my waterproof boots, but it was too late now.

I thought about what would happen when I saw him. I imagined myself striking him over the head and him going down. And then me running him through. Or maybe he'd bolt and I'd stab him in the back. I knew there was a chance that he wouldn't come out, especially on a night like tonight. But my father went fishing in all weathers, and some people like the rain. Miko used to walk in it for hours.

And that's what went by – hours. I started to think he wouldn't come. And then I knew he wouldn't. Because once again I saw him in the club in his suit. He looked like one of those people who hated the rain – hated being outdoors for that matter. No, he's not going to come out in this weather, of that I was sure. But then I heard a car.

I stood back as it passed and then I looked around the corner. The car took a right and went out of sight. It must have parked in a gap between the containers. Then I saw a man carrying a large plastic box towards the waterfront. He disappeared behind a small wooden shed and so I moved towards it. But I froze when I saw him heading back to the car. I couldn't see his face because he had his hood up. But when he reappeared he was carrying a fishing rod and a fold-up chair. It had to be him!

I kept my back to the containers until I was opposite the shed. Then, very slowly, I peeked around the side. He was trying to attach bait to a hook but he was having trouble because of the wind. And so he pulled down his hood so he could see better. When I saw Kako a calm came over me. I was almost relieved. But then the fear came and the adrenalin pumped. I opened the top of the bag and slid the sword from its mounting. Then making sure that the coast was clear I headed towards him. I gripped the sword in both hands and held it level in the *chudan* stance. He didn't know I was there until

I was standing right behind him. And then it was too late. He looked shocked, like he didn't know what was happening. But he looked more shocked when I pulled down my hood.

'Yukio!' He swallowed hard but he tried to smile. 'Don't tell me – you're going to kill me because I slept with Miko. I didn't know you were the jealous type.' He seemed calm, but he couldn't take his eyes off the sword. 'Listen, if it's a girl you're after, I know plenty. And they're a lot better than her!' He held my gaze for a second, and seeing his words had no effect he became angry. 'Come on, Yukio. She was a Buraku. They're dogs – they don't matter!'

She was dead and he was calling her a dog. He must have seen the hatred in my eyes because he fell apart then.

'Riko and Louise made me do it! It was all their doing!'

'Where do they live?'

His eyes widened with hope. 'They live by Aka-saka Palace!'

'Where?'

He held his head and tried to think. 'There's a blue glass building opposite the palace wall. Behind it is an office block called . . . Garden City! They live in the block next door. And they have the penthouse, Yukio! I can show you where it is, if you like.'

He looked like a scared little boy. I almost didn't want to do it. But then I saw Hiroshi being hit by the train! 'There's no need,' I said, and stepping forward I raised the sword. He cried out and raised his arm. The blade stuck in his elbow and cracked into the side of his skull. He started to scream. I swung the sword and it shattered his teeth. Then I thrust the blade into his stomach. When I ripped it out he dropped.

I slid the sword into its mounting and put it in the bag. Then I scurried back into the containers. All I wanted now was to get away. I took a right and a left but I couldn't see the fence. Then I took another right and hit a dead end. And then I just ran. I didn't know which way to turn. And then I came back to the waterfront.

'Help! Help!'

I couldn't believe it! Kako was on his feet and staggering around! I took out the sword and ran at him. Half slashing, half pushing, I shoved him into the water. There was a loud splash. Suddenly I was blinded by the spotlights of an incoming ship.

'There's someone in the water!' shouted a seaman.

Next thing I know, there were sirens wailing and dockers running towards me. I turned to run in the opposite direction, but two forklifts were coming my way. And there were men hanging off them. All of a sudden it had turned into Shinjuku station.

I ran through a path between the containers and came straight to the fence. I went along it looking for the gap, but I couldn't find it so I ran back the way I came, but I still couldn't see it. I put the sword in the bag and the bag over my shoulder. Then I charged at the fence and grabbed the top. I threw my arm over the wire but my feet slipped on the mesh and I fell. I tried again but but the fear had drained away my energy. Then I saw a flashlight coming down the path towards me. I didn't know whether to take out the sword or run. And so I ran. I sprinted along the fence as fast as I could. I took a right and ran down a long path between the containers. I ran all the way to the end, but that brought me to the gate. And there were two guards on it. They were looking in the direction the sirens were coming from. Then behind me I heard a man shout, 'There's been an accident!'

When both guards bolted towards the waterfront I pulled up my hood and walked through the gate.

I ran to the backstreet where I'd left the bike. I was panicking so much I almost ran past it. But I stopped quickly and searched for the keys. I couldn't find them! I must have dropped them! I was just about to run when I checked the ignition. There was a second of absolute joy and then I kick-started the engine and rode away.

I kept to the backstreets until I was away from the docks. Then I switched on the lights and headed out on to the main road. I was dreading the cops would come up behind me. And I felt cold and exhausted and I couldn't stop shaking. My stomach turned over and my mouth filled with saliva. I was just in time to raise my helmet before I threw up. Vomit splashed on my pants and sneakers, but I never stopped. I rode on and let the rain wash it away. All I wanted to do now was get home. I rode through Roppongi and Shibuya and headed up Omotesando. But I never thought about the ride. I only thought about the front door. And all of a sudden I was there. I switched off the engine and pushed the bike into the garden. I looked under the seat for the sword, but it wasn't there! Then I realized it was still on my back.

I opened the front door, and closing it I put my head against it. But then I heard something in the living room. I put the hall light on and looked into the shadows. There was someone moving around, but I couldn't see who it was. Then the Lump emerged from the darkness. She held that ugly severed head in one hand and her cellphone in the other. She checked it like she was awake but she wasn't. Her eyes were glazed and she was gazing into nothing. I'd just killed a man and I was holding a samurai sword. But I swear there was something about her when she sleepwalked that made my hair stand on end. I took her by the hand, and walking her up the stairs I showed her to her room. 'Go to sleep,' I whispered. She lay on her futon and held that horrible head so it was glaring at me. It was like it knew what I'd done and didn't like it. Boy did it give me the creeps! And so closing the door I left them in the dark. And in the dark is where I hoped they would stay.

7

I raised the blinds in my room to let in the light. Just another day, I thought. But it wasn't just another day. I'd changed, and everything around me seemed different. I suppose all the great swordsmen, even the likes of Musashi, felt different after their first kill, cold and empty inside, and disgusted. I can still see that look of horror on his face when I plunged the sword into his stomach. I suppose I'll never get that image out of my head. But it was nowhere near as horrific as the image of Miko hanging or Hiroshi being hit by the train.

I went downstairs and picked up the paper. 'Body Found in Tokyo Bay: The body of a young man believed to have been murdered was discovered by fishermen late last night. Who he is and who killed him is not yet known but . . .' I quickly scanned the article but there was nothing about me running away. Who knows, maybe I wasn't seen. Or maybe the police were keeping that information to themselves. Either way the word 'body' meant that he was dead. Then I saw another headline: 'Suicide Rate Rises with the Heat'. The suicide rate always rose in the summer, but this year it was higher than usual, or so the article claimed.

I looked up to see the Lump sitting in the living room. She sat so quietly you'd never know she was there. She was wearing her rucksack over her jacket like she was going somewhere. But she always dressed like she was going somewhere, even if she wasn't.

Then Yoshe came out the kitchen. 'Well, she's all ready!'

'Why, where's she going?'

'Wherever you're planning on taking her.'

'I can't look after her today. I have to go somewhere.'

Yoshe opened the front door and we stepped outside. 'I'm going in ten minutes. You have to look after her.'

'Can't she stay in the garden?'

'She could, if she was a dog! Look, Yukio, your

grandmother spoke to you about this. Every day you have to make plans to take her somewhere.'

'Where?'

'I don't know. Why don't you take her on a river cruise? She'd like that.'

'Why don't I just take her somewhere so she can't find her way back?'

Yoshe gave me a cold look. 'Your grandmother said you'd be like this and so she told me to give you a message: go out without her, and you'll be sleeping in the park with the peasants.'

The Lump appeared in the doorway. She looked a little embarrassed and so she checked her cell to hide it.

'Come on then!' I said, and stormed off.

'Have a nice time,' said Yoshe. And the Lump ran after me.

I was angry at Yoshe then, and I was never angry with her. It was the Lump's fault.

'Twins,' said the Lump as we passed their apartment.

I turned on her. I was just about to shout, but she looked sorry and so I didn't. I just headed up the hill to the shrine. That little fat lump wasn't getting the better of me. I'd leave her with Natsuko.

Then I heard her mumbling behind me. That was another annoying thing about the Lump. She couldn't put two words together but she mumbled like a maniac.

I turned quickly. 'What are you saying?'

The Lump looked up at me. 'Nothing.'

'I know you're talking about me! You'd better pack it in!'

But she didn't pack it in. All the way up to the shrine I could hear her talking to herself. She only stopped when we came to the temple and running up the steps she rang the bell. Then she clapped three times to summon the gods and bowed. I ignored her, and heading around the side of the temple I knocked on the nuns' house. But then I realized I hadn't seen Natsuko since I was sick. And now I felt awkward about asking her to look after the Lump. But it didn't matter anyway because no one was home.

The Lump was walking along the garden paths with her hands behind her back. She stopped every now and then to give a statue or a plant a good inspection. She always inspected things with her hands behind her back; she was strange like that. But then she spotted dozens of stone dogs at the side of the temple and ran towards them. They weren't the lion dogs that you see outside most temples. They were more fox-like and they each had a red cotton handkerchief wrapped around their neck. The Lump looked at them in absolute wonder. 'Beautiful!' she said as I came towards her. She always thought everything was beautiful. She was a real dummy.

'Listen,' I said.

She cringed as she looked up at me as though bracing herself for bad news.

'I'm going to leave you here for five minutes.'

'Leave me?'

'Just for five minutes. I'll be back soon.' I went to leave but the Lump followed. 'No, you stay here.'

'Hungry,' said the Lump.

'That's why I'm leaving. I'm going to get you something to eat.'

She seemed happy with this and wandered off to explore the grounds. I walked until I was out of sight and then I ran. I ran all the way back to the house and crept into the garden. I looked through the kitchen window, to make sure Yoshe had gone, and then I got on the bike and rode to Akasaka. I figured it would take me fifteen minutes to ride there, fifteen to find their apartment, and fifteen to ride back. The most the Lump would be left alone was an hour or so, and she'd seemed happy enough when I left her. But even if she wasn't, it didn't matter. This came first.

I rode through the Minato area and into Akasaka and then I rode around the stone wall that encircles Akasaka Palace. The palace is where heads of state stay when they visit Japan. But the royal family used to live here at one time and so the grounds are pretty big, and so are the walls that run around them. And the whole area's covered in office blocks and apartment blocks and I couldn't see a blue glass building to save my life.

I stopped and asked a cop did he know where the Garden City office block was, but he didn't and so I rode on. I guess I shouldn't have asked a cop for a location where I was going to kill someone, but it was too late now. I saw a traffic warden giving someone a ticket. I was just about to ask him when I saw this tall blue office block. It was a Sony Building, and just behind it was the Garden City skyscraper. Kako hadn't lied.

I parked the bike in front of the building and looked around. Kako said that the girls lived right next door, but there were three or four apartment blocks close by. It could have been any one of them. I walked across a wide walkway, which turned into a pedestrian bridge, and headed into a small concrete jungle. The Park Court Tower was definitely the closest and so I reckoned that was the one. But he'd also said that the girls had the penthouse, which was bad because the tower was at least thirty storeys high. There was a residents' board outside the entrance, and so I started to scan the names. But then I heard a voice behind me.

'Can someone get me a drink?'

I turned to see another apartment block, no more than six floors high. At the top was a penthouse with small trees and a rooftop garden. And leaning on the rail was Riko Tanaka! I jumped behind a concrete post as quick as I could and peered around the side of it. She had a patch over her blind eye and she was dressed in black. Maybe it was to show respect for her cousin Kako. She must have known by now that he was dead.

She stood there smoking a cigarette and admiring the sky, and then she looked down in my direction. It was like she was looking straight at me. I pulled my head in and waited a few seconds before looking out again. A man in a white vest handed her a drink and then they leaned on the rail and talked. He had a shaven head and his arms were covered in yakuza tattoos. I hated those tattoos, but not as much as I hated Riko. 'I'll throw you off that rooftop! You see if I don't!' But now that I knew where the girls lived I had to get back to the Lump. I could just see her wandering back to the house and Grandmother answering the door. Then there'd be hell to pay. But I couldn't take the chance of Riko seeing me, which she would if I walked back across the bridge while she was there. And so I had to wait.

At least half an hour went by before they made their way inside. 'Louise, I'm going!' shouted Riko. As soon as the coast was clear I ran across the bridge and bolted back to the bike. I put on my helmet, kick-started the engine and rode out on to the main road. It was a real piece of luck Riko coming out on the rooftop like that. Otherwise it might have taken me months to find them. But now I had to get back to the shrine. I rode at full throttle and whizzed between the traffic as quick as I could, but then I got held up by the lights. It's always the way when you're in a rush! A Mercedes jeep pulled up alongside me, and turning, I came face to face with Riko. And for some reason I couldn't look away.

She couldn't recognize me because I was wearing my helmet. But she didn't look happy. She said something to her broken-nosed bodyguard, who sat in the front seat, and then he turned around and gave me a look. I moved up to the front of the traffic and looked back at them in my mirror. 'Now's not the time. But soon!'

When the lights changed I turned on to the dual carriageway and followed it around to Omotesando. The lights stayed in my favour all the way to the park, and cutting across the tracks I headed up the hill to the shrine. As soon as I reached the top I parked and ran into the grounds. But I couldn't see the Lump anywhere. She must have gone home!

'Yukio.'

I turned to see Natsuko. She looked a little pained as she came towards me, as though remembering all the times I'd been there with the twins. And I felt a little sad myself when I saw her. She went to speak, but then something down the path caught her eye. 'Is that someone asleep?'

I was relieved when I saw the Lump. 'My cousin.'

Natsuko looked surprised. 'Oh yes, I remember her.'

We walked along the cool path, in the shade of

the trees, and headed towards the Lump. But we were both straining for something to say.

'So how are you?' asked Natsuko.

'Getting better,' I said. 'And stronger.'

'You've always been strong, Yukio. That's why people look up to you.'

I felt a surge of pride and my back straightened. 'And how are you?'

'It hurts me when I think of them, but I am weak. And I feel as though my faith is being tested. I mean, we talk about rebirth as though it's something to rejoice. But why would I rejoice at the twins' death?' She turned to me. 'Have you any idea why they did it?'

I felt like telling her who was responsible and how they were going to pay. And I felt like telling her how I'd killed Kako. But I didn't. Natsuko hated violence, even if it was justified.

'No,' I said. 'I have no idea.'

We came to the Lump, who was asleep on a bench. She had used her rolled-up coat for a pillow and she slept with her arms around a glass jar filled with wild flowers. I couldn't believe how shabbily she dressed. The soles of her sneakers were worn away and her faded T-shirt was ten times too small for her. It even had holes in it. I felt embarrassed that she was my cousin, but she didn't care. She was so dead to the world that a greenfinch perched on her shoulder.

Natsuko smiled when she saw her. 'She sleeps so peacefully. Sign of a clear conscience.'

The Lump's eyes opened and the bird flew away. She looked a little startled, and sitting up she put on her coat. Then she played with her palm-tree. 'Hungry,' she said.

'Oh, she's adorable!' said Natsuko.

The Lump liked this, and picking up the jar with the flowers she handed it to Natsuko.

'I made,' said the Lump. 'For you.'

'What a beautiful flower arrangement! Do you like ikebana?'

The Lump just sat there looking happy.

'She doesn't speak much,' I said. 'She's a little backward.'

The smile left the Lump's face and her head dropped in shame. Natsuko looked surprised, like she couldn't believe what I'd said. But I didn't think the Lump would understand, I really didn't.

'Nonsense, Yukio,' said Natsuko, kneeling in front of her. 'Appreciating beauty is the beginning of wisdom. And anyone who can create such a beautiful flower arrangement must be very wise.'

The Lump was happy then and the joy returned to her face.

'What do you want to be when you grow up?' asked Natsuko.

'A nun,' said the Lump.

Natsuko laughed. She had a nice laugh. 'I'm sure you'll make a wonderful nun.'

'Eight Fold Path,' said the Lump. And then she frowned like she was trying to remember. 'Do no harm!' she said.

Natsuko seemed touched by this. 'Do no harm,' she said in a soft voice. 'You see, Yukio, she is wise.'

But the Lump wasn't wise. She didn't even know what she was talking about. The Eight Fold Path was a set of eight Buddhist recommendations on how to live your life. There was something in there about harmlessness. But there was nothing that said 'do no harm'. And the Lump was looking so pleased with herself.

'Natsuko.' We turned to see the older nun by the temple.

'Coming,' said Natsuko. 'I have to help prepare the food for the homeless. But we're going to the temple next week to do the last of the repairs. The head priest here has been so kind, but I'm sure he'll be glad to see the back of us. You can come and help if you like. It has a great view of Fuji.'

'I will,' I said.

'When it's repaired the first mass I say will be for the twins.'

'Twins,' said the Lump in a serious way.

'Yes, the twins,' said Natsuko. She smiled, but her eyes became teary. 'I'll see you soon.'

Me and the Lump bowed to Natsuko as she walked away. And then I turned on her.

'Since when have you wanted to be a nun?'

'Always,' said the Lump.

'Always? You're only nine, you know!'

But the Lump turned stubborn. 'Always!' she said.

I just walked away. She didn't know what she was talking about.

The Lump followed on behind. 'Hungry,' she said.

The street was dark and quiet. But it was hot and there was no breeze, and the black hat I was wearing was making it hotter. And so I thought about the ancient samurai and what they had had to endure. And then I thought about Bokuden and his 'decisive first strike', which was important in battle when fighting more than one man. You aimed for the armpit, neck or wrist of the first opponent, slashing an artery or breaking a joint. You might not kill him immediately, but you finished him, meaning you could move on to the next man. I thought about this technique as I stood outside the Tanakas' apartment block. Because tonight I think I was going to need it.

But what was driving me crazy was waiting for them to come out. Once they did I could kill them at the entrance and run to the bike. But if they didn't come out I'd have to go up there. And they were up there, or someone was. I'd walked around the back earlier and taken a look. But who it was and how many I did not know.

But even if they did come out it could still be a problem, especially if they got picked up. To the left of the entrance, below the building, was a small underground car park. I'd watched a man in a Mini drive in there earlier. The steel mesh gate raised and he drove down a short slope and parked in front of a wall. If the Tanakas' driver drove in there to pick them up, I could do nothing. It's not that I couldn't get under the gate before it closed – I could, but it'd be a real risk. The place was well lit and there was nowhere to hide. The only other thing I could do was follow one of the tenants inside. But that didn't seem such a bright idea, considering I was dressed like a cat burglar and carrying a samurai sword.

I saw an old woman out with a dog. She was on the other side of the street but she homed in on me like I was the only person on the planet. I'd put the sword at the side of a tree, so she couldn't see it. But it was like she knew I was up to no good. And if that wasn't bad enough, her dog started to bark. Loud biting barks that echoed all over the place. I didn't know what to do. I was on the verge of screaming at it to shut up. 'What's his name?' I said. The barking stopped. The woman gave me a dirty look and pulled him away by the lead. Some people have got nothing better to do.

I saw the Mercedes jeep coming down the street. It was the driver and the bodyguard. I grabbed the sword from behind the tree and got ready. The driver stopped in front of the gate and the gate raised. The jeep rolled down into the car park. Just before the gate closed I ran across the street and slid underneath. I crouched low as the driver and the bodyguard got out of the jeep. If they looked back at the gate they'd see me, but they didn't. They went to the elevator and stood with their backs to me.

I pulled the sword from the mounting and moved quickly. But the broken-nosed bodyguard heard me coming and turned around. I thrust the sword through his chest before he could react. He clutched the blade with both hands, but I ripped it away and turned on the driver. He pulled out a pair of nunchakus and swung them frantically. He was so frightened he couldn't see he was out of range. I stood back, and lining him up I sprang forward. The blade struck his elbow and a bone came through his suit. He turned to run but he tripped on the bodyguard, who'd fallen behind him. Again I sprang forward and hacked deep into the side of his neck. His head hit the ground and blood gushed out of him.

I dragged his bleeding body behind the jeep and then went back for the bodyguard. He looked up at me with wild eyes and tried to speak, but he was too far gone. I heard the elevator chime. I left him next to the driver and ran for it, almost slipping on the trail of blood that had oozed like slime. I pressed the top button. The doors closed and the elevator rose. My heart was banging and sweat was running down my face, but I ignored it. I sucked up deep breaths and readied myself for battle. When the doors opened I stepped out ready to strike, but there was no one there. At the end of the hall there was a door slightly open and music was coming from inside. I used my shoulder to push back the door and then I entered the apartment. I walked down a long white corridor, heading towards the music. Coming to a living room, I peered around the corner. I saw a guy stripped to his waist. He was stocky and bald and his bare muscular back was covered in tattoos. He was fixing drinks on a trolley.

'Will you two hurry up?' he shouted.

I checked to make sure he was alone. Then moving quickly into the room I ran at him. He saw me in a mirror and reached for a bottle. But I brought down the sword on the back of his head and it cracked like an egg. He crashed to the floor with the trolley and the music fell silent. He must have knocked the plug from the stereo.

I heard one of the girls say, 'What the hell was that?'

High heels came down the corridor. I stood in front of the door and held the sword level, in the *chudan* stance. The heels got louder and then Louise appeared, but she turned so fast! I slashed at her and severed a triangle of hair. Then I chased her down the corridor. And as she ran she sprayed a line of red blood along the white wall. I must have caught a vein in her neck. She took a right and ran into a larger living room. And then, almost calmly, she sat in a chair. Her face drained of colour as the blood squirted out of her. She was dying and she knew it and so she gave me the finger. But then her body began to twitch and her hand fell into her lap. When the blood stopped squirting she froze like a statue.

I stood still and listened. The apartment was silent. I was just about to leave when I saw Miko's Prada bag on a table. 'That was Miko's birthday present!' I screamed. 'And she was such a decent person!' Without thinking I snatched the steel-tipped claw off her pinky and put it in my pocket. And then, as I left, I switched off the light and looked back. Louise sat by a wide window with Tokyo's bright lights blazing away behind her. Another image I'd never get out of my head.

As I walked back down the corridor I heard a

low buzzing sound. It was the intercom. I didn't know whether it had only just gone or had been going for a while. I was thinking of staying and catching Riko. But when I heard a car horn sound in the street all my senses told me to get out of there. I ran out of the apartment. The light above the elevator showed it was rising! I saw a door saying 'fire escape', and pushing it open I ran down the concrete steps. I passed the ground floor just as the door opened. I heard men's voices and then I heard them clambering up the steps, but I didn't stop. I opened the basement door, and running through the car park I picked up the mounting. I ran to the gate and looked for a switch to open it. But there wasn't one. I was trapped! Then through the mesh I saw car headlights. The gate rose. Three cars, full of yakuza, cruised in. They must have been having a wake for Kako. I was dying to run but I walked up the slope as calmly as I could. Some of them saw me but they didn't seemed concerned. But I saw a man looking at me from the back of a Lexus. I swear it was Uncle Benni.

I kept the sword at my side and walking out into the street I saw half a dozen yakuza going into the entrance. Then I heard a high-pitched scream. The men rushed inside. I turned to the car park just as the gate came down.

'I can see you!'

I looked up to see Riko on the rooftop and started to run.

'He's getting away!'

I looked back as I ran, but the street was empty.

'Get him! Someone get him!'

Riko's scream faded the further I got, but it never stopped.

I sprinted back to the bike. Jamming the sword under the seat I kick-started the engine. I stayed in the backstreets until I was well away from Akasaka and then I moved on to the dual carriageway. I tried to stay calm, but I kept thinking they were coming after me. But I couldn't believe I'd killed Louise. And I couldn't believe I'd made it out of there. Within ten minutes I was cutting through Shibuya and passing the park.

I only felt safe once I'd crossed the tracks and riding up the hill I turned into my street. But suddenly I had to swerve! Someone was in the road. I looked back and saw the Lump! She was wearing her pyjamas and she was carrying that severed head by its hair. I must have forgotten to lock the door. I got off the bike and went back to get her. She looked up at the twins' apartment and climbing halfway up she sat on the steps.

She looked so peaceful I didn't want to startle her. And so I gently took her by the hand and brought her down the steps. She stopped when we got to the bottom and looked up at the apartment.

'Twins,' she said in a sleepy voice. 'Beautiful twins.'

All the adrenalin and anger left me then. I felt so bad for her. The twins were probably the only friends she'd ever had. 'Yes, beautiful twins,' I said. And very slowly I walked her back to the house.

There was screaming in my nightmare and then I woke to more screaming. I went out on the balcony with my heart banging and looked down to see the Lump tormenting Yoshe's baby boy. He'd only just learned how to walk, and he was chasing the Lump around the plants on the patio and around the small pond that's shaped like a fish. But she was staying just out of reach and he didn't like it, and so she stopped and gave him a swing. He was happy then and he laughed and the Lump laughed with him.

'Breakfast's ready,' shouted Yoshe.

I went downstairs and picking up the paper I went into the kitchen. Yoshe put her baby boy in a high chair and the Lump took a seat. I already knew what the headlines would be before I saw them, and I was right. 'Benni Tanaka's Niece Slain by Assassin', was on the front page. And when I looked inside the headline read: 'Psycho Killer Slays Four'. I scanned the article to find out why they called me that. Apparently 'Psycho Killer' was the song playing on the stereo when the victims were murdered. I don't remember what was playing, but it wasn't important and so I read on. It said that Kako, who was Louise Tanaka's cousin, was killed the previous night. And it said, 'While reports are unconfirmed, it's likely that the victims were killed by the same sword.' One cop said it could be the work of a vigilante. It was also rumoured that Uncle Benni had a hit squad on standby.

So it had begun. Killing Kako was nothing because he was a nobody. I bet Uncle Benni never even batted an eyelid over him. But killing his niece was a whole different ball game. You see, the yakuza are the largest criminal organization in the world. There are fifteen hundred gangs in Japan, with close to ninety thousand members, and that's not counting the creeps who work for them. It has a hierarchy like that of an army or a corporation. They have trainees who work for years to become soldiers. Some rise to become officers and executives, who are also known as lieutenants. Ranking alongside the executives are the clan's advisers. Then comes the head of a clan, the *oyabun*, or family boss. He employs lawyers, accountants and administrators to help him run his section of the operation. And the yakuza's tentacles are everywhere. They work from street level to corporate boardrooms. They even have politicians on the payroll. Some of their business is legitimate, but mostly they deal in drugs, gambling and girls. And everyone answers to the big boss Uncle Benni. That meant that he had an army at his disposal. And by now every one of them would know that Louise Tanaka was dead. The news would have spread as far south as Nagasaki and as far north as Sapporo. It would spread to other criminal organizations in China and Korea. Condolences would be sent. Offers of loyalty renewed. Her father in prison would have been informed. Word would have been sent to Tomi Yamamoto in Osaka. He would have sent a message to his sister, and their stepmother, Matsu, who was doing time in a mental hospital. Yakuza gang leaders would have been woken up in the middle of the night. There would be meetings, phone calls and conversations. Uncle Benni's enforcers would be kicking down doors and the cops would be dragging people out of bed. Fear and paranoia would spread throughout the organization. And they'd all be asking the same question: who killed Louise Tanaka? I had all this on my mind and I still had to listen to the Lump slurp her noodles! 'Does she have to do that?'

'What?' asked Yoshe. 'Eat?' She put some tea in front of me. 'Would you like breakfast?'

'No, I'm going for a run,' I said. But I couldn't take my eyes off the paper. The Lump slurped her noodles again and I gave her a look to make her stop, but she didn't.

'She was sleepwalking last night! And the night before!'

The Lump stopped in mid-slurp, strings of noodles running from her mouth to the bowl.

Yoshe looked a little worried. 'She can't help it. And she'll be OK once she settles in.'

The noodles shot up into the Lump's mouth and she sat there looking smug. She wasn't scared of me any more. I didn't like that. And when Yoshe's baby boy started slurping his noodles I liked it even less.

I went upstairs to get changed and then I left the house in my running gear.

But then Yoshe came out of the garden. 'Aren't you forgetting someone?'

'I'm going for a run!'

'We've thought about that.'

She held open the steel door and the Lump rode out on my old bike. She was wearing my old black skateboard helmet. She looked like a little fat traffic cop.

'Well, come on then, if you're coming!' I said.

'Watch out for her on the road,' shouted Yoshe.

I watched out for her on the road and on the train tracks. But once we were in the park I ran up the ramp and left the Lump struggling to pedal upwards. I bet she didn't even have the good sense to lower the gears.

I ran around the inner road of the park while thinking about last night. But when the road curved I saw the Lump coming after me, and she was gaining. I ran faster, but the Lump wasn't easy to lose. She had a serious frown on her face and her small legs were spinning like a clockwork toy. I came off the road and ran on the common. She tried to follow, but she couldn't ride as fast on the grass and I left her behind. I ran right across the common and through the trees and then I got back on the road that ran around the inside of the park. But then I saw the Lump riding towards me. She must have remembered that the road was a circle and ridden back the way she'd come. She was really starting to annoy me!

I sat on a bench beneath the shade of a tree and got my breath back. The Lump rode up, and putting the bike on its stand she took a seat. She looked more than a little uncomfortable; she must have known I'd tried to lose her. Then she noticed the dirty look I was giving her and she started to whistle. But she couldn't and so she checked her cell instead. She never stops checking that damn cell! 'Who ever calls you on that? Go on, tell me!'

She tried to speak but the words wouldn't come. It happens that way sometimes, especially when she's under pressure. I suppose that's why she only says a few words at a time. But I have to admit I felt bad then. 'It doesn't matter,' I said. 'Forget about it.'

But the Lump took a deep breath and tried again. 'Mum and Dad and sister, Hatsu,' she said.

She looked away so I couldn't see her face, but I knew she was lying. No one ever calls her. She stayed here for a whole month last May and she checked that cell ten times a day. But she never got so much as a text message. I'm not surprised. Her mother's selfish, her father's a phoney and that sister of hers is spoilt rotten. They couldn't care less about her. And they certainly didn't care enough to call her. They never even bought her the cell – she won it in a school raffle. She put the cell in her rucksack and pulling out that shrunken head she smoothed back its black hair.

'What is that?'

The Lump held up the head and looked at it lovingly. 'Om,' she said.

'Om?'

'Best friend Om!' said the Lump. Then something caught her eye. 'Ants!' she shouted. She jumped off the bench and squatted on the ground. That was another thing about the Lump. She has this thing for ants. They kind of amaze her.

'Thirty-two,' said the Lump.

It drove me insane when she did that. You'd never know if she was right or not and so you'd end up trying to count them. One time she told me there were twenty-four. And it really looked like there were twenty-four. But you couldn't tell because they kept moving around.

Another ant came out of a hole. 'Thirty-three,'

said the Lump. And then she tiptoed out of them to make sure she didn't stand on any.

'Come on,' I said, and walked back to the house. I had a lot on my mind and the Lump was confusing things.

'Cherry blossoms,' said the Lump.

'The season's over.'

'Cherry blossoms,' she said and pointed. And there, among the trees, was one small cherry tree just beginning to blossom. I couldn't understand it. They only blossomed for ten days a year and the season had ended a month ago. When I looked at the Lump she was looking kind of pleased with herself.

'Come on,' I said, and walked away.

By the time we got back to the house Yoshe had gone. The Lump pushed the bike into the garden and I went to my room to think about my next move. I was still determined to kill Riko. But I knew the yakuza would be on guard now and so there was nothing I could do. Not for the moment anyway. And so I went out on the balcony to see what the Lump was up to. She was inspecting things in the garden. She gazed at the lotus blossoms in the pond and the plants on the patio. She even stared at a rusty old watering can for a time. Then a big blue butterfly fluttered into the garden. The Lump got on to it straight away and followed it around, wide-eyed, like she was blown away by its beauty. But then it fluttered upwards and flew over the wall. She waited to see if it would come back, but it didn't, and so she sat on the bench and checked her cell.

I felt kind of sorry for her then, she looked so alone. But I don't think she felt sorry for herself. She looked happy to sit and wait for the next big thing to happen, and then it did. One of Grandmother's cats came out. The Lump tried to befriend it, but it was the fat ginger cat that was friends with no one. It just climbed on top of the shed and went to sleep in the sun, which is all it ever did. And so the Lump returned to the bench.

I felt a little stressed over last night's killings, and as I had nothing better to do I decided to get a shinai from the shed and do some katas. If I couldn't battle I might as well train. I went downstairs, and cutting through the kitchen I went out into the garden. As soon as the Lump saw me she jumped up like we were going somewhere. But I just ignored her, and taking a shinai from the shed I did some stretching. I didn't need to warm up because it was so hot, but I did some stretches just in case. Then I did the power exercises. I squatted on my legs and jumping forward I struck with the shinai. It was a hard exercise but it built my thigh muscles and taught me balance. Balance is important in kendo, because if you lose your balance you've lost control. I did the strikes and the katas from the different stances and then I started to move fast, jumping forward and thrusting at an imaginary opponent.

The Lump looked amazed. Her eyes were wide and her head was twitching from side to side. 'Me!' she said.

'No.'

'Me!' said the Lump.

She was so annoying. 'There's another one in the shed.'

The Lump scurried into the shed and came out with a shinai. She screamed as loud as she could and started slashing the air like a little barbarian.

'Stop that!' She stopped and looked up at me. 'Stand behind me.' The Lump stood behind me and to the left. 'Now watch.' I held the shinai in the *chudan* stance and screaming I struck straight ahead, stamping my foot as I did so. 'Now you.'

As she raised her shinai the Lump looked deadly serious. Then with a loud scream she struck straight ahead and froze in the stance. It was a solid strike. She even stamped her foot at the right time. I walked around her and looked for a fault in her stance but I couldn't find one. She even stayed stone-faced and looked straight ahead.

'OK, watch this.' I moved across the patio doing all the strikes, blocks and blows you could do from the *chudan* stance. Then turning quickly I came back, striking and thrusting as I came. I stopped when I reached the plants and turned to her. 'Now you.'

The Lump was buzzing. Even her palm tree looked electrified. Crying out she struck and thrust her way to the wall. She did every single move the same as me. Then she spun around and crying out she came back. She was frighteningly good! She even flicked the shinai with her wrists rather than striking with a heavy blow. And I never even told her to do that. She came to a stop and looked up at me.

'You've done kendo before!'

'No,' said the Lump.

I glared at her but she never looked away. I think she was telling the truth.

'Go and put that helmet on.'

The Lump bolted in the shed and came out wearing the helmet.

'If I hit you on the helmet I score a point. If you hit me anywhere you score a point. Understand?'

The Lump nodded.

I bowed to the Lump and she bowed back. Then she cried out and charged. I wasn't expecting such a ferocious attack. She hacked and stabbed with all her might. Then she whacked me on the ankle. I nearly fell in the pond.

'Stop! You can't hit someone's feet!'

'Why?' asked the Lump.

'Because I said. Now step back.'

She'd got lucky because I'd never fought someone so small. But I was away from the pond now, and I had space. We eyed each other up and circled the patio. I struck her on the helmet. I did it again. And then again. The Lump was livid but she couldn't do anything about it. I hadn't taught her how to block. But then she hit my big toe. And I was in my bare feet too!

'I said not on the feet. You did that on purpose.'

But the Lump ignored me. Then crying out she attacked. But I blocked her blows with ease.

Her eyes went shifty and she moved around me

in a sneaky way. She was looking for an opening, I could tell. I'd met her type before. But then she kicked something at my feet. I looked down to see what it was. Suddenly she thrust the shinai into my face. The rubber end struck the tip of my nose, bringing tears to my eyes. Then she whacked me on the head. I stumbled over the flowerpots and fell into the plants.

'What the hell are you doing?'

'Accident,' said the Lump.

'You liar! I try to teach you something and this is how you behave!' I got to my feet. 'You little fat lump! No wonder you've got no friends!'

Her head went down like she felt bad. But I'd had enough of her. I threw the shinai on the patio and went upstairs to my room. Then I went out on the balcony. I was expecting to see her sulking on the bench, but she wasn't. She was practising with the shinai and she looked like she was having fun. She'd only pretended to feel bad! I ran into the bathroom and grabbing the plastic bucket I filled it with water. Then I went out on the balcony and called her. 'Come here, you. And take that stupid helmet off.' She took it off and came running over. Then she looked up at me like a real dummy. Before she had a chance to move I dumped the bucket and drenched her. Then I laughed out loud. 'That'll teach you!'

The Lump looked livid. She grabbed the shinai and ran in the house. When I heard her coming up the stairs I locked my door and lay on my bedroll laughing. I heard her bang into it. 'It's locked, you dummy!' I laughed some more and she kicked the door and walked away. It felt good to laugh. I hadn't laughed since the twins . . . but then I felt tired. I didn't sleep well last night because of the killings. And when I did sleep the nightmares came. I kept dreaming I was trapped in the car park and I couldn't get out. Either that or I was having a conversation with Louise's corpse. But when my eyes closed the sunshine and the warmth sent me to sleep. It was such a beautiful sleep too. I could feel myself falling deeper and deeper and then . . .

'Argh!!!' I couldn't breathe! The shock and the cold were too much! I saw the plastic bucket hit the floor and feet running. As I got up I stood on ice cubes. She'd put ice cubes in it!

'You're dead!' I ran to her room and tried to get in, but she'd locked the door. 'Let me in!'

'No.'

'Are you laughing?'

'No.'

But she was laughing – I could hear her! 'I'll get even with you! You see if I don't!' I slapped the door and went back to my room. There were ice cubes everywhere, and the futon and the bedroll were soaked. I hung them on the balcony and then I stood there, puzzled. I'd locked the door. I know I had. She couldn't have got in, not unless she had a key. I went back to her room. 'Open up, you!'

'No.'

'Are you hungry? There's chocolate cake in the fridge.' She never answered but I knew her tiny mind was ticking away. 'Yoshe made it specially. She makes the best chocolate cake in the world.'

'You'll get me.'

'No, I won't. Look, I soaked you and you soaked me. We're quits.'

I heard the door unlock. As soon as it opened I grabbed her arm. 'You tell me how you got in my room, you annoying little lump!'

'Chocolate cake.'

'Tell me first!'

'No!' The Lump got aggressive. 'Cake first!'

I let her go. 'One piece. That's all you're getting. And then you better tell me!'

We went downstairs and I took the cake from the fridge. The Lump sat at the kitchen table smiling like it was her birthday. But I cut the smallest, thinnest slice possible, and putting it on a plate I pushed it towards her.

The Lump looked disgusted. 'Small! Very small!'

I laughed. 'Tell me and I'll cut you a bigger piece. You found a key, right?'

'Drainpipe,' said the Lump.

'You liar!'

'Drainpipe,' said the Lump, and reached for the cake.

But I pulled it away. 'Let me see you climb it.'

'Cake!'

'Climb it and you can have all the cake you want!'

The Lump was out of that chair so fast. I ran upstairs and went out on the balcony. She came into the garden and took hold of the drainpipe. But she never climbed it. She just looked up at me.

'I knew you were lying.'

Then I could hardly believe my eyes! The Lump climbed that drainpipe as fast as a monkey. She clambered over on to the balcony, ran through my bedroom and back downstairs. 'Chocolate cake!'

I was kind of dumbfounded so I never said

anything. I couldn't even climb it that fast. The Lump was turning out to be a sneaky person. Very sneaky. Maybe I could use her in my fight against the yakuza.

It had just turned dark as I came out of the east exit of Shinjuku station. The whole area was swarming with people and there were hundreds of teenagers gathered in groups. There were bright lights and billboards, and huge TV screens advertising the latest must-haves. And it was so humid the air felt sticky. I made my way through the masses of people and headed down to the Kabukicho, which is like Tokyo's version of a red-light district. Kane had once told me that Riko managed some massage parlours there, and I was hoping to bump into her. But I hadn't brought the sword with me; this was just a scouting trip – I'd brought the Lump instead.

'Lights!' said the Lump.

I figured if the yakuza were looking for a single assassin, it'd be best not to go alone. And the Lump would make a good decoy. After all, who brings a kid with them when they go to kill someone? That said, I wouldn't put the Lump in any real danger. She was my cousin after all.

I looked down at her and she went to speak. But then her hands dropped to her sides as though the wonder of it all had taken away the only word she was going to say. She looked a little pained that she couldn't express herself. But then she blurted it out. 'Beautiful!' she said. I'll say one thing for the Lump – she never minced her words.

We headed into the bustle of the Kabukicho, where the lights shone bright and the music blasted from the bars. The streets were lined with touts, in suits, enticing girls into various places, and there were girls dressed like geishas enticing guys into various clubs. I was glad the place was packed so I could lose myself in the crowd, but then I lost sight of the Lump. You couldn't take your eyes off her for a second! And then I saw her trying to dance to the music. The Lump couldn't dance a step, but she danced every chance she got. Then she danced after this group of girls who were heading into a nightclub. But I grabbed her before she could go through the door. 'Where are you going?'

'Music,' said the Lump.

'Forget about the music, you dummy, and stop wandering off!'

The Lump looked a little disappointed, but she

soon became amazed by something else. And then we passed a FamilyMart.

'Hot,' said the Lump.

It was hot as well.

'Ice cream,' said the Lump.

'You've just had ice cream!'

'Ice cream again,' said the Lump.

She was starting to get on my nerves. I gave her some money and she ran into the FamilyMart. That's the thing with Tokyo – there're snack shops everywhere. There's a Lawson, a 7-Eleven or a FamilyMart on every corner. And every time we neared one, the Lump got hungry. No wonder she was fat.

She came out eating the ice cream and we headed further into the Kabukicho. Further into the bars, clubs and massage parlours owned by the yakuza. We passed the boy clubs and the love hotels, and crossing the road we stood outside the Hotel Siena and watched the goings-on. I couldn't see Riko or any of her crew anywhere, but the night was still young. But when I looked at the Lump she seemed kind of tired. 'You OK?'

'Hungry,' said the Lump.

I just shook my head. 'OK, wait here.'

I went to a Lawson and roamed the air-conditioned aisles grabbing biscuits and crisps. I bought myself a Coke and got the Lump a can of hot coffee. We'd only be out another hour or so, but I didn't want her falling asleep.

When I went back she was sitting on the steps at the side of the hotel. She looked relieved when she saw me. As though she thought I might have gone off and left her.

'Here.' I gave her the coffee and the snacks.

'Coffee!' said the Lump.

You should have seen the look she was giving me. You'd think I'd just kicked her in the leg.

'You don't like coffee? Here!' I swapped her the coffee for the Coke. She took it but she started mumbling. She'd turned into a real grouch all of a sudden.

'What are you saying?'

'Nothing,' said the Lump. But she was still scowling.

'I'm just going to take a look around. OK?'

The Lump looked up at me while munching on a mouthful of crisps. And she didn't look happy.

'I'll only be gone five minutes. And listen, while I'm gone, you keep a lookout for a one-eyed girl.'

The Lump looked puzzled. 'One-eyed?'

'A girl with one eye, you dummy!'

The Lump gave me a dirty look. Then I realized that's how she communicated. She never used words so much. She used facial expressions. The Lump has more facial expressions than the Noh theatre has masks. And this one was saying, 'Don't talk to me like that or I'm going home!'

'Look, I'll only be gone five minutes, OK?'

She didn't say anything. Not even with her face.

I looked back at her once I was across the street. She was stuffing her face and staring at the passers-by. She looked happy enough, and so I wandered around looking for Riko.

I looked in the bars and the coffee shops and I scanned the streets until my eyes hurt. But the area was packed and more people were pouring into it all the time. How I was going to find her among this crowd I didn't know. I couldn't even see anyone who looked like yakuza. The only person I did see was my green-eyed English teacher, Viviana, who was out with her bald boyfriend. But she wasn't English, she was Mexican.

'Hi, Miss Santiesteban.'

She gave me a big smile. 'Hi, Yukio!'

I looked back at her as I walked up to the station. She was really nice. What she saw in him I don't know.

I came back down a different street, but I saw no one and so I went back for the Lump. She was still where I left her, but she was leaning against a post and she was fast asleep. I gave her a shove and she woke up. 'Some lookout you are.'

'Tired,' said the Lump.

'That's because you sleepwalk. Come on, let's go.'

The Lump got her energy back on the way to the station and so she was in no rush to get home. She kept stopping and looking at things. 'Will you hurry up?' But she wouldn't hurry up. She was taking her sweet time and she was doing it on purpose. And when we passed a club I caught her dancing to the music. 'Stop that,' I said. She did stop, but she started again when I walked on. I could see her reflection in a window.

Then I saw someone heading down a side street. It wasn't Riko or any of her crew. It was that Korean creep who used to live by us, and I absolutely hated him! 'Follow me!' I said. The Lump looked excited. She knew something was happening and she ran to keep up. I followed the Korean down a dark backstreet but I never got too close, which was good because he stopped to talk to someone. Me and the Lump jumped in a doorway and stood back. Then the Lump peeked around the corner. She must have thought we were playing a game. But it was no game as far as I was concerned.

You see, I hated that Korean creep as much as I hated the Tanakas, and I'll tell you why. No more than a month after my dad died, Mum bought me a puppy. She knew that I was missing Dad and she thought that a dog would be company. Tito was his name and he was a little bundle of joy. One evening we took him over to Yoyogi Park so he could run around. We threw him sticks and chased him, and he chased us. I remember trying to seem happier than I was so as to cheer Mum up. And I think she was doing the same for me. But when it got dark we decided to head home. But then I had to pee and so I ran to one of the toilets in the park.

But when I came out I got the shock of my life! A man had Mum up against a tree. He was kissing her and groping her and she was trying to get away!

'Leave my mum alone!' I shouted, and kicked him in the leg.

When he turned I saw it was the Korean who lived in our street. He kept hold of my mother by her coat and pushed me to the ground. Then he went back to abusing her.

'Help!' I shouted. But there was no one around. I got up and tried to pull him away. And Tito bit at his ankles. Suddenly the Korean turned and kicked him hard. Tito started screaming in pain.

'What's going on there?' asked a jogger, coming to a stop.

The Korean told the guy to get lost. And then he started saying the most terrible things to my mother. It was as though hatred was drooling from his drunken mouth.

He spat in her face and staggered away. Mum grabbed me and Tito and held us tight, and then we rushed back to the house. When we got through the door she broke down. But she wouldn't call the police and she told me not to tell anyone about what had happened. But she was terrified, and it wasn't just that night. For weeks after she was scared to go out of the house. She made sure that Yoshe was with her and she never went out after dark. I wished Dad was still alive. He was never a violent man, but he had honour. And I'm sure he would have killed that

Korean for what he'd done. But Dad was dead, and the Korean must have known that.

The Lump looked out again. 'Clear,' she said.

We followed him down a quiet backstreet on the outskirts of the Kabukicho. He stopped outside a massage parlour and me and the Lump jumped into another doorway. A girl walked past and he said something to her. I could tell by her face that it was something sleazy. And then, sucking up, he spat in the street like a pig.

I heard a thumping sound and a guy pulled up on a chopper. I could tell by his tattooed arms that he was yakuza. I stood back in the shadows and watched. The Korean went in the massage parlour and coming out he handed the biker a white envelope. The biker put it in his jacket pocket and rode away without a word.

'Motorbike,' said the Lump.

I was only a little kid when that Korean assaulted my mother. But I wasn't a little kid now. And I was determined to defend my family's honour. I was going to kill that Korean the first chance I got! In fact, if I'd had the sword with me then I'd –

'Do no harm!' said the Lump.

I kind of froze. Then I looked down to see the

Lump glaring up at me. It was like she knew what I was thinking! The Lump had turned into a little fat mind reader! She was freaking me out!

'Look, here's a hundred yen. Go and get yourself something to eat!'

The Lump took the money and headed to a 7-Eleven. But she turned and scowled at me. Then she smiled at the money and ran into the shop. I swear, that Lump was getting stranger by the second!

9

We were cruising on the motorway in the early-morning mist. The monk who was driving the van had got us up so early and I felt really tired. That's the thing with monks – they get up early, and they think everyone else should get up early as well. I'd tried to start a conversation with him when we started out, but he wasn't much of a talker. In fact, you'd think he'd took a vow of silence, the way he hung on to his words. He was worse than the Lump.

When I looked behind me she was staring excitedly into a comic. I couldn't believe how excited she looked. I'd told her she could have all my old manga and she'd carried every one of them to her room; there must have been a hundred. She never even read the words, she just speed-scanned the pictures. Her head twitched from side to side and her eyes flickered over the images. And as they did her facial expressions changed. She went from being happy to sad and from angry to scared. It was like watching a computerized emoticon flick through its whole range of expressions. Then her face froze into a 'what the hell's going on here?' look, and then she glared at me like it was my fault.

'What?' I said.

But she never answered. She just turned the page and breathed out a dramatic little sigh.

Then Mount Fuji came into view. I was always impressed when I saw it, but it looked especially good today. Its base looked bronze while its snow-capped peak was bathed red by the rising sun. I turned to the Lump. 'Here's Fuji,' I said. But she never even looked up. She was lost in a cartoon world.

The van rolled off the freeway and curved around a bend. We followed a side road lined with orange groves, and then we bumped down a dirt road that ran alongside a river. We headed through some pine trees, and coming out in a clearing we pulled up in front of a wide field of wheat. And there was Fuji, as big as I'd ever seen it. From where I sat it looked like the wheat ran all the way to its base, but I knew the mountain was miles away.

The side door slid back and the Lump jumped out. She was excited about being in the countryside, but that was no surprise. She got excited if you took her to the supermarket. I got out and stretched and breathed in the air, which was cool and smelled of the country. I had a look around. There was a large wooden temple with an unfinished roof, and there was a wide stone courtyard in front of it. To the side of the temple there were shocking-pink plum trees and towering above them was a three-storey pagoda. It had four black roofs that were wider than its base, and rising from its peak was a coiled bronze spire called a *sorin*. I like pagodas. They're nice to look at and you always get a good view from the top.

'I'm glad you could come, Yukio.'

I turned to see Natsuko with her arm around the Lump. I almost didn't recognize her. She was wearing a T-shirt and overalls with paint on them. And she had a scarf around her head. She looked just like a normal woman.

'I'm glad too,' I said. But I felt a bit embarrassed,

seeing her that way, and so I went around to the back of the van.

Me and the monk unloaded the wood and the paint and the rest of the supplies, while the Lump looked on. 'You're supposed to be helping, you know.' Then I saw the shinais. 'How did they get here?'

'Me,' said the Lump.

'What did you bring them for?'

She picked up a box and headed to the temple. 'Practice,' she said.

I took two and followed her. 'Practice? We're here to work.'

'Birds!' said the Lump.

Shaded under a Japanese maple, and surrounded by bonsai trees, was a lilied pond with cranes in it. They crept through the water on their long legs, inching towards the large green dragonflies that hovered above the reeds.

'Fish!' said the Lump.

Huge koi carp came to the surface with their mouths open, as though they were expecting us to feed them.

'Beautiful fish!' said the Lump.

I just rolled my eyes and walked away. The Lump

ran to catch up and we passed a huge bronze bell, housed under its own roof. We crossed the leafy courtyard, and taking off our shoes we followed Natsuko up the temple steps. As soon as we entered we saw a statue of Buddha in the form of a woman. She was holding a flower in one hand and a golden staff in the other, and she was so tall her head reached up to the ceiling.

'The statue's been here since the temple was built,' said Natsuko. 'It was damaged by the fire, but the craftsmen have done a good job repairing her.'

I put down the boxes and turned to see the Lump praying at the altar. She bowed to the Buddha and came over to us. 'Beautiful,' she said.

'Yes, she is beautiful,' said Natsuko, and smiling she put her arm around the Lump again. I didn't like that. I found myself feeling a little jealous.

'What would you like me to do?' I asked.

'Well, the floor needs brushing and mopping,' said Natsuko. 'And the courtyard needs sweeping. Nothing exciting, I'm afraid.'

'I'll get started,' I said.

I went to take a brush but the Lump beat me to it. She started brushing like mad. She was just showing off. Then somewhere an electric saw started up.

Banging and hammering followed. Natsuko rubbed the side of her head, as though the noise hurt her, and I could see that she still wasn't well. When she noticed me looking she tried to smile.

'It's just a headache,' she said. 'Now, I have to get on with the painting. I'll see you two at lunch.'

Me and the Lump bowed to Natsuko as she walked away. Then I turned to her. 'You're such a little show-off.' I said. But the Lump ignored me, and looking smug she started to brush the floor. And so I went to find another brush.

We worked side by side to get the temple floor clean and we worked well. I thought the Lump would wander off once Natsuko had gone but she didn't. She helped me brush all the wooden shavings and the sawdust into one pile and then we scooped it up. Then we got some mops and buckets and mopped the entire floor, except for behind the altar, where we weren't allowed to go. But the floor looked funny when we'd finished – it was a mixture of old and new planks. A dark-skinned labourer appeared with a big tin of varnish and a couple of brushes.

'You want to do it?' he asked.

'Sure,' I said.

'Me as well!' said the Lump.

'Of course you as well!' said the labourer. And he laughed as he walked away.

'This is my job,' I said to her. 'You go and look for something to clean.'

'No!' said the Lump.

She grabbed a paintbrush and held it to her chest. I knew I wouldn't get it back without a fight and so I gave in. 'OK, but you'd better not make a mess!'

We knelt over a couple of new planks and started to paint. The varnish was the same brown colour as the old planks, and as soon as we put it on it blended in. I kept my eye on the Lump at first. I was sure she was going to drip varnish everywhere or end up working on the wrong planks, but she didn't. She worked slowly and patiently, like an artist painting a picture. Except that artists don't have their tongues out when they paint.

It took hours to do, but it was easy work, and when we were finished we were proud that we'd done a good job.

'Let's get started outside,' I said.

The Lump bowed to the Buddha and ran to get the witches' brooms. She handed one to me and we brushed up the leaves in the courtyard. It felt nice being in the sunshine after the gloom of the temple, and we had a great view. Fuji's white peak was brilliant against the blue sky, while its base was green with beech trees. Red maples ran around the hills and cedars lined the field of wheat, which had turned golden with the mid-morning sun. The whole place made me feel kind of tranquil. But most Buddhist temples do that. It's a Zen thing.

The Lump looked up at the sky. 'Dolphin,' she said.

Like an idiot I looked up as well. Then I gave her a look to let her know to stop bothering me.

'Dolphin,' said the Lump, and pointed.

I saw a fluffy cloud that was shaped like a dolphin. It even had a dolphin's face and a dolphin's smile. I don't know why I hadn't seen it in the first place. But it was just like the Lump to see things that other people don't. It's like she's living in a different world.

It took us the rest of the morning to get the courtyard clean. And then, taking the garbage bags, we followed the dirt path down to the incinerator. I took two of the larger bags and the Lump took a small one, but she looked like she was struggling with it.

'You want me to take that?'

'No,' said the Lump, looking determined.

'You're very strong,' I said.

'Very strong,' said the Lump.

She sort of made me smile then and I felt sorry for her. 'So why do these kids pick on you?'

'Mean,' said the Lump.

'Well, you should be mean to them.'

'No,' said the Lump. 'Don't wanna be mean.'

'Well, they'll just keep picking on you.'

The Lump pondered this all the way to the incinerator. Then she looked up at me. 'Don't wanna be mean,' she said.

You could never reason with the Lump and so I never tried. One of the nuns came over a low hill. 'Lunch is ready.'

'Lunch!' said the Lump, and dropping everything she ran back down the path.

I followed her, and rinsing my hands under a tap at the side of the temple, I headed down to the field of wheat. A table had been placed in front of it and there were a dozen people sitting down. They were the labourers and the nuns, and the monk who'd driven us there.

The Lump took a seat at the head of the table

and sat there as happy as a princess. As soon as I sat down Natsuko said a short prayer, and when she'd finished the bowls and plates were passed. I took a bowl of ramen noodles in a miso broth. It contained a thick slice of pork, a whole egg and a square of seaweed. The Lump took a bowl of thick white udon noodles, which she drowned in soy sauce and slurped until they were gone. She drank the broth from the bowl before picking up her chopsticks and starting on her beef fried rice. The Lump was so happy eating she was dancing a little in her seat. She didn't notice she was entertaining the dark-skinned labourers. They smiled at each other and then one of them passed her a plate of sushi, which she took with a small bow and devoured in a matter of minutes.

'Good appetite,' said the labourer.

We finished by drinking green tea in the heat with the warm wind blowing around us. And when the labourers were done they gave a dignified bow and went back to work. Natsuko and the nuns took the dishes away and the Lump helped them. Then Natsuko and the Lump came back carrying apple juice and the Lump took a seat and pushed a glass towards me.

'What do you want me to do now?' I asked.

'The roofer needs a hand, if you're not scared of heights,' said Natsuko.

'I'm not.'

'You know, Mikazuki was just telling me how much she likes Tokyo.'

I couldn't remember the nuns' names and so I didn't know who she was talking about.

'Which one's Mikazuki?' I asked.

Natsuko gave me a disapproving look. I turned to see the Lump with her arms folded. She had a 'you didn't even know my name!' look slapped all over her face. I couldn't help but laugh. It wasn't that I didn't know her name. It was just that the twins used to call her Mika. And I hadn't remembered the name Mikazuki because it never suited her.

'Don't pay him any attention, Mikazuki, he's just teasing,' said Natsuko, and took the last of the dishes to the kitchen.

But the Lump wasn't buying into it. She glared at me like I'd just insulted her ancestors. And so I looked at the temple to avoid her gaze. 'We did a good job on that floor, didn't we?' I said, but she still wasn't happy. I laughed again. 'I was just joking! Of course I know your name.' But the Lump knew I was lying. She climbed down from the table, while still giving me the dirty look, and mumbling she walked away. I laughed as I drank my juice, but then I felt a shinai tap my shoulder.

'Fight,' said the Lump, and put a shinai next to me.

'No, it's too hot.'

'Fight,' she said, and poked me in the ribs.

'No!'

'Coward!'

I jumped up and grabbed the shinai. The Lump screamed and laughed and fled to the field and so I chased her through the wheat, which cracked and snapped around us. The Lump couldn't run as fast as I could, but she ran faster in circles than anyone I'd ever seen. And she had the advantage because the wheat was as tall as she was. But I soon gained on her, and raising the shinai I got ready to strike. But all of a sudden I tripped and fell. The sneaky Lump doubled back and started whacking me. I blocked her blows with my arm, but she was so aggressive she made me laugh. 'Pack it in!' I said. But she wouldn't and so I got up and chased her again. Suddenly the Lump turned and going down on one knee she whacked my leg. I tripped and fell, but I was ready for the counter. But she didn't attack. I stood up, but I couldn't see her. I couldn't even see her trail in the wheat. 'Who's the coward now?' I shouted. But she was hiding and she wouldn't come out. I stood still for a minute, hoping she'd give herself away, but all I could hear was the wind hissing in the wheat. 'You want some cake?' I shouted, but she still wouldn't show herself and so I left. But I had to admire those tactics. Making me chase her into the wheat where she had the advantage. Then fighting when she wanted to and retreating when she didn't. For a kid who was supposed to be slow, the Lump was turning out to be as sneaky as a ninja.

I walked around the side of the temple and climbing a ladder I helped the old roofer. Which meant I passed him a tile whenever he needed one. It was really hot on the roof, and so I did like he did and put a scarf around my head. But I liked being up high. I've always liked heights and it had a great view of Fuji. And I could see all the surrounding land, and down into the valley where the town was. There was a huge blue lake, way in the distance, and beyond that I could see the bullet train blasting through the countryside. I looked at the field every now and then, to see if I could see the Lump, but I couldn't. She was either staying hidden or she'd fallen asleep.

It was hours before she surfaced, or rather her palm tree did. It looked like a little black bird floating above the wheat. Then she raised her shinai and it moved through the field like a periscope at sea. The Lump gave out a war cry and her shinai crashed into the wheat and disappeared. And that's the way she spent the rest of the afternoon: battling imaginary armies who she'd beat to death by whacking the wheat. And every time she cried out the old roofer chuckled to himself. 'Sister?'

'Cousin,' I said.

'Nice kid.'

The Lump was all right in small doses, I suppose. And the day had been better for her being there. So much so that I hadn't thought about Riko or the rest of the yakuza gangsters that I was at war with. But listening to the Lump's war cries brought it back. And when it came it hit me hard because my guard was down. But battle had to be done. The twins had to be avenged, and the yakuza had to know that there were people who'd stand up to them.

'Done,' said the old roofer with a satisfied smile, and we both climbed down.

And then, as if a bell had sounded, everyone began to pack up. Tools were put in the van and the sweating labourers washed under the tap. Natsuko changed back into her usual robes and then she came towards me dressed in white. 'Where's the little one?'

Just then we heard a war cry and the Lump burst through the wheat with her shinai raised.

She looked around as though surprised to be out in the open. The labourers laughed and the nuns laughed too. The Lump's face was flushed and her hair was covered in wheat seeds.

'Come on, little one,' said Natsuko. 'Time to go home.'

We all got in the van and headed back to Tokyo. It was full then and so I sat in the back with the Lump. She put her head against my shoulder and returned to reading her manga. But I knew that before long she'd be asleep. I rolled down the window and took one last look at Fuji, whose peak was tinted red by the dying sun. I felt a pang of fear and a touch of sadness then. Because I knew I was returning to the battlefield. And part of me really didn't want to.

But there was another part that couldn't wait to be back. And by the time the sun had set that would be the only part that mattered.

It was a hot night and there was a lot of traffic on the road. I'd ridden my bike all over Tokyo but I hadn't seen a single yakuza. And I really wanted to find one. I'd already been to the Kabukicho, but that Korean creep wasn't there. And I'd spent an hour staking out the clubs in Shibuya, but again I couldn't find anyone. And what made it worse was that Tokyo wasn't a city with an uptown and downtown. It was like five cities rolled into one. Shinjuku, Shibuya and Ikebukuro were like cities. And Ginza and Ueno were cities as well. And so finding someone was damn near impossible. Especially when you didn't know where they hung out.

But as I rode I thought about fate. Both my father and my grandmother had taught me the importance of duty and self-sacrifice. I was practically brought up on the seven virtues of the bushido code, and I've being doing kendo since I was four. And now I was living by the code and using my skills to fight the yakuza. I was actually starting to think that all of this was meant to happen. I mean, I'd gone into the Tanakas' apartment and left them for dead. And I'd got out of there even though the place was surrounded. And a feeling came over me when I thought about it. I felt powerful. It's as though there really was an energy force flowing through me.

But the Lump messed things up. When I was with her I never felt like war. I don't know why, because she irritated me most of the time. You'd think she'd have the opposite effect, but she didn't. She had this horrible habit of dragging me into her own little world where there were dolphins and ants and things. And I didn't want to be there. Maybe I should stay away from her.

I slowed by Akasaka Palace, and turning away from the stone wall I headed down the narrow road that went by the Tanakas' apartment block. They say a criminal always returns to the scene of the crime, but in my mind I wasn't a criminal. And I wasn't returning; I was just passing by. I expected to see cops or yakuza gangsters watching from the rooftop, but the street was surprisingly empty. I knew then that Riko wasn't there. Because if she had been, her bodyguards would have been outside.

I passed the Imperial Palace, and heading into the heart of Ginza I saw that the pavements were swarming with late-night shoppers. I never realized that Ginza was such a night city, and a city of lights at that. Bright lights and billboards were blazing everywhere and spotlit posters were advertising the latest clothes. There were more lights when I turned a corner, but they belonged to the cops.

I pulled up to see a woman crying next to her totalled Toyota and a guy in a Nissan sitting behind a smashed screen. Lights flashed from digital cameras and cellphones as the crowd captured the image. I heard a droning sound and a helicopter hovered above us, no doubt taking its own pictures. Then sirens sounded and an ambulance came to the scene. I was just about to move off when someone tapped my helmet. I turned to see one of the girls from school. She smiled and gave me a quick wave, and then she ran to a group of girls who waved as well. I was debating on finding a place to park but a whistle blew. 'Don't stop there,' shouted a cop, and he waved me on.

I cut through the Ginza Crossing, and turning down one of its fancy backstreets I started a grid search. There were lots of sushi bars and restaurants, and a sax blasting from a phoney jazz bar. And there were lots of fancy stores where women in designer clothes were waiting for someone to come in. Not exactly a yakuza hangout, but you never know.

I passed the packed Apple Store and turned off at the gold-coloured Cartier building to continue my search. I took a turn around the Conrad and Peninsular hotels but all I saw was well-dressed rich people. I'd heard that Riko hung out in Ginza sometimes, but I couldn't imagine her in those places; she had no class.

When I got hungry I cruised across the Sumida River and pulling up outside a FamilyMart I bought a couple of pieces of fried chicken. I ate them while walking back towards Ginza and the river. There were brightly lit barges on the water and tourist boats going by. I could hear a tour guide's smooth voice and see the flashes from the cameras reflected in the water. Downriver was the bustling fish market where I used to go with my father as a boy, and beyond that were Ginza's huge hotels. It was a nice night and there was a cool breeze by the river.

My mind kind of mellowed then, and I tried to think of the name of the girl who'd tapped my helmet. She had a really nice face and good teeth. I like girls with good teeth. I remember seeing her talking to Miko one time. I even think she was at the funeral.

Maybe she was interested in me. It would be nice if she was. But then I felt so guilty I sank. Miko's ashes were still warm and I was thinking of someone else. And what sort of girl was she anyway? Tapping on my helmet when she knew what Miko had meant to me! I felt so angry when I thought about it. And where the hell are these yakuza cowards who were responsible for her death? I swear I wanted to find one so badly . . . Then a thought came to me. The only place I hadn't been to was the florist where Hiroshi threw the brick.

I went back to the bike, and kick-starting the engine I rode back across the bridge. All the way to the florist's I kept telling myself that no one would be there. But I kept the bike at full throttle all the same, and I was soon passing through Roppongi. I stayed on the outskirts of Shibuya to avoid the heavy traffic. Then crossing the tracks at Uehara station I headed down the long, narrow road that led to the shop. As I neared it I saw there was a light on and so I pulled up behind a parked car.

The street was badly lit and walled in with apartment blocks. There were shops on the ground floor, but they were all shut and the street itself was almost deserted. I took the nylon bag from under the seat and made my way down to the florist's. I held the sword close to my side, in case anyone came, and I kept my helmet on because I'd left my hat at home.

I stopped on the opposite side of the road and peered into the store. All the flowers had gone, but there were two men sitting inside. They were eating a takeaway. One of them was dressed in a suit and tie, and he must have been about sixty. The other was in his twenties and he was wearing a T-shirt that showed off his muscles. I could see them talking, but I couldn't make out what they were saying.

There was a blind alley next to the florist's and the back door was open. If I could hear what they were saying I'd know if they were yakuza or not. I crept down the alley, but just as I neared the door I heard them coming out. I jumped into a doorway and hid in the shadows.

'How long do you think it will take me to become a soldier?'

'You've only been a trainee for a year.'

I was sure they were yakuza. I peered around the corner. Light from the doorway was shining on the two men, who were lighting up cigarettes.

The younger guy leaned on a parked car and took

a long drag. 'But with your guidance, Basho, I'll get there. I want to be a soldier by the time I'm twenty-five. You know Suzuki made lieutenant by then.'

'Yes, but he was Yoshio Kodama's grandson,' said the older man.

'And even that didn't stop him from being killed.'

The old man looked away. 'Suzuki wasn't killed.'

'No. How did he die? Can you tell me?'

'Sure. It's no secret,' said the old man. 'He started dating Takahashi's daughter. It's always a mistake to date a boss's daughter. Then he made an even bigger mistake: he dumped her. Takahashi, taking it as a slight upon himself, had him kicked out. And Suzuki, with nowhere else to go, fell on his sword.'

'He committed suicide? Couldn't he have done something else?'

'What was he going to do, serve sushi? No, you can have a good career in the yakuza. But it doesn't prepare you for anything else.'

As soon as I heard those words the butterflies came. I slid the sword from its mounting and gripped it tight. I was just about to step out when I heard . . .

'And what about this Psycho Killer? You think he's an assassin sent by Tomi Yamamoto?'

The older man sounded bewildered. 'Why would

Tomi Yamamoto kill Uncle Benni's niece? It serves no purpose.'

'I suppose not,' said the younger guy, and sucked on his cigarette. 'You ever meet Louise Tanaka? I heard she was a bit of a psycho herself.'

'I never met her or any of the Tanakas. And I've never so much as spoken to Uncle Benni. The only person I ever meet is my lieutenant. And he doesn't say much when I do.'

I was considering leaving it. They weren't exactly big shots. But it was obvious that they'd taken over the florist's, which meant that the owner had paid off his son's debts by giving them the place . . . No, I couldn't leave it. They were the enemy.

The young guy suddenly perked up. 'Tell me, Basho, who do you think is the greater godfather – Uncle Benni or Yoshio Kodama?'

'I don't know,' said the old man, sounding bored. 'They're from different generations.' He stamped on his cigarette. 'Come on, let's lock up.'

I could feel my legs quivering as I stepped out of the doorway. Both men kind of froze when they saw me. And then they saw the sword.

'It's him!' shouted the old man, and ran for the door.

I beat him to it and stabbed him through the back. Then I turned, expecting an attack. But the younger guy had jumped in the car and locked the doors. He was searching frantically for the keys but he couldn't find them. 'Basho! Basho!' he shouted. 'If you've killed Basho, I'll kill you!'

'You'll have to get out the car first!'

'Basho!' He started to cry.

'You'll never make lieutenant blubbering like that!' I shouted. But I knew I couldn't get him and so I walked away.

'You think that helmet hides your face, but it doesn't!' he screamed. 'I'll remember you!'

I froze with my back to him. I couldn't leave him alive! I looked for something to break the window with, but there was nothing. I tried to kick in the glass but my sneakers were too soft. He started shouting into his cell. Then he looked at me. 'There's a crew on the way! You'd better get out of here!'

I saw a lighter on the ground. I ran to the old man and took off his tie.

'Please . . . tell my daughter I loved her.'

I ignored him, and ripping off the petrol cap I shoved the tie inside. Then I lit it. I tried to run

184

before it exploded, but BOOM! It was like a bomb had gone off! The car filled up with fire and smoke, and the guy just sat there burning.

I grabbed the mounting and bolted back down the alley. I put the sword in the nylon bag and walked out on to the street. Lights were going on all over the place and windows were opening.

'What happened?' asked an old woman from her window.

A man in a kimono came to his door. 'Sounded like a gas explosion.'

A young woman with a baby pointed from her balcony. 'There's a fire down the alley!'

I kept the sword at my left side and slipped it under the seat. I was about to ride away, but there were too many people by then; it would have looked suspicious. And so I rode back towards the scene and pulled up like a passer-by. The car was ablaze and black smoke billowed from the burning rubber. People were running towards it with water. Men were shouting and a woman began to scream. I watched two silhouettes drag the young guy's burning body from the car. Then I noticed dozens more people standing in their nightclothes, their faces lit up by the flames. They stared in wonder at the bodies and the burning car. Some of them seemed terrified but others looked on like happy children watching a horror show.

And there I stood in the aftermath of battle like so many samurai before me, but the feeling of power that I'd felt earlier had gone. I took no pleasure in killing the old guy. And I'd have sooner killed his apprentice quickly, with the sword, rather than blow him up. But then I remembered something that my father once told me when he was talking about the Warring States period. He said that war wasn't always waged against evil people. Sometimes it was simply waged against someone from the opposite side. I watched the flames until I heard the sirens. And then slowly I cruised away.

10

The dojo became loud with screams and shouts and the sound of bamboo cracking against bamboo. I watched Akeno closely. He was very slowly inching to my left. So slowly, in fact, that you could hardly see him move. And then he screamed, '*men!*' to indicate he was going to strike my head, and stamping his foot on the floor he struck. I blocked the blow and tried to counter but he was too fast. He attacked again. Our shinais rose and pushed against each other and then we pushed away. I tried to strike his *men* as he was going back but I barely caught his shoulder. Then we both struck at the same time. Our shinais cracked with such force that a section of bamboo broke off.

We stopped and circled each other. Without

thinking I jumped forward and struck his right *kote*. It was a perfect strike and Sensei Kubo raised his hand to indicate a point. Akeno came again and I struck his torso, or *do*. But I was off balance and so there wasn't enough power to score a point. Then with two lightning strikes he struck my *do* and *men*. They were so fast I never saw either. He wasn't national champion for nothing. He made another forward thrust to my throat, but I dodged it. I caught his *kote* as he backed away, but it didn't count. Then we both leaped forward at the same time. I made a perfect strike to his *do*, but screaming, '*Men!*' he struck my head.

'Enough!' said Sensei Kubo. 'Well done, you two.'

My final blow had been good, but he was the winner overall. That said, I'd never done so well against him. We knelt on the wooden floor and bowed to each other. Then taking off my *men* and head towel I stood up.

'Well done, Yukio,' said Akeno. 'Your skill is really starting to show.'

'Thank you, Akeno.' I was so happy to hear him say this I bowed again.

He left to fight Alex the Austrian, and Sensei Kubo came and stood next to me. He didn't say anything, but he had a satisfied look on his face, proud that his protégé was doing well.

We watched the Lump fight G.I. Joe on the other side of the dojo. She looked funny in her kendo armour, like a miniature warrior. And what made her funnier was how aggressive she was. She screamed and attacked like a demon and she was so quick on her feet! She scurried around in circles so fast that G.I. Joe looked under pressure. I mean, he was only joking, but I could tell he was finding it difficult to line her up. Then she dropped on to one knee and struck his ankle. He pretended to be angry and complained to Anna, who was refereeing the bout. And so Anna explained the rules to the Lump. But the Lump kept peering around her shoulder; she was dying to attack G.I. Joe. And as soon as Anna was out of the way, she did.

'She's like a bee attacking a bear,' said Sensei Kubo. 'And she seems to have a natural talent. Maybe it runs in your family,' he said and went over to watch the bout.

I felt good then. He rarely paid compliments, and when he did you knew he meant it.

Then everyone in the dojo was lining up to fight the Lump. Akeno took G.I. Joe's place and pretended to take it seriously. The others shouted advice as they fought and laughed and joked as she attacked. They really took to the Lump, and for the first time I was proud that she was my cousin.

When I was done for the day I got changed and waited for her at the entrance. It was a good ten minutes before she turned up. She came trotting down the stairs with her rucksack on her back.

'Where have you been?'

'Talking,' said the Lump.

'Like you ever talk.' I was just about to tell her off but Sensei Kubo came out.

'It was a pleasure meeting you, Mikazuki,' he said with a slight bow. 'I hope you will come again.'

The Lump bowed with more than a little ceremony. You'd think she was bowing to the emperor or someone.

'Yes, make sure you bring her again, Yukio,' said G.I. Joe. 'I want to get even for some of those blows I took.'

The Lump laughed a little as she followed me to the subway. Then she pretended to be calm, but I knew she was buzzing. Her palm tree was tingling with static and her eyes were shining bright. I decided to put her in her place. 'You did OK, I suppose. But don't let it go to your head.'

'No,' said the Lump.

I gave her a hard look but she held my gaze. I walked on for a bit, then stopped. 'They want me to bring you again, and I will. But you have to stop hitting your opponent's feet. It's bad manners.'

The Lump looked up at me. 'OK.'

I walked on, but I stopped again. 'It reflects badly on me if you fight dirty. You understand?'

'Understand,' said the Lump.

But I don't think she did understand. She was just humouring me.

We changed trains at Ikebukuro and then we took the Yamanote line down to Shinjuku. It was packed with people, but we managed to get seats, at least I did. The Lump squashed herself in between me and some guy and made us both uncomfortable. I was going to tell her to get up, but then I saw the newspaper headlines: 'Psycho Killer Strikes Again'. And underneath the photograph of the two bodies in the alley it asked: 'Serial Killer, Vigilante or Assassin?

'Hungry,' said the Lump.

I looked down at her. 'When aren't you hungry?'

'Always hungry,' said the Lump.

'Come on. Here's our stop.'

It was hot and sunny when we came out of the station, and I wanted to get home. But I'd bought the Lump an ice cream and so she was in no rush. At least three times I had to tell her to catch up, but she kept stopping to stare at things. And it didn't have to be anything special. A tree or a plant or a tin can. One time I turned around and she was staring at a common daisy that had grown between the cracks in the pavement.

'Will you hurry up?'

But as we turned into our street I saw a man outside the house. He was wearing a suit and he had something in his hand. He could be a yakuza hit man! But they couldn't know who I was or where I lived. Don't get paranoid, I thought. But just because you're paranoid that doesn't mean that they're not after you.

'Listen – you go straight into the house, OK?'

'OK,' said the Lump, and pushing open the steel door she ran into the garden.

The man was short and slim and the thing in his hand was a notebook. His face was glum and his greying black hair was combed back tight, making a perfect rectangle of his forehead. 'Yukio Takeda?' he asked.

The fact that he knew my name was enough to start my heart pounding. 'Yes.'

'My name is Detective Maki. I'd like to ask you a few questions. Is there somewhere we can talk?'

My mind ran into a frenzy and my stomach turned, but I tried to stay calm. 'Sure,' I said, and held open the steel door. But as soon as I did I realized my mistake. The bike was in the garden and the sword was under the seat! He'll see it! We passed a spade. For an insane second it crossed my mind to kill him.

He took off his suit jacket and put it over one of the iron chairs. Then taking a seat he put his notebook on the iron table. 'Such a beautiful garden,' he said. 'And so much space.'

I looked at the bike and froze. The sword had gone.

'Do you mind?' When I turned to him he was showing me a pack of cigarettes.

'No,' I said, and took a seat. I was panicking inside but I tried to relax.

He lit up a cigarette and sat back. 'You were friends with the Kobayashi twins, yes?'

'Yes.'

He checked his notebook. 'And you also knew Goro Kakomo, known to all as Kako?'

I decided not to lie. 'Yes.'

'We've discovered two things that connect Miko Kobayashi and Kako. One we are not going to divulge. The other is you.'

I watched a wasp crawling around the table. I had a sudden urge to crush it.

'Tell me something.'

'What?' I asked.

'Tell me anything.'

'We don't know why the twins . . . did what they did. And all I know about Kako is what I read in the paper.'

'When was the last time you saw him?'

'In a club called Paradise, a few weeks back.'

He pointed at our small pond. 'What sort of flowers are they?'

The question threw me. 'I don't know.'

'Of course you do. They're lotus blossoms.' He stood up and examined them more closely.

'You know what they say about lotus blossoms? They grow at the bottom of the pond in complete darkness. Their darkness reflects man's ignorance because he can't see the truth. The seed grows towards the sunlight, just as man grows towards the light of the truth . . . Miko was your girlfriend, was she not?'

I could tell by the way his back stiffened that he was no longer concerned with the lotus blossoms. 'No,' I said.

'Funny, because I hear she was.' He sat down and took a long drag on his cigarette. And as he did he glared at me. 'Of course she wasn't. She was a Buraku after all. A young man from a good family, like yourself, would never get involved with that sort. Am I right?'

I could have killed him! Right there and then! But I knew he was baiting me.

'Miko was not my girlfriend, but she was a friend. And a finer person you'll never meet. If you're going to insult her, you'll have to leave.'

'Sorry, kid. Just doing my job.' He made a note in his notebook. 'On the night Kako was killed, where were you?'

'Here probably.'

'What about last night?'

'With me.'

I turned to see the Lump, who bowed to the detective.

He chuckled when he saw her. 'What? All night?'

'Tummy trouble,' said the Lump, who'd never had tummy trouble in her life.

'Yes,' said the detective in a weary way. 'There's a lot of that going around.'

Yoshe came out. 'Oh, I didn't know you had company, Yukio.'

The detective stood up and gave a short bow. 'Mrs Takeda?'

'No, she's inside. Would you like to see her?'

'If I may.'

'One moment,' said Yoshe, and went inside to ask. Then she came back. 'If you'd like to follow me . . .'

The detective stepped on his cigarette and went inside. It was quiet then, and the silence was worse than having him sitting in front of me. I had a sickening feeling in my stomach and I was finding it hard not to fidget. But when I heard voices coming from Grandmother's room I had to stand up. The Lump didn't look happy either. She stood with her back to the wall and bit her lip. And she stayed that way until she heard the detective say goodbye. He came out and picked up his jacket.

'Thank you for your time, Yukio.' He looked at the Lump. 'And I hope your tummy gets better.'

'Would you like tea, detective, before you leave?' asked Yoshe.

'I would, but I have a dozen people to interview today and it's already noon.'

Yoshe bowed and went back in the kitchen.

I opened the steel door for him and he stepped through. 'I don't think I'll be bothering you again, Yukio. But let me ask you one last question: did you like Kako?'

'No,' I said.

He looked satisfied. 'No, nobody did.' He put on his jacket and looked down the street. 'What about Louise Tanaka?'

'I never knew her,' I said. 'Is this to do with the—'

'Sorry, I'm not allowed to discuss an ongoing case. Enjoy the rest of your day.'

I watched him walk away and then I closed the steel door. 'Where is it?'

'No!' said the Lump.

She tried to run but I grabbed her. 'Where?'

'Not telling!'

But then I saw the sword hidden in the plants. 'You dummy!' I pushed her away and grabbing it I went inside. I made sure Yoshe wasn't there before running upstairs.

But she came out of the kitchen. 'Yukio . . . ?' She cringed a little, as if she didn't like to ask. 'Was that about the twins?'

I kept the sword hidden. 'Yes.'

'I'm glad they're looking into it. There was something not quite right about the whole business.'

'Does Grandmother want to see me?'

Yoshe looked puzzled. 'She never said anything.'

I went to my room and hid the sword in the cupboard. Then I went out on the balcony to make sure the detective had gone. But I saw him peering through the window of the twins' apartment. I didn't think he suspected me of the killings. I mean, he'd left after talking to Grandmother. But I didn't think I'd seen the last of him either.

I heard the Lump going to her room. I had to think about what to say to her. She was as devious as that detective when she wanted to be. I mean, I knew she knew nothing, but she sensed things, which was even worse. When I looked in her room she was sitting on her bedroll pretending to read, but she wasn't. Her eyes were fixed on one spot and her facial expression was blank, except that she looked a little upset. I felt bad then. Somehow she'd sensed I was in trouble and tried to help.

'You hungry?'

The Lump ignored me.

'Listen, a terrible thing happened to the twins. And the people responsible—'

The Lump gave me the stop sign. 'Do no harm!' she said.

'Hey, you're my cousin! You're supposed to be on my side!'

The Lump looked down at her comic and sulked. 'Do no harm.'

'You dummy. I don't know why I bother with you!'

I went back to my room and out on the balcony. I was relieved when I saw the detective walking down the street. He'd given me quite a scare. But there's no way he was going to stop me from carrying out my duty! And neither was the Lump. She came out in the garden and sat in a chair with her arms folded. She wasn't speaking to me and she wanted me to know. Then she started mumbling like a real grouch.

'First sign of madness,' I called. But she stuck her nose in the air and looked away. 'You won't ignore me when you're hungry.' And she wouldn't either. A bowl of beef fried rice would put things right. She was easily bought.

I stood in the doorway, which stunk of pee, and watched the Korean trying to entice people into his massage parlour, which stood at the end of a brightly lit road. Most people turned back before they reached the Korean's place, because it was on the outskirts of the Kabukicho and all the streets after it were dark. But some didn't – they came all the way to the end, and when they did the Korean would approach them. He'd hold out his hand to foreign tourists, and if they took it he'd hold on to it. Or if they were Japanese he'd bow and follow them for a bit. No one was interested, but he didn't care; he was a real creep.

I liked it that the Korean was connected to the yakuza. I mean, assaulting my mother was a good enough reason to kill him, but working for the yakuza made him more of a legitimate target. But the question now was how to get away once it was done. If I attacked him in the street it would be a quick bolt back to the bike, which was parked down a side street. But that meant that people would see, and some might give chase. If I waited for him to go inside, which he did from time to time, I could follow him in. But just like with the Tanakas' place, I didn't know who else was in there.

I scanned the outside of the massage parlour. It looked like a small shop except that there was a curtain drawn across the window. I figured there wouldn't be much room inside to swing the sword, and so I thought about a kendo term called *ma-ai*. In general it refers to the distance between the tips of the opponents' shinais when held in the *chudan* stance, but it also refers to space. The swordsman needs to assess his surroundings and place himself in a position where he has the advantage. If I followed the Korean inside, the first thing I'd have to do was check the height of the ceiling. If it was too low, I wouldn't be able to raise the sword. And I'd have to look out for things like posts and lamps and anything else that could get in the way.

He spat and went inside. I pulled my hood over my head, and keeping the sword close I crossed the street. Before I knew it I was opening the door and stepping inside. It felt strange, like being in a dream, but the first thing I noticed was that the place was empty. I drew the sword and held both pieces behind my right leg. Then I went down three steps and stood there with my heart banging. It was like a basement inside and the ceiling was low, but there was plenty of space otherwise.

There were racks of smutty DVDs and magazines against the wall, and there was a counter by the window. And there were partitioned cubicles with beds in them and curtains at the side. When I heard someone coming down a flight of stairs my stomach turned. A bookcase moved and the Korean came from behind it. 'Welcome, welcome. Take a seat and let's see what we can do for you!'

I should have killed him then, but I hesitated and he moved behind the counter. He looked more creepy close up. He had a bit of a beard, because he couldn't be bothered to shave, and his skin was as greasy as his hair.

'You're a bit young, aren't you? Is that why you have your hood up, trying to hide your age? Don't worry, everyone has to start somewhere.' He peered under my hood. 'I know you from somewhere, right?' The smile left his face. 'What's that you've got behind your back?'

I felt dizzy. For a second I thought I was going to faint. He came out from behind the counter.

'Who are you? What is that?'

'A sword,' I said.

His face froze into a puzzled look. 'Is this a joke?'

Suddenly I dropped the mounting and took the sword in both hands. He turned to run, but I jumped forward and slashed down. The blade hacked into his back and cracked his ribs. He dropped on to one knee. I heard someone scream behind me. I swung the sword as I turned. A woman raised her hand and her fingers fell to the floor. Her eyes widened as she looked in horror at her missing digits. She collapsed and clutched her bleeding hand. Then a guy came through the front door. I hit him with the back of the sword and he cried out and cowered. Then another guy came in. How many perverts does Tokyo have? I beat him with the sword and he roared and ran out. Then the woman without the fingers started to scream. I heard an almighty crash and the Korean jumped through the window. I grabbed the mounting and ran outside. The Korean had collapsed on the pavement. People were running to his rescue. Then that yakuza biker pulled up on his chopper. A woman screamed and a man tried to grab me. I pushed him away and ran.

I sprinted down the street, and taking a right I ran down a darkened road. But then I heard the chopper coming after me. I put the mounting on a bonnet, and standing between two parked cars I got ready. And then, just as he passed, I swung the sword. I spun around and landed on the bonnet of the car. But the rider was still going down the street. The blade hadn't made contact! But then I noticed blood, as fine as mist, spraying from his neck.

The sirens were far away at first and then they were close. I grabbed the mounting and ran for the bike. I pushed the sword under the seat, jammed on my helmet and rode away. Then I heard a crash, and reaching the lights I saw what it was. The biker's mangled body was crushed between a car and his chopper. The shocked driver held his head in his hands, while a woman threw up at the side of the road.

I cut through Shinjuku, where thousands of revellers were enjoying their night out, and passed by Shinjuku station, where a long-haired band was blasting away. I followed the overhead down towards Sangubashi station. Before I knew it I was riding into my street.

I stopped before I reached my house, and turning off the engine I pushed the bike into the garden. The air crackled with electricity and a bolt of lightning lit up the sky. I opened the front door, and climbing the stairs I went straight to my room. I never even got undressed. I just threw down the bedroll and pulled the duvet over my head. Then I lay there, shocked and shivering. I didn't want to think about the woman without fingers, or the biker crushed under the car. But they were all I could think of. And then thunder rocked around the sky. It was like the gods were angry at me. And if that wasn't bad enough, I started to feel like someone was watching me. Slowly I pulled the duvet from my head. A flash of lightning lit up the room.

'Argh! What the hell are you doing?'

'Lightning!' said the Lump.

'You scared the hell out of me, you dummy!'

The Lump stroked the Om's ugly head. 'Don't like!'

I sat up and held my head in my hands. Could this night get any scarier? 'OK, put your stuff over there and go to sleep.'

She ran out, and coming back with her bedding she laid it out at the far end of the room. A loud clap of thunder sent her diving under the duvet. Then her hand came out and she placed that ugly head so it was facing me.

'Night, Om,' said the Lump.

I pulled the duvet over my head and tried to sleep. And I found myself wishing I'd never wake up. And I mean never.

11

I threw the paper on the seat in front of me and watched the land go by. But I could still see the headlines. 'More Killings in the Kabukicho . . . Dead Biker Rides into Traffic . . .' The article said that the woman who'd lost her fingers was a poor Chinese girl, and that they'd already been sewn back on. I was relieved that she was going to be OK. I really was. But I still felt agitated. I'd slept badly, and when I did I had bad dreams. And they revolved around that Korean. I thought I'd be glad that I killed him, but I wasn't, and I couldn't understand why. But then once again I saw him assault my mother. 'You should be proud, Yukio, that you defended your family's honour. Stop being weak.'

There were a lot of eyewitness accounts, but no

one had seen my face. One guy guessed my age at about thirty-five. Another guy said I was only five foot six. How could they get it so wrong? And the police had nothing else to go on because there was no CCTV inside the massage parlour. But now they were saying that the Psycho Killer was starting to look like a vigilante. They must have known that the biker was yakuza, and that the Korean was connected to them.

There was another headline as well: 'Summertime of the Dead'. It was about the suicide rate, which was still rising. One psychiatrist said that it was because Japanese people saw suicide as an honourable death. But the head of the Rinzai school, which is a Buddhist sect, said that it was because people were having trouble seeing their true identity in today's fast-moving society. He said that most people live their whole lives lost. I don't know if they do, but the headline stuck in my mind because it summed up what the summer was turning into. And what it meant to me. It really was the summertime of the dead.

As the train rolled into the station the Lump pressed her face to the glass. I'd decided to take her to Kamakura for the day. Partly because I was supposed to take her places, and partly because I wanted to get out of the city. I felt under pressure now that the killings were getting so much attention. They were on every TV channel and radio station and on the front page of every paper.

Kamakura was Japan's capital at one time and it was a real tourist trap. Thousands of people came here and I couldn't stand the crowds. But I knew the Lump would like it. There were dozens of temples and shrines and she was dying to see the Great Buddha, which was a bronze statue as big as a house. So much so that she'd put on her rucksack three stops back and as soon as the train stopped she was off.

We made our way through the old station, which was packed with school trips and day trippers, and headed down to the Great Buddha, which was only a mile or so away. But the Lump couldn't wait to get there. She kept running ahead and looking back, irritated because I wouldn't hurry up. Then, crying out, she ran behind me and pushed me to make me go faster. But I just laughed.

When we got to the site we paid to enter, and as soon as we did we saw the Great Buddha of Kamakura. I was always impressed when I saw him.

He had broad shoulders and a big head and he was meditating in the lotus position. And he had such a tranquil face that he made you feel calm. What's more, he was highlighted by the green hills behind him. It was like he'd been placed there for that purpose, which he probably had. Zen monks always think of things like that.

The grounds were packed with picnicking families and tourists taking photographs, but the Lump didn't care. She bolted in front of the Great Buddha, and bowing her head she started to pray. I took a seat on one of the large rocks and waited for her. But then I saw a group of girls laughing at her. They were older and mean-looking, and I could tell by their faces that they were saying nasty things. I saw then why she was bullied at school. It wasn't because she was slow or stupid. It was because she was different. And people don't like it when you're different. I think it frightens them.

I gave the girls a look and put my hand on the Lump's shoulder. Her eyes opened and she looked at me. 'Praying,' she said.

'I know, but I was getting bored by myself. Come sit next to me.'

The Lump liked this, and sitting on the rock we looked at the Great Buddha.

'Smiling,' said the Lump.

She was right. I'd seen that Buddha a dozen times before, but it was only then that I saw he was smiling. The Lump was strange like that. She could make you see things that you hadn't seen before. She pulled the Om from her rucksack and placed him on the rock so he too could see the Great Buddha. 'Om very happy,' said the Lump.

'Why is he?' I asked.

The Lump folded her arms and studied him. Then she looked up at me. 'Just is,' she said.

She made me laugh sometimes. 'Well, we have a lot of temples to see today. Shall we take him to see some others?'

The Lump's face grimaced at the thought of leaving the Great Buddha.

'I'll take you to see him again,' I said. 'Next time you visit.'

The Lump was happy at the thought of more visits. 'OK,' she said, and we moved on.

The next temple we went to was up the side of a hill with a view of the sea. There were two golden Buddhas housed in their own temples, and outside there were hundreds of small Buddhas lined up like soldiers. They were to show that anyone could become a Buddha. And where there was one Buddha, hundreds more would spring from him. At least that's what the monk told my class the last time we were here.

I followed the Lump as she strolled around the gardens with her hands behind her back. There was nothing she didn't stop to inspect. She looked up at the sunlight that was shining through the leaves in the trees. Then she stepped across the stepping stones to watch the water run down the rocks. She frowned as it bubbled in the perfectly shaped pond and she smiled at the fish that were floating there. After the fish the flower beds caught her attention. She gazed at the yellow, orange and blue flowers and at the bees that were buzzing inside them. And then she held out her hand for a bee to land on.

'Don't blame me if it stings you,' I said.

'It won't,' said the Lump, and it didn't. It just crawled around for a bit and then it flew away.

'Come on.'

The Lump scurried after me and we climbed up the decaying stone steps that went up the hill. The path cut through a clump of trees, and through the foliage we could see stone statues with faded faces. They looked as if they'd been there for hundreds of years. Further up we saw small lizards clambering up trees and we saw scary spiders waiting in their webs. It was like being in a small jungle.

It was a hard climb in the heat, but we got a great view once we reached the top. We could see the sea and the town, and the Great Buddha, who was now as small as a snail. And we saw red fishing boats on the beach. And in the distance we could see the coastline like a rocky arm reaching out to the sea.

'Thirsty,' said the Lump.

We made our way back down to the temple, and getting a couple of Cokes from the cafe we sat in the plastic chairs. I could never understand why they made such an effort with the temple and then put out cheap plastic chairs for people to sit on. And they were hot in the heat.

'Why don't you take off your coat?' I asked.

'Don't want,' said the Lump. She drank her Coke and checked her cell. And then she frowned at it before putting it away.

'What do you want to do now?'

The Lump smiled. 'Beach,' she said.

We headed down the hill and followed the road

to the sea. But when we got to the beach it was bad. The water was more brown than blue, and the dirty sand smelled of oil. Not only that, but there were wooden shacks that looked like they were falling apart. No wonder it was deserted.

But the Lump couldn't see it. She was running around like she was stomping on the golden sands of Okinawa. And she was staring at dirty shells like they were jewels. But I found it depressing and so I imagined Kamakura in the old days, when the beach was beautiful and geishas strolled along its shores.

'Castle,' said the Lump.

The Lump had found an old bucket, and kneeling in the sand she'd made a castle, leastways she'd made a mound. And there she was looking for praise.

'Are you kidding? That's the worst castle I've ever seen! Here, this is how you do it.'

I grabbed the bucket and made four mounds. Then I built a wall between them, to keep out the enemy, and then I put shells in the towers for windows. I took a brick out the centre and threw it away, but it hit the Lump's castle and a section came down. The Lump looked at me like I'd done it on purpose. She picked up the brick and threw it at my castle, but she missed. And so I threw it back at hers, which then collapsed. The Lump looked livid. She jumped up and stamping on my castle she ran down the beach.

'You're dead!' I said.

The Lump laughed as she ran and I laughed as I chased her. And there we were like a couple of madmen running around in the heat.

When we were tired of the beach we went to the tunnels. They were cut into the rock with caves and candles inside, and they'd been turned into a sort of shrine. The last time I was here our teacher told us that an old hermit had made them. If that was the case, I wish he'd made them bigger. I had to stoop really low inside, but the Lump was like a gopher. She ran down one tunnel and appeared in another. Then she'd make sure she could see me before running away again. But I didn't like the tunnels so much and I was tired of having to stoop. 'Come on. Let's go,' I shouted.

The Lump ran around a bit more and then she followed me outside.

We headed up to the river and followed it upstream. Sometimes we'd have to walk on the road, but other times we could use the stepping stones to continue along its banks. There were small brown fish in the shallow water and brightly coloured dragonflies hovering above it. The Lump liked the dragonflies and she stopped to stare at them, but then she'd end up daydreaming.

'Will you hurry up?'

She ran past me then, with her rucksack bouncing, and scouted ahead.

We crossed a stone bridge and headed up into the trees and the hills, and the hiking trail than ran over them. We couldn't see much once we were up there because the foliage was so thick. But every now and then it cleared and we got a good view. But the Lump didn't care about the view. She only cared about running along the trail, which went up and down like waves. She'd run to the top of one peak and wait for me to catch up. Then running to the next she'd wait again. When the trail was blocked by fallen trees she took great joy in clambering over them. It was fun to watch her, and before long I forgot about things. My war with the yakuza seemed far away and the thought of killing someone seemed obscene. And so I didn't think about it. I just watched the Lump having fun.

We came down from the hiking trail and rejoined the road that ran alongside the river. But as we did it started to rain. It was only drizzle, but the clouds were getting darker and the wind was picking up. I turned to see the Lump with her mouth open. She was trying to catch raindrops. 'Hurry up.'

'Thirsty,' she said.

We followed the river up to the Bamboo Garden, which was my favourite place in Kamakura. I paid the admission fee and then I paid a little extra so we could have tea. And then, making our way along a boardwalk, we entered a forest of bamboo. It was pretty dark inside because of the clouds and the tall shoots, but it made the place more magical. The Lump was immediately amazed and wandered around like she'd entered an enchanted garden. She gazed up at the green shoots while turning in circles.

'Beautiful!' she said.

But then it poured down and so we scurried to the cabin at the far end of the forest. There was a light on inside and there were two women wearing kimonos. I gave one of the women the tickets and they started to make the tea. The Lump watched them closely as they whisked the green powder into a thick broth and then, when it was as thick as pea soup, they handed us the cups. The women smiled at the Lump and one of them gave her a cookie, and the Lump smiled back as she took it.

We took a seat and drank the tea while watching the rain soak the small forest. I felt cosy then and my mind mellowed, but suddenly we heard ringing. Me and the Lump looked at each other. Then it came to us: the phone! I laughed as she scrambled to take off her rucksack. And then she couldn't get it open fast enough. 'Hello. Mikazuki speaking! . . .' But then she cringed a little and the joy left her face. 'OK.' Slowly she put down the phone. I knew then it was a wrong number, and she'd waited all that time.

The women behind the counter looked concerned. 'Is she OK?' they asked.

As I turned to answer them the Lump ran out of the hut. I grabbed her rucksack and cell and ran after her. I sprinted down the boardwalk and out into the street, and then I chased her through the rain.

She was heading to the river! And she was running as fast as she could. I tore through those streets, and grabbing her jacket I pulled her up!

'It's OK,' I said.

She held her head in her hands. She tried to speak

but the words wouldn't come. And she was in so much pain! She reminded me of Hiroshi on that horrible night. And it absolutely killed me to see her that way! All she wanted was one lousy phone call to tell her that they loved her. But they didn't love her and so they'd never call.

'You don't need them. You've got me! When you go home I'll call you. I promise!'

The Lump was almost crying. 'But you —' she fought to get the words out — 'don't care!'

'Of course I care!'

She shook her head. 'No. Retard, you say — dummy!'

I felt so bad then I couldn't speak myself. I sank to my knees. 'I shouldn't have said those things, but I do care. I didn't at first, but I do now.'

'No!'

'Of course I do! I'm going to ask Grandmother if you can stay with us for good!'

The Lump looked at me to see if it was true. Then she threw her arms around my neck and hugged me tight. And when I thought about it, it was true. I didn't want her going back to those phoney parents. I liked having her around.

'I'll tell you what. Let's stop off at Yokohama

on the way home. They've got a funfair by the sea. We'll have a great time – just you and me.'

I put my hand on her shoulder and walked her back to the station. And by the time we got there she was happy again. But that was the Lump for you. She lived in the moment and she left bad things in the past. I was starting to realize that there were some truly great things about my cousin. And that was just one of them.

The rain had stopped by the time we got off the train but the sun was starting to set. We made our way down to the waterfront, where Yokohama's stylist skyscrapers fought for attention. There was the triangular Pan Pacific, the sail-shaped Grand and the rocket-shaped Royal Park. But the Lump wasn't interested in architecture. Her eyes were fixed on the Ferris wheel and the roller coaster that ran around it. And so we crossed the canals and headed along the footbridge that led to the amusement park, which was built over the old docks. But the Lump stopped when she saw the sailing ship with the huge sails. She looked at it like she wanted to run around on its decks. Then she saw the small kids screaming in the go-carts and the passenger ship that was taking people to faraway lands. She was so excited she didn't know which way to turn. But the screams from the amusement park put her back on track and she ran towards it.

She lined up for the roller coaster while rocking her body in time to the techno music. The other kids gave her a funny look as she tried to dance, but the Lump was too happy to notice. But her face soured when I gave her the ticket and walked away.

'You!' she said.

To be honest, I was kind of scared of roller coasters, and my life had become scary enough.

'I'll watch,' I said, and sat on a bench.

The Lump looked worried then and so I gave her some candy to take her mind off things. But when it was time to get on board she made the mistake of sitting in the front, which was always the scariest seat. And she looked glum as the guy brought down the restraint. And when the roller coaster started to move she started to mumble. And then she gave me a dirty look. It was like I'd deserted her in her hour of need. The roller coaster crawled to the top and then there was clattering and screaming and she disappeared. I heard the Lump scream above the blasting music. Then suddenly she flew by with her face frozen with fear. I couldn't help but laugh. She went by again and looked to me for help. But there was nothing I could do and so I laughed some more. I caught more glimpses of her in between my laughter and then the roller coaster came to a stop. I thought she'd jump out and attack me but she stayed in her seat. 'Again!' she said.

'Are you sure?'

'Again!' said the Lump.

I gave her a ticket and stood back. Slowly the roller coaster moved away, only this time the Lump's head was bobbing with the music. She even danced a little in her seat. But she stopped as it reached the top and, raising her arms in the air, she dropped. There was that clattering sound and she shot by laughing her little Lump head off. She was such a madman.

She wanted to stay on again and so I gave her a ticket and left her to it. But then another girl came along and sat next to her. And funnily enough she looked just like the Lump. She was short and round and she had the same sort of face. The only thing that was missing was the palm tree. They looked at each other and smiled and then they sat there as content as two eggs in a tray. The Lump had made a little friend.

But I thought about what I'd said when I sat on the bench. And I realized I shouldn't have said it. It wasn't that I didn't want the Lump living with us – I did. But Grandmother might not want her there. And I had the war to think of. I mean, I could be killed or arrested. Or the yakuza might find out where I lived and the Lump could get hurt. Then my mind turned dark with bad thoughts and I imagined how I'd butcher anyone who hurt her!

The ride finished and Lump and her little friend came running over. The Lump looked nervous as she introduced me. 'Uncle Yukio.' It was the first time she'd used my name and it sounded nice when she said it. The girl bowed a little and I bowed back. Then the Lump stood there looking awkward, but I knew what she was after. 'Here.' I gave her a stack of five-hundred-yen coins and she smiled as she collected them. Then they ran to a woman on a bench with a baby, who must have been the girl's mother. And then they ran back to the funfair.

They went on all the rides, running from one

to the other, and then they went back on the roller coaster and stayed on it until the money ran out. The girl's mother packed up her things and called her. The girl and the Lump looked hurt then, like they didn't want to part. And so they gave each other a hug before saying goodbye. The girl walked away with her mother while looking back at the Lump. The Lump smiled and waved and the girl waved back. But the Lump looked a little down when she'd gone. And so I went over to her.

'Hungry?'

'Hungry,' said the Lump. And the joy returned to her face.

We went into the World Port building, which had been turned into a shopping mall, and taking the escalator to the food court we wandered around deciding what to eat. I was thinking of having *domburi*, which is a bowl of rice served with beef and egg. But the Lump stopped at a pizza place and never moved on. So we got a large pizza, with a couple of extra-large Cokes, and we ate it until we were stuffed. I sat there thinking about what a good day it had been, but then I saw Uncle Benni on a TV screen!

He came out of a large house and got into a Mercedes while being snapped by photographers. I stood up and went to the TV just in time to see Riko! She was wearing sunglasses and a short dress, and as she got in the car the lights flashed around her. And then in my mind I saw her that night in the club. She was seething because Miko was better-looking than her. And so, like an evil spider, she'd trapped her in her web. And when I thought about it I was boiling with hatred! But then I realized. That must be his house. I stood closer and scanned the screen. The car drove down a driveway and two bodyguards pulled back the iron-barred gates. There were golden lion dogs, on posts, either side of the entrance. And as the Mercedes drove down the street I saw Tokyo Tower in the distance. It could only have been two or three miles away.

The camera turned to a woman with a mic. 'Benni Tanaka, godfather of Tokyo, has taken on extra bodyguards now that more of his crew have been killed. But who is behind these killings? And when will they strike again? These are the questions that all of Tokyo is asking. This is Anna Takahashi reporting live for *Tokyo on Five*.'

Extra bodyguards! They'll need them! Because I'm going to find that house and when I do . . .

'Water,' said the Lump.

I knew she'd be able to read my face. And so I froze for a second before looking down at her.

'You want water?'

'To see the sea,' said the Lump.

'Oh. Come on then.'

I tried to get the bad thoughts out of my head as we went down the escalator. Otherwise the Lump would sense something. But she seemed happy enough. She spun around as we headed down to the waterfront, and she ran to the sea as soon as she saw it. It was dark then and the rain had come back, but it was only drizzle and it felt nice with the night being so hot.

Yokohama Bay Bridge was lit up and so was the passenger terminal. And when we turned we saw the skyscrapers lighting up the low clouds, and the Ferris wheel reflected in the water. A white ship cruised into the bay with well-dressed people on board. We could hear their conversations and their glasses clinking. Then fireworks flew up from the ship and the sky exploded in colour. I watched for a while and then I turned to the Lump, who was smiling. I smiled back, but really I felt bad inside. I was torn between the hatred I felt for the Tanakas and the affection I felt for the Lump. And both those feelings were so strong they put me in pain.

'Beautiful!' said the Lump.

But I did my best to seem happy. 'Yes, beautiful,' I said.

12

I heard the Lump coming upstairs for the second time and then she knocked on the door and came in. 'Up!' I opened my eyes. 'Up!' she said, and slamming the door she disappeared. The Lump was taking liberties now that we were friends and I wasn't happy about it. All night I'd had bad dreams that revolved around the Buddhist festival of Obon, which is when we traditionally honour our ancestors. We go to their graves and clean them and pray, and on that day the spirits of the dead are said to revisit the household altars. The twins were not my ancestors and they never had a family altar. But we do, downstairs, and I dreamt that they came to it. But it turned into a nightmare because in my dream they were being held by Hungry Ghosts. Hungry Ghosts were evil people in their previous lives, and having built up so much bad karma they're tortured through hunger, thirst and heat. Even the moon scorches their skin. I dreamt that Louise and Kako and the other yakuza I'd killed had turned into Hungry Ghosts and they had hold of the twins. The twins were pleading with me to get them away, but I couldn't. Every time I grabbed hold of a Hungry Ghost their skin would melt through my fingers. In the end I ran upstairs but they were all over the house. Some were drinking water from the toilet. Others were crying in corners. It was such a horrific nightmare. But now in the light of day I felt ashamed that I'd run away. I should never have left the twins when they needed me. Not even in a dream.

I heard the Lump running upstairs and then the door opened again. 'Up!'

I pulled the covers over my head. 'Go away, you dummy.'

'Dummy!' I heard her small feet shuffle and then she started hitting me over the head with a pillow.

'Pack it in!'

She wouldn't and so I threw my pillow at her, but she was too fast. The door slammed and I heard her laughing as she ran downstairs. Then I heard Yoshe.

'Yukio, you have to get up.'

I did have to get up as well. Not only because it was Obon, but because Natsuko was going to be saying a small mass over the twins' graves.

I showered and dressed in a white shirt and black pants, and then I trotted downstairs. The paper was on the hall table, and picking it up I looked for news of the killings. But I didn't like what I saw. Turns out that old yakuza I'd killed had a daughter in a wheelchair. 'Tell my daughter I love her.' That was what he'd said. He probably did love his daughter, and he didn't seem like such a bad guy. But I'd bet he'd done plenty of damage in his day. And I'd bet he had something to do with entrapping the twins. So to hell with him!

Yoshe came into the hall with the Lump and the baby. 'You head over with Mikazuki. I'll get a taxi when I'm done.'

'You're coming?'

Yoshe looked surprised. 'Yes, I loved the twins. I couldn't be at the funeral because—'

'Sorry, Yoshe, I didn't mean anything by it . . . Would you like me to help you with your housework? That way we can all go together.'

'That's OK. But you can take the baby if you want!'

I looked at the baby and he looked at me. 'Sure,' I said. But I'd never so much as taken him to the park.

The Lump's face lit up. 'I'll push!' she said.

Yoshe put the baby in his buggy and we stepped outside. Then she kissed his face. 'Look after him.'

'I will.' I put on my dark sunglasses and started to push him away.

'And try to keep him clean,' shouted Yoshe.

We crossed the tracks and the road, and running up the ramp we cut through the park. I pulled back the buggy until the front wheels came up and the baby was lying flat, and he liked it and laughed.

'No,' said the Lump, looking concerned.

But I did it again.

'Get sick,' said the Lump.

'No, he won't.' And he didn't. The Lump was just jealous because the baby liked me. But then she started mumbling and so I felt bad and gave her the buggy. She was happy then and she pushed him proudly through the park.

But then something scary happened. I heard the

clanging sound that the barrier makes when the train's coming. But we were well away from the crossing.

'Can you hear ringing?'

'Ringing? No,' said the Lump.

That meant I was hearing it in my head! I sank down on a bench and covered my ears. But it wouldn't stop! All of a sudden I felt frightened.

Then the Lump screamed. 'Ants!'

She scared the hell out of me! 'Do you have to shout like that?'

The Lump pushed the buggy towards the trees. 'Ants,' she whispered, and pointed them out to the baby. The baby leaned forward in his buggy until he saw what she saw. 'Onts,' he said. The Lump and the baby laughed, but I still felt frightened. How could I hear something that wasn't real?

'Sixteen,' said the Lump.

That got to me! I jumped up, and snatching off my sunglasses I started to count. 'One, two, three . . . There're only fifteen!' I said.

'Tree,' said the Lump.

And sure enough there was an ant crawling up the trunk of the tree.

'Ant and the rubber-tree plant,' said the Lump.

And then she sang. 'Whoops, there goes another rubber-tree plant.'

I froze for a second. Then the ringing stopped. Then I burst out laughing and the baby joined in. 'You lunatic!' I said, and grabbing the buggy I pretended to run her down. The Lump screamed and laughed and ran away, and me and the baby chased her all the way to the gate.

On our way down Omotesando I bought a few stacks of flowers and I bought the Lump and the baby an ice cream each. I didn't think about what Yoshe had said about keeping him clean until we were in the cemetery. But when I looked into the buggy I almost died. It was like he'd washed himself in ice cream just to spite me. I grabbed some wipes and started to clean him. But then I saw the twins' grandad getting out of a taxi. I had known he was going to be there and I was dreading seeing him. I still felt guilty over their deaths, and I was sure that he blamed me in some way.

Then I saw Natsuko walking through the graves in her white robes. She shielded her eyes from the sun and then she came towards us. She must have sensed I was feeling nervous.

'It'll be OK,' she said. That warm feeling came from her then and I knew that it would be.

'And how is my little Mikazuki?' asked Natsuko. The Lump bowed. 'Good,' she said.

'And you've brought a friend!'

'Baby!' said the Lump, looking proud.

Natsuko smiled and caressed the baby's hand. 'How beautiful.' Then she looked at me. 'Shall we begin?'

We headed over to the twins' grandad, who was gazing down at their graves. He looked so tired and his face was creased with pain. I'd known this old man all my life and not once had he ever said a bad word to me. And to see him now lost and alone was so sad. But he looked relieved when he saw me.

'Yukio!' He put his hand on my shoulder. 'I'm so glad you could come!'

I saw then that he never did blame me for the twins' deaths. He was probably just disappointed because he had depended on me to look after them.

'I'm glad too,' I said.

We knelt at the side of the grave and started to clean. We took the dead flowers from the metal vase and ripped up the weeds that had already started to grow. He picked up the twigs and the leaves that were lying on the path, while I got a cloth from under the buggy and wiped the black marble tombstone until it shone. All the hate and sorrow flowed out of me as I worked, and I started to feel good.

When we were finished the Lump knelt down and arranged the fresh flowers in the vase. She worked carefully, arranging one flower so it highlighted another. It was as if she'd been doing ikebana all her life. And when she'd finished we saw a flower arrangement as beautiful as it could be. I was grateful to her for doing a good job and I put my arm around her to show it. I noticed other families cleaning tombstones or making their way to graves. Some of the men wore black suits, as though once again they were going to the funeral. But some of the women wore brightly coloured kimonos, which was another way of showing respect. And I felt glad then that I was here on this day. Because showing respect was what it was about.

A taxi pulled up and Yoshe got out. She was dressed in a black dress and she looked as smart as I'd ever seen her. She kissed the baby, and opening a parasol she stood as erect as a soldier. Natsuko came to the head of the grave and rang a small gold bell. We bowed our heads and she started praying in a singing voice. The baby must have liked it because he joined in, but Yoshe soon shushed him. And then, when Natsuko had stopped praying, she turned her attention to us.

'I've seen a lot of death and suffering this year. And when I returned to Japan I was praying for peace and tranquillity. But then I heard that the twins had died. I consoled myself with the fact that they were no longer suffering, only we who are left behind are suffering. But through that suffering we celebrate what great spirits they were. I truly believe they found Nirvana and that they are finally free from the constant cycle of rebirth and death. And that they are now in heaven.'

Natsuko bowed to the twins' grandad and he stepped forward. He looked a little frail, but he started to speak. 'Thank you, and thank you all for coming. There were things that I wanted to say at their funeral, but I was too devastated to speak. And now I am at a loss for the right words. But let me say this: the twins made my world beautiful! I know that Miko and Hiroshi are in a better place. I only hope that when my time comes I will be with them.' His eyes filled with tears then and he kind of lost his way. 'I'm sorry. Maybe their best friend, Yukio, would like to say a few words.'

I was already feeling pretty emotional, but I had to say something, and so I did. 'Miko once told me that there were no bad people and no good people. There were only people with good and bad in them. But she was wrong. Her and Hiroshi never had a bad thought in their heads for anyone. Not in all the time I knew them.'

Yoshe looked a little teary. 'Well said, Yukio.'

It was over then. There was no more to be said. The twins' grandad bowed to everyone and we bowed back. And then taking his arm I walked him to a taxi.

'If we never meet again, Yukio, remember that I always thought of you fondly. The twins could not have asked for a better friend.' The door closed and I bowed as the taxi drove away. But I felt so sorry for him. Because wherever that taxi was taking him, he'd be there alone. The Lump came over, and linking her arm through mine she walked me back to the others. But then she stopped.

'Policeman.'

I could see a man at the base of a tree, but the branches blocked his face.

'How do you know it's the policeman?'

'Shoes,' she said.

'Shoes. Are you kidding?'

'No,' said the Lump.

I kept my eye on the man as I walked back to the others. Yoshe put the buggy in the trunk of a taxi and turned to us. 'Would you like a ride home?'

'We'll walk,' I said.

She gave me a hug, and bowing to Natsuko she got in the taxi. Natsuko waved to her as she drove away and then she turned to us. 'Come and see me soon, Yukio. I really miss your visits.'

'Me too?' said the Lump.

Natsuko smiled. 'Of course you too.'

We bowed to Natsuko and she headed back through the graves. Then I saw ravens flying up from the tree and turning I saw Detective Maki walk away.

'So it was him.'

'Policeman,' said the Lump.

I still felt a little hatred for him for what he'd said about Miko. And I knew he'd seen that tape. And now, on Obon, when we were here to pay respects to our dead he'd turned up! He was more of a dog than a detective! I tried not to hate him because in many ways we were on the same side. But I didn't know what I'd do if he got too close. I really didn't.

I sat at the kitchen table scanning a map. I opened the compass to one inch, and putting the point on Tokyo Tower I drew a circle. One inch represented one mile. I didn't think Uncle Benni's house could be much closer. I opened it to three inches, because I didn't think it could be any further away than that, and drew another circle. Then I saw the problem. The area within the two circles was only small on the map but it'd be a huge area to cover. The outer circle touched Harajuku, Omotesando and the cemetery. It encompassed the Imperial Palace and went down as far south as Shinagawa station, not to mention most of the port. It would take me forever to find the house. But find it I would.

I heard the Lump coming down the stairs. She came in the kitchen in her pyjamas and sat down like it was Saturday afternoon. Then, putting the Om on the table, she yawned and looked around. 'Hungry,' she said.

I could tell by her eyes she wasn't sleepwalking. 'Do you know what time it is?'

The Lump had a think. 'No.'

'Well, it's late. Go back to bed.'

I put the map in my pocket and got ready to go out.

'I come,' said the Lump.

I didn't pay her much attention. 'I'm going on the bike.'

She ran upstairs and I went out into the garden. I wasn't taking the sword. There was no point if I didn't know where the house was. This was just another scouting trip.

I pushed the bike into the street and closed the steel door. But then I got a fright! 'What are you doing?'

'I come,' said the Lump.

She was wearing her jacket over her pyjamas and she had that black helmet on her head.

'There's not enough room.'

The Lump looked at the seat. 'There's room.'

I don't know why I was trying to reason with her. It was well gone midnight. 'Go back to bed,' I said, and pushed the bike away.

'Please!'

'No!'

I kick-started the engine and rode away, but

I felt bad. And when I looked back she was still standing there. I couldn't leave her. She might end up sleepwalking to Shinjuku.

I rode back and pulled over.

'Don't blame me if we get stopped by the cops.'

The Lump couldn't climb up fast enough. 'I won't!' she said.

We took the backstreets to the dual carriageway, and then pulling back on the throttle we zoomed away. Suddenly the Lump started screaming! I went to pull over. 'What's wrong?'

'Happy!' she shouted.

The Lump was a lunatic, but she made me laugh.

'Faster!' she shouted.

I pulled back on the throttle.

'Faster!' shouted the Lump.

'This is as fast as it goes, you dummy!'

She chuckled all the way around the park and screamed down Omotesando Boulevard. And with every corner we took there was a cackle of excitement. But then, as we rode in between two rows of traffic, she pushed her head against my back. 'Frightened!' she shouted. But she laughed like a madman when we were in the clear, and then she went back to screaming. The Lump was having more fun than she did on the roller coaster.

When we got in sight of Tokyo Tower I pulled up and turned to her. 'Listen. You have to look out for lion dogs, OK?'

'Lion dogs?'

'Yes, we're looking for a big house with iron-barred gates and golden lion dogs.'

'I find,' said the Lump.

We circled the tower once and then we circled it again. And with every turn we took we got further away. But it was a lot more difficult than I'd thought it'd be. Sometimes we'd end up going down a dead end. Other times we'd find ourselves heading back towards the tower when we wanted to head away. And once we got on a dual carriageway that would have taken us home. I did a cheeky turn, much to the Lump's joy, and we continued our search. We rode around until we were dizzy and the tower was in the distance, but we couldn't find it. And then we lost sight of the tower. And then we were just lost. I was riding around a park that I thought was Shiba Park, but I couldn't be sure. And I was starting to feel tired.

'You OK?'

'Hungry,' said the Lump.

I was just debating whether to stop at a snack shop or head home when the Lump shouted, 'Golden lion dogs!'

'Where?'

'We passed.'

I turned the bike around and rode back. Lion dogs are a common sight on the entrances of Tokyo's houses and so I didn't have my hopes built up, but when I pulled up on the opposite side of the street I couldn't believe it! It was the house all right. There were the lion dogs and the iron-barred gates, and there was Tokyo Tower in the distance. I'd even parked right on the spot where the journalist must have stood. I took off my helmet and looked around.

The street was long and narrow and as quiet as a country road. The stone wall of the park was on one side of it, and the high-walled houses were on the other. I could tell by the size of them that it was a well-to-do neighbourhood. And the spikes on the walls told me that they didn't like intruders.

Uncle Benni's house had the highest walls with the sharpest spikes. It was one of those old-style traditional houses with the double rooftop decorated with demons and gargoyles. It reminded me of a fortress built to intimidate, and it did. But I felt sure Riko was staying there and I was determined to take a look.

'Jump down.'

I switched off the engine and the Lump climbed down. I fumbled to get my black hat from the bag under the seat. And while I did I thought about what I'd say to her.

'Listen, I think a friend of mine lives there. I'm just going to climb over the wall and take a look.'

But the Lump's eyes were fixed on the iron-barred gates. Or rather on what was behind them.

'What is it?' I asked.

But the Lump didn't answer. I stood up and tried to see what she was looking at, but all I could see was a short driveway and some trees. But then the Lump took a step back.

'Frightened!' she said.

She looked frightened too. She was starting to scare me.

'There's no one there,' I said.

But then, through the bars of the gate, I saw a shadow move. The shadow grew in size until a large man appeared at the gate. He grabbed the bars with his big hands and looked at us. But not like we were a couple of kids out for a ride. He looked at us like we were possible assassins. And he had the eyes of a tosa ready to attack.

'Very frightened!' said the Lump.

I never told the Lump we were leaving. I didn't have to. I just put on my helmet, kick-started the engine and tore away.

'Scary man!' she shouted.

The Lump had never spoken a truer word. Because I knew who that man was. His name was Yama and he was an absolute maniac! There are two Yamas. One's from Buddhist mythology. He's the god of the dead, the ruler of the underworld. And he did some terrible things to some terrible people. But he was nowhere near as bad as this Yama. He was Uncle Benni's most feared enforcer and it was rumoured that he drank the blood of the dead. And the worst thing was, it might be true.

You see, the triads, who are the yakuza's equivalent in China, were having trouble this one time with a rebel crew. They asked Uncle Benni to sort the situation and he sent in Yama. Afterwards they found the triad crew in a basement – leastways they found their body parts. And the Hong Kong papers reported that some of the body parts had been eaten. Yama was arrested and held in custody for two years, but they couldn't make the charges stick and so he was released. When he came back to Tokyo one journalist made the mistake of saying, 'A beast like Yama shouldn't be allowed on the street.' Three days later the journalist's body was found in a dumpster. But he had no tongue; someone had bitten it off. After that nobody said a word about him.

Like the Lump said, he was a very scary man. And just the thought of him standing in the shadows was enough to give me the creeps.

'Hungry,' said the Lump.

I couldn't believe how lucky I was bringing her with me! I would have been dead otherwise. Yama might have been able to hide from me, but nothing escapes my cousin.

'When we get home, my little Mikazuki, I'll cook you whatever you want. I don't care how late it is.'

It was silent as we sat at the kitchen table. I drank some green tea and concentrated on the paper. The Lump drank her hot chocolate and concentrated on her cookies. Then we heard a noise coming from the hall. Me and the Lump looked into the darkness and saw an image like a ghost. Then Grandmother came in and took a seat. It was rare to see her out of bed. And she was still wearing her night dress.

'You OK, Grandmother?'

She held her head in her hands, like she'd had a bad dream, and so I put some tea in front of her. The Lump looked concerned. Getting down from the table she gave Grandmother the last of her cookies. Grandmother sat up then as though coming to her senses.

'And how are you, Mikazuki?'

'Good,' said the Lump.

'I hope my grandson has been treating you well.' She gave me a strange look. 'He can be selfish at times, but he is a brave warrior to be sure. Even our ancestors would be proud of him.'

For just a second I thought that Grandmother knew! But then she looked away.

'Tell me, Mikazuki, what do you think of your Uncle Yukio?'

The Lump looked at me. 'Very nice man,' she said.

'And have you enjoyed your stay?'

'Very much!' said the Lump.

'Well, your sister's tour finishes soon. So you'll be able to go home.'

The Lump's face clouded over. She gave me a look and I knew I had to say something. 'Could she not stay with us, Grandmother?'

The Lump's eyes shot to Grandmother. But Grandmother looked confused. 'She is staying with us.'

'For good, I mean.'

Then it sank in. 'Well, well, well. Who'd have thought that you two would end up being friends?' Grandmother had a chuckle to herself. But then she stared into nothing and seemed far away.

The Lump gave me another look.

'Well, can she?'

Grandmother didn't look happy then. 'Of course she can't. Her family will miss her.'

I could have said something about that, but I didn't. But the Lump saw it was no good and her head went down. But Grandmother's face softened.

'I'll tell you what – I'll ask her mother if she can stay with us every time she has a school holiday. And every time Hatsu goes on tour. Not only that,' said Grandmother with some formality, 'I will request that she comes and lives with us when she's a little older. So she can be educated here in Tokyo. And I'm pretty sure she'll agree, if it's put properly.'

'Thank you, Grandmother,' I said.

When I looked at the Lump she was finding it hard to control her joy. She got down from her chair. I thought she was going to bow to Grandmother, but she ran into her lap and threw her arms around her. Grandmother was taken aback at first, but then she stroked the Lump's head. She even looked a little touched. 'OK, that's enough, let me get back to bed.' She got up and headed to her room. 'Don't you two stay up too late.'

'We won't,' I said, even though it was late already.

The Lump took a seat and drank the last of her hot chocolate. In all my life I'd never seen anyone look so pleased.

'Very happy!' said the Lump.

She made me laugh. 'Me too,' I said.

13

I sat on a bench in the park with the newspaper in my hands. I'd read the article a few times and each time it was a little more painful. And so I stopped reading it and watched the ravens bicker over a piece of bread. It must be nice to be a bird or a small animal, something that doesn't have problems. Because my problems had just got a lot worse. That yakuza I'd killed on the chopper, the one who rode into an oncoming car, well, he wasn't a yakuza at all. He was an undercover cop, and the police were vowing to hunt down his killer. His chief said that he was a dedicated officer respected by his colleagues and that he would be sorely missed. He wasn't married and had no children. But his mother said that there was a girl he was fond of, but she married someone else. She also said that ever since he was a small boy, all he wanted to do was help people. And now that he was dead she wanted to die herself.

I put the paper in the garbage and headed back to the house. As soon as I opened the door the Lump was there. She was sitting in the hall with her rucksack on her back. She stood up and smiled when she saw me and I smiled back, but she sensed that something was wrong. 'OK, Yukio?'

'I'm not feeling too good. We'll go out later, I promise.'

I went to my room and closed the door and then I stood there feeling as lost as I'd ever felt. And I was so tired – it was like all my chi energy had drained away. I'd started out to avenge the twins, defend the weak and live by the bushido code. I'd wanted to live with honour or die an honourable death. But I'd ended up killing an innocent cop, which is such a dishonourable thing to do. But ashamed as I was, I took a deep breath and tried to get my mind straight. Because tonight I was going to Uncle Benni's house to kill Riko. And there was a good chance I wouldn't make it out. They say karma always catches up with you in the end, and so I suppose if I'm killed tonight then that will be justice for the cop. But then the thought of death sank into my mind and saddened me, and I had no right to feel sad. I've taken life and therefore I should be willing to face death. But it wasn't death I was afraid of. There were animals in that house, and I knew if they caught me I wouldn't die quickly. 'I have to train!'

I took off my shirt and took the sword from the wardrobe. There was enough space, as long as I didn't raise it in the *jodan* stance. And so I started the katas from the *chudan* stance. I imagined there was an opponent in front of me and I thrust the sword into his throat, stabbed at his torso and struck at his shoulders. I stooped and jammed the sword into his armpit. I hacked at his hands and fingers and I chopped at his elbows.

I kept performing the katas until I was sweating and the room was spinning. But then something strange happened. It was as if my mind went into a trance. I started to see real people in front of me. It was like I was being attacked by an army of tattooed men, and the more that came the harder I fought. I struck their skulls, gashed their throats and stabbed at their eyes. I could feel the sword breaking bones and severing arteries. And I could see the men falling in agony around me. I hacked at their raised hands, and their fingers fell to the floor. Blood spattered on the bedroom walls and dripped from the ceiling. I could feel its warmth running down my back. But then I stumbled on the screaming bodies and the body parts and the heads that were staring up at me. And then I fell to the floor, which was swaying like a rolling ship. The screaming turned into that clanging sound. It got louder and louder until it was so painful I had to cover my ears but that didn't help. I looked up at the statue of the Buddha and I begged him to make it stop.

Next thing I knew, the Lump was there. She said something, but I couldn't understand her. She pulled my hands away and put her hands over my ears. Suddenly the ringing stopped. 'Poor Yukio,' she said, and she looked so worried. She took the sword from me, and putting it in the wardrobe she piled pillows on top of it. I just sat there in a daze like the shocked survivor of a train crash. I even looked around the room searching for body parts, but of course there weren't any. I felt frightened then, and sad, because I knew I was changing, and I liked the person I used to be.

The Lump took my arm and helped me to my

feet. My whole body was aching and shivering and I felt exhausted.

'Come, Yukio,' she said, and handed me my shirt.

I put it on and followed her downstairs and then she opened the door and led me outside. She wanted to lead me down the street but I pulled away. I don't know where she was trying to take me, but I didn't want to go. But the Lump grabbed my arm. 'Please, Yukio!' I was too weak to argue and so I went along. She led me over the tracks, and across the road, and pulling me up the concrete ramp she led me into the park. She walked me through the trees, and all the time her eyes were searching. It was like she was looking for something and she seemed desperate to find it. Then she stopped. 'Ants! Look, Yukio, beautiful ants!' I looked down at them just to please her, but they were just ants. She saw a butterfly land on a plant. 'Look, Yukio, beautiful butterfly!' It was a big butterfly with emerald-coloured wings. It fluttered upwards and I watched it go. 'And look, beautiful trees!' said the Lump. I looked up at the trees. The golden sunlight made the leaves see-through and it warmed my face. The Lump took my hand and we came out on the common. There were families having picnics and there were small children running around. An old woman with a camera smiled as she took photographs, and a proud dad was teaching his small son to fly a kite. To me it all seemed as unreal as the bodies in my room.

A couple of common sparrows landed on the ground. The Lump pointed at them. 'And look, Yukio, beautiful birds as well!' She held out her hands and cringed as though the beauty of it all pained her. 'Beautiful park! And beautiful people! And beautiful sky!' Then she looked up at me. 'And beautiful Yukio!'

That killed me! A pain came into my heart and I collapsed to my knees! I tried to be strong, but for the second time in that park I broke down. I cried for the twins and the cop and the girl with no fingers. And I cried for Yoshe's baby and Grandmother and for the Lump, who thought everything was beautiful. I felt so pathetic but I couldn't stop. And so the Lump put her arm around me and hugged me and wiped away the tears. Then she knelt next to me and held my hand. I felt peaceful in my head then, just the way I did before all of this started.

We watched children chase each other around the trees and we watched a mum with her little girl as she rode her bike for the first time. We smiled at the small boy as he ran with his red kite and we flinched when he fell down. But he got up and laughed, and then we got up and headed home.

The Lump linked arms with me as she walked me back to the house. And as soon as we were through the door she ran to my room. I knew what she was after, and sure enough she came out carrying the swords.

'Hide,' she said.

I climbed the steep steps into the loft and the Lump followed. She looked around and seeing only the chest she opened it. She started to take out all my grandfather's things – his books and his medals and his uniforms. I helped her, and when we were done she put the swords at the bottom. Then, very quickly, she started piling the other things on top. She kept going until the chest was full and then she closed the lid and stood back. She scowled at it, as if she didn't like it, and then she turned to me.

'It's OK,' I said. 'It's over.' I was so relieved when I said those words. I felt like a soldier on a battlefield, ready to make a suicide attack, only to be told that the war was over. The Lump had saved me and now I didn't know what to say to her.

'Hungry?'

'Hungry,' said the Lump.

As soon as we went downstairs Grandmother came out of her room. She had a letter in her hand. 'Mikazuki, your parents are home. You will be leaving us tonight on the sleeper to Sapporo.'

The Lump looked sad and so did I.

'Don't worry, Yukio,' said Grandmother. 'She'll be back soon enough . . . Now you get packed, Mikazuki, and I'll have your things sent to the station. Then, if your uncle so wishes, he can take you somewhere nice for dinner. Would you like that, Yukio?

'Yes, Grandmother, I would.'

The Lump went upstairs to pack and I went in the kitchen and sat at the table. Yoshe put tea in front of me, without being asked, and then she took a seat.

'You look so pale, Yukio. Are you OK?'

'Sure,' I said.

'It was nice you looking after her while she was here. I think she really enjoyed herself.'

'I'm going to buy her a present before she goes. What do you think she'd like?'

'I don't know. She's so . . . different. Maybe you should ask her.'

We heard her coming downstairs and went out into the hall.

Grandmother came out of her room. 'Where're your clothes and your suitcase?' she asked.

The Lump looked a little embarrassed. 'Rucksack,' she said.

I knew then why she always wore that jacket. It was to hide those worn-out T-shirts. All the rest of her clothes she could fit into that tiny rucksack. Those phoney parents of hers must have spent all their money on themselves and their piano-playing daughter. No wonder the kids at school picked on her.

Grandmother looked taken aback but she tried to hide it. 'Well, it's always good to travel light,' she said. Then she nodded to Yoshe and they both went into her room.

'I'd like to buy you a present before you leave,' I said. 'What would you like?'

The Lump had a think. 'Shinai,' she said.

'No, you can have anything you want.'

The Lump had another think. 'Shinai.'

I went upstairs and came down with the best shinai I had.

'Wrapped up,' said the Lump.

'Wrapping paper? . . . I know there's some in the kitchen.'

But then Yoshe came out of Grandmother's room. 'Mikazuki, how would you like to come shopping with me?'

'Shopping?'

Yoshe smiled. 'Yes, just us two girls.'

The Lump's eyes lit up.

I heard someone knocking on the door and my eyes opened.

'Yukio.' Yoshe looked in. 'If you're going to take Mikazuki to dinner, you'll have to get up.'

It was like I'd only been asleep ten minutes, but I could tell by the light that the sun had set. I got showered and dressed and went downstairs, and there I got the shock of my life. The Lump was wearing a kimono! It was cream-coloured and covered with long-legged cranes and lotus blossoms. And it had long sleeves and a wide waistband. She was even wearing the straw sandals and the white socks that geishas wore. My cousin Mikazuki looked like a lump in everything she wore, but she looked like a superstar in a kimono. Yoshe was smiling while Grandmother was trying to hide how proud she felt. But the Lump was biting her lip. It was like she was waiting for my approval.

'You look great,' I said.

Her face beamed into a smile and she looked down at herself, with her arms out, as though proud of her own appearance.

Grandmother glared at me. 'Jeans and T-shirt? I think not! Now go and get changed!'

I ran upstairs, put on pants and a proper shirt and ran back down.

Yoshe was holding a camera. 'Quick, Yukio, before the taxi comes.'

I stood next to Grandmother, and the Lump stood in front of us. I put my hand on her shoulder and we all looked as proud as we could. Yoshe took the photograph. 'It's a great shot!' We heard a horn outside and Yoshe opened the door. 'Taxi's here.'

Grandmother looked a little sad now that it was time for the Lump to leave. 'You're family, Mikazuki. And family is important in this house. Know that you are always welcome here.' Then, with more than a little ceremony, Grandmother bowed to the Lump.

The Lump bowed back. 'Thank you, Grandmother.'

We went outside and got in the taxi. Yoshe came

out and handed the Lump a silk fan. 'Don't forget this . . . Now, I'll meet you at Tokyo station with her luggage. Don't be late.'

'I won't,' I said.

The Lump waved at Yoshe and the taxi drove away. Then she sat back and smiled.

Strange – earlier that day I was training to kill someone. Then I went insane. And then the Lump brought me back to my senses. If she hadn't I would have been on my way to Uncle Benni's house, where I definitely would have been killed. But that was the Lump for you. She mightn't have been able to put two sentences together, but she saw a world that other people didn't. And when she showed it to me all the bad things seem to fade away.

We pulled up opposite the seriously crowded Shinjuku station and stepped on to Shinjuku Terrace: a smooth pedestrian walkway that ran below the skyscrapers and above the train tracks. It was lined with trees, cafes and coffee shops and a lot of people came here to people-watch. And they were getting a treat tonight. The Lump linked her arm through mine and we walked along the terrace with an audience watching us. I felt a little embarrassed at first, because of the attention. But then I saw how pleased the people were when they saw her. They pointed her out to their friends, and they'd point her out to other people. Then an American came out of Starbucks.

'May I?' he asked, holding up his camera.

I stood to one side and stooping like a professional he lined her up. The Lump never smiled or posed but she stood as tall as she could.

'Can you open your fan?' asked the American.

She opened up her fan and held it in front of her. The man took one picture and then another. And then cellphones raised as more people came to capture the image. And then I thought about the photographs on Grandmother's wall. And how, in a hundred years' time, the Lump might be on someone's wall. And the people would look back to this period and wonder who she was and where she came from. Well, she was my cousin and I was proud of her.

I put my arm through hers, and passing the trees we crossed the wide pedestrian footbridge that led to Takashimaya Times Square, a huge building that sold everything from camping gear to designer clothes. But we weren't interested in shopping. We took the outside elevator to the top, and as we rose the Lump put her head to the glass. She watched the trains, and the terrace, and the people who shrunk to the size of ants. Then the bell for the doors chimed and we stepped out on to a floor filled with fancy restaurants.

It was a nice place with big couches and balconies and rooftop walkways. And I knew the Lump would like it, and she did. She smiled as we strolled around, but she barely looked at the restaurants, even though we were there to eat.

'What about this place?' I asked.

It was a steak place that my mother had taken me to one time. It had soft lights and candles on the tables and they served the steaks with knives and forks. We went inside and got shown to a table by the window. The smiling waiter pulled back the chair so the Lump could sit down. 'You look very nice,' he said. And then taking our order he moved away.

It felt warm and cosy inside and everyone seemed happy. They were mainly couples, talking and laughing. But there were a group of older women as well and they all seemed to be smiling at the Lump.

'Everyone watching,' she said.

'It's because you look good,' I said.

The Lump was pleased with this, but trying not to show it she looked at the view. It was a great view too. We could see all of Shinjuku's skyscrapers and tall buildings blazing away in lights, and they seemed to go on forever. I'm not kidding – we could see five miles or more, but they never seemed to end. And they all had these flashing red warning lights at the top to stop the helicopters crashing into them. It was like looking at a thousand red stars. And the whole thing looked like a futuristic city from a scientific world.

'Happy,' said the Lump in a soft voice. It was like she was talking to herself.

'Me too,' I said.

We didn't say much after that. We didn't have to. And when the food came the Lump ate slowly and delicately. It wasn't so important to her any more. Maybe all she wanted was somebody to care for her, and now she'd found three people who did. And that's not counting the baby.

When we were finished we had ice cream and then tea. And then we stepped out on to the rooftop terrace and strolled around like we were in a park. The Lump never got bored of the blazing lights.

They were magical to her and she watched them as we walked.

'Beautiful!' she said.

When it was time to go we strolled back along Shinjuku Terrace and once again we ran the gauntlet of the photographers. The cameras were still flashing as we got into the taxi. It was like we were a pair of celebrities for the night.

'Famous,' said the Lump.

I laughed then. And we had a nice drive to the station. I even gave the Lump a bit of a tour. And when the taxi pulled up outside Tokyo station the first people we saw were Yoshe and the baby. 'I wanted him to say goodbye,' said Yoshe, 'but he fell asleep.'

The Lump put on her rucksack, and leaning into the buggy she kissed him on the cheek. And then she touched his face affectionately. I could see she was sad about leaving him.

'He'll miss you a lot,' said Yoshe. 'We all will.' She gave the Lump a hug and a kiss. 'Goodbye, Mikazuki. Come back soon.'

She handed her a dozen bags from different department stores and of course I knew what was in them. Grandmother might have been as mean as a mountain monkey, but she was always generous with money.

'Bye, Yoshe,' said the Lump. But then she looked like she didn't want to go.

'You'd better get going,' said Yoshe in a gentle way. 'Don't want to miss your train.'

I put my hand on her shoulder. 'Come on,' I said.

I took the shinai, and some of her bags, and we made our way inside. We weaved around the people, and showing the guard her ticket we went through the gate. I heard an announcement for the sleeper train to Sapporo. And looking up at the screen I saw which platform it was leaving from.

We took the escalator up to the busy platform just in time to see the sleek-bodied bullet train gliding into the station. It was snub-nosed, like a plane, and it seemed to go on for miles. I checked the Lump's ticket and we scurried around the piles of luggage to get to her compartment.

'Well, this is it,' I said.

I gave her the bags, and going inside she put them above her seat. I looked down the platform, at all the people who were saying goodbye. They seemed happy, but I wasn't because I knew she didn't want to go. And I didn't want her to go either. But I tried to smile when she came out and I handed her the shinai, which I'd wrapped in gift paper.

'You can beat those kids with it if they try to bully you.'

The Lump looked worried then.

Suddenly I was seething! 'Hey, you tell those kids if they go near you I'll—'

'Do no harm,' said the Lump. And then she got on the train.

Was that it? She wasn't going to say goodbye? I could see her putting the shinai on the seat and then she took something from her rucksack. I looked at the clock. Only two minutes left! She'd have to get off now if she wanted to say goodbye! I was relieved when she did. She opened a silver tin containing homemade cards, every one a different colour. And she frowned as she looked at them as though wondering what colour to give me. It was a difficult decision.

'For you,' she said, and handed me an orange card. It said her full name: Mikazuki Mia Takeda. And her cell number was below.

We just stood there then, feeling a little shy. The Lump wasn't much of a talker and I was lost for words. And so I knelt down in front of her and we hugged. 'I'll call you. I promise.'

'Best friend, Yukio!' said the Lump.

When we heard the whistle she got on the train and sat by the window. There was a chiming sound to indicate that the doors would close and then they did.

'Have a safe trip,' I said.

When the train started to pull away I walked after it. The Lump put her hand on the window as if to touch my hand. And then I saw she was crying.

'It'll be OK!' I said. 'You can come back any time!'

But then the train shot away and she was gone. I felt so alone then. But then a worse feeling came over me. It was like I was never going to see her again.

'It's just a feeling,' I said. 'It doesn't mean anything.'

After a while I turned around and walked down the empty platform. I was going home to a house where there was only Grandmother, who rarely came out of her room. The train wasn't even out of Tokyo and I was missing her already.

14

A month had passed since the Lump had left. For the first week I was sure that the cops were going to come through the door. In the second week I was less sure. And by the end of the third week I was almost sure they weren't coming. I mean, I never saw that Detective Maki, not once. And if he suspected me he'd no doubt have come snooping around. And so in the end I stopped worrying. I even started to feel happy again. In a way I didn't want to feel happy. I still felt guilty over some of the killings, especially the cop. But that's how I was feeling all the same.

I trotted downstairs and passed the paper but I never picked it up. Articles on the Psycho Killer were moved to the middle pages and then they disappeared altogether. The last I read he was rumoured to be a foreign assassin who had returned to his own country. Another article said, in something of a whisper, that he'd been killed by the yakuza and they'd disposed of his body. The headlines returned to the suicide rate, which was now out of control. It had become a nationwide problem and was being debated in the House of Representatives, but they didn't seem able to do anything about it. But how anyone could think of suicide on a day like today was beyond me. It was such a beautiful day.

I went into the kitchen, which smelled of bacon and eggs, and took a seat. Yoshe's baby boy put an egg soldier in his ear and laughed. Then he scowled at me. 'Mikazuki!' he said. And he said it like I'd taken her away from him. I just ignored him – he got on my nerves some days. But I couldn't believe that he'd remembered the Lump's name. He didn't even know my name.

Yoshe came in with Grandmother's breakfast dishes and put them in the sink. Then she saw the state of the baby. 'You naughty boy!' The baby laughed and rubbed egg into the table until Yoshe stopped him. She put some breakfast in front of me and started to clean him up. 'You look well,' she said.

'It's all the training.'

'I'm glad you're back to your old self. You know, some of your school friends came by yesterday. They said they'd see you in the park around ten. And they said Shiomi would be with them!' She smiled and waited for me to say something, but I just carried on eating. 'Well, who is she?'

Shiomi was the girl who'd tapped on my helmet. I'd bumped into some of the guys in the park last week and we'd played soccer. And she'd been there with some of her friends. I caught her looking at me a few times, and when I was leaving she walked me to the gate.

'Don't tell me then,' said Yoshe, raising her eyebrows.

'OK, I won't.' I put my dishes in the sink and went to leave.

'You know, Yukio, I'm sure Miko wouldn't want you to be alone.'

'No,' I said.

'You should invite her round. And invite your school friends as well. You spend too much time by yourself.'

'I'll think about it.'

'And have you called your cousin yet?'

'No. I keep meaning to, but I forget.'

'Well, call her today. Your grandmother's just told me that she'll be spending the whole of September with us. She'll like that.'

'She will too.' I could just see the joy on the Lump's face when she gets off the train. 'I'll see you later, Yoshe.'

'Mikazuki!' said the baby, still accusing me of hiding her.

Yoshe laughed. 'Yes, Mikazuki's coming!'

I didn't want to look at the paper because I was in such a good mood. But it was on the hall table and I saw the headline: 'Yakuza Suspected Over Murder of Prominent Politician'. The article said that Mr Itou, who was leading an investigation into illegal gambling, hadn't wanted to go along with things and so he was gunned down outside his family home. His wife said that he was a loving husband and a good father. She said he was a brave and decent man who'd stood up to the yakuza and he'd paid the price. And what made her angry was that he was the only one. She accused his colleagues of being cowards. And suggested that some of them were on the yakuza payroll.

I went out into the sunshine. It wasn't my war

any more and I wasn't going to get involved. But there was still a twinge of guilt. Part of me felt like a deserter who'd run away from a battle. But then I didn't care and I started to run. I wanted to be in the park playing games with my friends! I didn't care what games they were, as long as we were playing something. And I wanted Shiomi to be there!

I ran across the tracks and the road, and sprinting up the concrete ramp I went into the park. I had so much energy I felt as if I could run for days. I ran through the trees and past a homeless guy as he sat up on a bench.

'Morning!'

'Morning,' he said, scratching his head.

I kept going until I was past the trees and then I looked around for the guys. I saw them at the far end of the common, sitting on the grass. There was Kane, whose father was a cop, and Oki, who was appearing in a soap opera next summer. And then there were the brothers Hiro and Hiroto, whose mother owned the Blue Fin, one of the best sushi restaurants in Tokyo. And behind them sat Jin and his sour-faced girlfriend, Fumi, whose lip curled every time she spoke. And then I saw Shiomi sitting in the centre. I was happy she was there, but trying not to show it I strolled over to join them.

'Here he is!' said Oki.

''Bout time,' said Fumi.

Shiomi stood up. 'We didn't want to start until you were here.'

'*You* didn't!' said the sour-faced Fumi.

Hiro kicked the ball in the air. 'Well, he's here now – let's play.'

'We called yesterday,' said Shiomi. Then she looked a little shy. 'Is it OK that we called?'

She had a really pretty face. 'You can call any time,' I said. She smiled and I did too. And then we looked away from each other.

'Why are you blushing, Shiomi?' asked Fumi in a sly sort of way.

Kane came over. 'Hey, Yukio! You looking forward to going back to school?'

'I suppose,' I said. And when I thought about it I was.

'I'm joining the police cadets in the autumn. Why don't you join with me?'

The thought of becoming a cop when I left school flashed through my mind. And there was something about it that seemed right. Maybe, in some small way, I could make up for the cop that I'd killed.

'OK, I will. Just let me know when you're going.'

'Great!' said Kane. He came closer and lowered his voice. 'Dad's told me some things about the Psycho Killer murders. I'll fill you in later.'

Then Hiro handed me a flyer. 'We're thinking of going to this club. What do you think, Yukio?'

I couldn't believe it! It was like a black cloud had blocked out the sunshine. It was an advertisement for a night out in Paradise, age group fourteen to seventeen. So once again Riko was opening the club!

'Will you come?' asked Shiomi.

'No, I won't. And you shouldn't go either!'

She looked a little startled.

'Yukio's right,' said Kane. 'My dad said that place is owned by the yakuza. They use the profit to deal in drugs. None of us should go.'

'Well, my uncle's in the yakuza,' said Fumi, 'and he doesn't sell drugs.'

'That's beside the point!' said Kane.

'No, it's not!' insisted Fumi.

'Forget about it,' said Hiro. 'I didn't want to go anyway. Now let's play ball.'

Everyone relaxed then and we started kicking the ball around. But I felt that seething hatred come back. And even though I fought against it, it wouldn't go away. Just the thought of Riko opening that club made me sick. And for that age group as well! And then it dawned on me: she was probably looking for girls to work in Uncle Benni's massage parlours. I wonder how many other girls had gone through what Miko did, only to end up dead. I kicked the ball back to Kane and turned to Shiomi. 'Listen, promise me you won't go to that club.'

'I won't,' she said, looking slightly hurt. 'I was only going if you were going.'

'Forget about it, Yukio,' said Kane. 'No one wants to go anyway.' He kicked the ball towards me but I missed it.

'Come on, Yukio!' said Hiroto. 'You're not concentrating.'

As I turned to go after the ball an orange frisbee hit my chest. I was so shocked I couldn't move. Then I dropped to my knees and took it in my hands. My eyes filled with tears as once again I saw Miko laughing and Hiroshi running to catch it. When I looked up a small girl was standing in front of me. She looked like Miko in the photograph on my bedroom wall. Slowly she took it from me, and then she ran back to her parents. I swear, it was like I was being summoned by my dead friends to avenge them. And avenge them I would!

'Are you getting the ball or what?' asked Fumi.

'I'm leaving,' I said, and walked away.

'What's wrong?' asked Kane.

Shiomi ran after me and put her hand on my shoulder, but I pushed it away and kept walking.

'Yukio!' she shouted.

But I was already gone. Games were for children. My place was on the battlefield.

The full moon was as big as I'd ever seen it and the ground was covered in mist. And it was silent. Silence is such a rare thing to hear in Tokyo. But this was the resting place of the dead and so it should be silent.

'It seems like such a long time since we've spoken. But I wanted to tell you that I still look at you as my best friends, even though you are not here. And I miss you so much. Earlier today I thought you were summoning me for revenge. But you were such good kids that you'd never want me to hurt anybody, no matter what they'd done. And my cousin Mikazuki is the same. You were right, Miko. She really is a great kid. She got me to put down the sword. "Do no harm," she said, and she's right in a way. But if I stand by, more harm will be done. And so once again I have taken up the sword and now I'm going into battle. But I have to admit that I feel more frightened than I've ever felt! And so I ask both you and my ancestors to watch over me and make sure I come to no harm. But if I am to die, then please let it be quick! . . . I love you both.'

I bowed once, and getting on the bike I rode away. As I headed towards Uncle Benni's house I thought about the Lump. She would be so sad if she came in September and I wasn't there. I could just see her sitting in the park by herself. And then I imagined her with the Om, sleepwalking all the way to my grave. I loved the Lump and I should have told her. But she's smart – she knows things without having to be told.

But I had to put her out of my mind now because I was nearing the park where Uncle Benni lived. Then I was on the road that ran around it. It wasn't long before I came to the house, and as I slowed I was sickened to see three yakuza standing guard at the gate. But Yama wasn't one of them, and the gate was open; at least that was something.

I pulled into the first street I came to, and parking

the bike I put on my ski mask. I took the sword from its mounting and walked back down the street. I kept close to the park wall, so as to stay out of the street lights. And then, as I neared the house, I moved into the shadows beneath a tree.

The guards were not young men but they were stocky and fit-looking and dressed in tight-fitting suits. And they had short haircuts and hard faces. Everything about them seemed sharp. But these were Uncle Benni's bodyguards, so what did I expect? They talked from time to time, but even then they looked around. One of them lit up a cigarette and before long I could smell the smoke.

If I walked out, they'd see me coming. I'd have to wait for them to step back. I had to have surprise on my side, otherwise I was dead. Just the thought of death filled me with a sickening fear. I took a deep breath and tried to stop shaking. 'You are a samurai. You live by the bushido code!' But the words were of little comfort. There was no chi energy flowing through my body. Even the hatred had deserted me. But if it was death, then so be it. Because these animals weren't getting away with what they'd done to the twins! And when I thought about it, I'd sooner die tonight with Riko than let her live!

The sky crackled with electricity and thunder followed. Somewhere I heard a bell toll. It echoed in the night like a ghostly foghorn. Then I heard chanting. There must have been a temple close by. And then, in my mind, I saw Riko dancing in that club. And I heard the song 'Psycho Killer'. The song merged with the chanting and a booming drumbeat played over it. I got goose pimples when I thought about all the great battles that had begun with the beating of the drums. And then I felt the chi energy flow through my body and my courage came back! I felt like roaring a battle cry and charging the gate. But I didn't because the men moved back into the driveway. I stepped out of the shadows and headed towards the entrance. And as I did the drumbeat grew louder, and the bell boomed, and that clanging sound rang in my ears. But it was too late to bother me now! I could hear the men talking. And then I saw them! My attack was like the rising of the wind. I went through them and never looked back. But I could hear them dying. One of them tried to shout but his throat was cut. Another tried to stay on his feet, but there was a hollow thud and his head hit the tarmac. The third was dead before he hit the ground. I headed towards a side entrance, away from the main door, and as I neared it, it opened. I thrust the sword straight into the man's chest. Then I pushed him back against a wall. I closed the door and climbed a spiral staircase. When I reached the top I heard him drop and the noise in my head fell silent.

I moved down a dark corridor and came out on a well-lit landing. Below was the main entranceway, and looking over the banister I saw the double doors that led to the driveway. And I could hear a thudding sound coming from a room a couple of doors down. Someone was using a punchbag. As I stepped towards the room the sound of the pounding grew louder. I peeked around the corner. It was a large wide room walled in mirrors, and bare except for some weightlifting equipment. Looking in a little further I saw a red punchbag and the person who was pounding it. It was Yama! He had his shirt off and his thick, muscular torso was covered in tattoos. He attacked the bag with furious left and right hooks. But powerful as they were, they were nothing to the karate kicks that followed. His huge bare feet slammed the bag with enough power to knock down a horse. It crossed my mind to get out of there. Before the fear got to me, I entered the room.

I came up slowly behind him. I wanted to strike him down with a surprise attack, but he saw me in the mirror. And what was worse was that he pretended not to notice me. He threw a few more punches, and then taking off his gloves he hung them on a hook.

'So we meet at last, Psycho Killer. I knew you'd come.'

His voice threw me. It was calm and soft like a girl's. He turned to face me. His body was covered in demons, but none of them was as demonic-looking as he was. His broad battle-scarred face was something to behold. And his sunken pale eyes made him look insane. And when he smiled I knew that he was.

'Are you not going to take off the mask? . . . Never mind. I'll rip it from your dead body.'

Fear got the better of me, and raising the sword I attacked. But it struck the low ceiling and I had to step back. Suddenly a karate kick thumped into my chest and sent me flying. I was winded, but I got to my feet. By that time he was holding a fat aluminium baseball bat. Suddenly he swung at my head. All I could do was duck. I couldn't even block the blow. If the bat broke the sword I was dead! He swung again and I jumped back. He moved quickly for a big man and he was fast on his feet. If I couldn't control my mind, I was done for!

'What's it like to know you're going to die?' he said.

A sickening fear flowed through me and my heart pounded painfully. Suddenly he sprang forward and swung. I jerked my head back and the bat swished past my nose. Another inch and I would have been in too much pain to continue. He swung again and I tried to block it. But the bat smashed the sword to one side. It was almost knocked out of my hands. For a second I thought it had broken. I started backing away and he followed. Then I saw that I was backing into a corner. I was going to die! Then in my mind I saw the Lump in her kendo gear. Suddenly I dropped on to one knee and hacked at his left foot. The blade cracked his ankle and slashed his Achilles tendon. Before he could club me I did a forward roll and jumped up. I saw bone sticking from his ankle and blood pouring from the severed tendon. It was a serious wound and he knew it. But with all the discipline he could muster he placed his damaged foot on the floor and limped after me. He swung the bat but missed. When he swung again I saw his side was completely open. I waited for his next swing. As he turned with the blow I stabbed him through the armpit. Blood ran down his side like a waterfall, and as it did the colour left his face. He looked to the door. For a second I thought he was going to shout, but he didn't. He turned towards me and came on. I was still backing away but my mind was calm. I lined up his left wrist and judged the distance. Crying out I jumped forward and struck the target. The blade severed his left hand with a surgical cut and he looked at his stump in amazement. Then he looked on the floor. But his hand was still clinging to the baseball bat, which he held in his right. He tried to take it with his stump but he realized he couldn't. Screaming, he charged. I thrust the sword through his chest but it had no effect! He dropped the bat, and grabbing my throat he pushed me against a wall. I couldn't get him off. And I couldn't breathe! He started clubbing me with his stump and then he tried to bite my face. With all my strength I pushed back his big head. And as I did his eyes filled with blood. He started to weaken, and so with one last shove I pushed him away. He fell to the floor, face first, and I fell with him. I knelt there choking and sucking up deep breaths. Then I heard someone running up the stairs.

'Benni! The guards are dead! The Psycho Killer's in the house!'

It was Riko.

I heard Uncle Benni. 'Yama! Yama!'

I tried to turn him over so I could get the sword, but he was too heavy. And so I grabbed his arm and pulled him on to his back. Ripping out the sword, I ran on to the landing.

It was silent but I sensed victory! But then I remembered *zanshin,* a kendo term that refers to staying alert. Never drop your guard! And it was good that I remembered it. Because if I hadn't I wouldn't have heard the man sneaking up behind me in his bare feet. I turned as fast as I'd ever turned and thrust the sword through his bare chest. He dropped his raised hatchet. And when I pulled out the sword he dropped next to it. His body was covered in yakuza tattoos. But he wasn't Japanese. He was a white Westerner.

I moved cautiously along the landing. I wanted to wipe the sweat from my eyes but I kept both hands on my sword. Then I looked around a corner. And there was Uncle Benni standing in what looked like a library. He pulled a samurai sword from its mounting and threw the mounting away.

'Come on then, Psycho Killer. Let's see what you've got.'

He was wearing a man's kimono and he must have been about sixty. But fear wasn't built into Uncle Benni. His face was as hard as granite and his eyes were calm and clear. If I underestimated this man he'd kill me. And I knew Riko was around somewhere. I pushed the door flat against the wall to make sure she wasn't behind it. I scanned the room. It was empty. And so I turned to face Uncle Benni.

He held his sword in both hands. 'Come – what are you waiting for?'

I raised my sword and moved closer. Suddenly he dropped on to one knee! 'Now!' he shouted. Riko rose up behind him, but I was already running. There were two loud bangs and bullets cracked into the door frame. There was another bang just before I jumped over the banister. I crashed on to the hall table, which broke into pieces, and then I bolted for the double doors. More shots shattered the woodwork. But I wrenched the doors open and ran down the drive. I heard a pinging sound as bullets ricocheted off the iron-barred gates.

'Leave it, Riko!' shouted Uncle Benni.

I jumped over the guards' dead bodies, and dodging Riko's bullets I ran for the bike.

There was no time to put the sword away and so I held it across the handlebars. I put on my helmet, kick-started the engine and pulled back on the throttle. But I rode straight into a dead end! I turned around and rode back. But Riko came around the corner blazing away. I put my head down and kept going. She stopped and scurried to change clips. She took aim but she hesitated, and then she turned and ran. I pulled back on the throttle, and taking the sword in my right hand I struck her down. I braked hard at the end of the street and looked back. She was on the ground and she wasn't moving. I rode back towards her and got off the bike. Her eyes were open but blood was oozing out the back of her skull. It formed into a dark pool and the full moon appeared in it. For a second I felt hypnotized.

'Riko! Riko!'

I put the sword away and grabbed the gun from her hand. Then snatching the silver claws from her severed pinkies, I put them in my pocket.

As I rode away I saw Uncle Benni in the mirror. He ran down the side street. Then I heard him scream. But I laughed as I rode because I knew it was the Lump's move that had saved me. I don't know how many times I'd told her she couldn't hit someone's feet, but she never listened. And I was so glad she didn't.

15

I ran down to Shibuya while the morning was still fresh, and heading into the Cafe Veloce I bought a coffee. I looked around for a seat, but the place was packed and so I had to sit in the smoking section. Normally I wouldn't sit there because it was full of smokers coughing and I couldn't stand that, but I was dying to read the news and so I took a seat and spread the paper out on the table. 'Bloodbath at Uncle Benni's. Six bodyguards were butchered at Benni Tanaka's house last night in an attempt on the godfather's life. Although the attempt failed, his most feared enforcer, Yama, was killed and so was his beloved niece Riko Tanaka.'

An old guy with yellowish skin sat next to me, and lighting up a cigarette he started to cough. I gave him a look in the hope that he'd move away, but he ignored me and stared at the TV. I saw that the news was on. One of the Mitsubishi directors was heading into work with half a dozen journalists in pursuit. He was the one caught in the photograph with Uncle Benni that time. And I remember Kane telling me that a lot of directors like to be seen with yakuza bosses, especially if they want to intimidate directors from rival corporations. But that was old news. Now he was being accused of money laundering.

'Are you the yakuza's banker?' asked one of the journalists. But he ignored her.

'Can you account for your three houses?' asked another. But he ignored him as well.

And so one of them shouted, 'Isn't it a little late to be going into work?'

He didn't like that and he turned on them. 'I work twelve hours a day! Some nights I'm here until midnight!' He pushed away the camera and stormed inside. The crew tried to follow, but the security stopped them. And then, when the camera pulled back, I saw it was the Mitsubishi Building in Ginza.

'Terrible,' said the old guy without taking his eyes off the TV. 'So much corruption.'

I ignored him and carried on reading. 'And while police are withholding many details, they did reveal that the victims were killed with a samurai sword. It goes without saying that the Psycho Killer is back.' I turned the page to see an old photograph of Yama surrounded by cops. He was in handcuffs, but he still looked scary. Then in my mind I saw him in that mirrored room. 'What's it like to know you're going to die?' I felt that fear flow through me again. But then I saw that dumbfounded look on his face when he realized I'd cut off his hand. 'Not so scary now, are you?'

But he still came forward. He never called for help or tried to run. And what about Uncle Benni? There was definitely something of the shogun about him. I could just see him commanding an army in a war zone. Bodies falling around him, and there he'd stand, stone-faced and fearless. He wasn't godfather for nothing. And what great tactics, having Riko stand behind him like that and then drawing me in. I found myself feeling more than a little respect for Uncle Benni.

But I'd finally got Riko. She'd had to die for what she'd done to the twins. But witch that she was, she was no coward either. But she let her rage get the better of her. Uncle Benni should have taught her the samurai sayings. Then she would have known what he knew: that you must never chase the enemy too far.

I turned the page and saw an old photograph of her and Louise. Riko must have been about six and Louise about five. They're dressed in kimonos, like the one the Lump wore, and they're standing in a park on a summer's day. I'd only ever seen them as monsters that I wanted to murder, but now . . . You've never seen two happier kids. They have their arms around each other and they're smiling. It's like there's a real bond between them, just like there was between me and the twins. And it's like they really love each other . . . But they grew up to become scum and they showed Miko no mercy!

Then Uncle Benni's house came on the TV. There were a dozen bodyguards standing at the gates, and then the camera switched to a woman reporter.

'Tokyo woke up this morning to news of a bloodbath. Osaka woke up to the same.'

The footage switched to Osaka. There were bodies under sheets and cops all over the place. But I couldn't understand why.

'Tomi Yamamoto and his brother Benji were

gunned down late last night as they came out of the Hemiji Casino. Several men in two cars were seen spraying automatic weapons. Tomi Yamamoto is said to have been hit two dozen times. A bodyguard and three members of the public were also killed. But these were not the only killings to take place in Osaka last night.'

The footage switched to fire engines hosing a smouldering house.

'In the early hours of the morning what is believed to have been a bomb was pushed through Miki Kimura's letter box, killing him and three others. Miki Kimura was the Yamamoto clan's main adviser and his brothers have vowed revenge. But to add to their troubles they'll be missing their main henchman, Hama Hamasaki. Hamasaki, who served fifteen years for a double homicide, will kill no more. His headless body was found floating in Osaka Harbour.'

The footage switched back to the reporter outside Uncle Benni's house.

'Did a certain person believe the Psycho Killer to be a super-assassin in the employment of the late Tomi Yamamoto. And if so, was a hit squad sent down from Tokyo? You can't help but fear that this is the beginnings of a full-scale gang war. And if that's the case, how long will it last? This is Anna Takahashi reporting live for *Tokyo on Five*.'

My mind started racing in ten different directions. I had to get out of there!

'You forgot your paper,' said the old smoker.

'I've read it,' I said.

I went outside and tried to sprint, but the crowds at the Shibuya Crossing held me up. I was seething. I had to stand there and wait for the lights to change. Then I watched them clash on the crossing like opposing armies. But they weren't holding weapons; they were carrying shopping bags. Prada bags and iPods. CDs and designer clothes! They were nothing but sheep shopping for trinkets! How many of them would go into a house full of gangsters not knowing if they would come out alive? I wonder what my grandfather would have thought. He'd charged the marines with an empty rifle and he'd been sold down the line for an American iPod. There's no honour in an iPod. These people should wake up, and something needed to happen to wake them. But it was nothing to do with me. I had my own war to think of . . . But then I realized that my war was over. Riko was dead. But this can't end. Not now.

I mean, I'll admit I was on a huge high over last night's victory. It made me feel powerful. I've never felt as powerful in my life. But it wasn't just that. I was more convinced than ever that all of this was meant to happen. I was meant to take up the sword and live by the bushido code. And I truly believed that the chi energy flowed through me.

'No, the war has to continue.'

I ran down a side street and headed home. I couldn't believe they were killing each other. And when I thought about it I was as happy as a drunken monk. I considered what my next move should be. Maybe I could make an attempt on Uncle Benni's life. But no, he'd be too well protected now. Maybe I could take out one of his crew, someone high up in the organization. I could even think about killing one of the heads of the other clans. That would really stir things up. But suddenly my energy left me and I stopped. I realized that anything I did now would only be seen as part of a gangland war, because the Psycho Killer was seen as an assassin. And what difference did it make who I killed if they were killing each other? It served no purpose. *I* served no purpose.

I walked on for a bit but I couldn't think what

to do. This was my life now, but if I wanted it to continue I'd have to think of a new strategy. Then it came to me. That Mitsubishi director who was linked to money laundering. It was said that he was the yakuza's banker, but I'd bet he'd never be charged. Those people get away with everything. They never get their hands dirty, but they make millions from ill-gotten gains. No, he should be made to pay. I could even use Riko's gun. And I could leave the girls' claws at the scene. It would send a powerful message to corporations, telling them not to associate with criminals. And then they'd see that I wasn't just an assassin.

But then everything went blurry and the ground I was walking on started to sway. For a second I thought I was going to faint. I clung to a lamp post and waited for the dizziness to pass, and then I stood up straight. Maybe it was because I hadn't eaten. 'You have to eat, Yukio. You have to stay strong.'

I felt better when I walked on, but then the doubts came. It wasn't that I didn't want to do it, I did. But I couldn't justify it, not really. He wasn't even yakuza. He's nothing more than a banker, and he was in no way connected to the twins' death. But it's not about the twins any more. It's a war against the yakuza and . . . the people who associate with them! Or maybe I was doing it for the Buraku. They've been persecuted in Japan for centuries, and now someone was standing up for them. That's it! I was doing it for the Buraku. Then I was so amazed with the way things fell into place that I stopped dead. The twins were Buraku. So I was doing it for them as well!

I felt relieved now that I'd made the connection. And that being the case I'd better stake out the place. I ran all the way home, and going inside I started to run up the stairs. But then Yoshe came out of the kitchen.

'Yukio, can I ask you a favour?'

'What?'

She came to the foot of the stairs. 'I have a dental appointment. I hate to ask, but can you look after the baby?'

'I can't. I'm going to Ginza.'

'You can take him with you.'

'I'm going on the bike.'

Yoshe looked disappointed. 'OK, doesn't matter.'

I went up to my room and took Riko's gun from the top shelf of the wardrobe. It was a small black Smith & Wesson automatic. When I pressed a button the clip came out. It had six holes running down the side, and for every hole there was a bullet. I pushed the clip back in and aimed it at myself in the mirror. I didn't mind using a gun. The samurai used firearms when it suited them.

I put it next to the girls' claws and put on a clean T-shirt. Then I trotted downstairs and took a few rice cakes from the kitchen. But then I felt bad about Yoshe. The baby's father was a bit of a baby himself and she couldn't get him to do anything, not even look for a job. And she always did things for me. 'I'll take him,' I said.

'You don't have to.'

'I want to. I like the baby. And I don't mind taking the subway.'

'That's great, because I think he's starting to like you too.'

Yoshe looked happy then. I suppose me taking the baby meant something more to her than missing a dental appointment; it showed that I looked at him as family, which I did.

She put the baby in his buggy and put on his baby baseball cap. He smiled then because he knew he was going out and he liked to go out. And he looked so cute in his cap.

Yoshe gave him a kiss. 'You're going out with Uncle Yukio!'

'Kio!' said the baby.

It was the first time he'd said my name!

'Oh, before I forget,' said Yoshe, wheeling him outside. 'The nun came by. She asked if you could call round and see her.'

'I'll go on my way back,' I said, and headed off to the subway.

'There's a bottle and wipes under the seat,' shouted Yoshe. 'And don't let him get too much sun!'

'I won't.'

I pushed the baby down to Yoyogi station and took the Chiyoda line over to Ginza. The baby didn't like being underground and he didn't like being on the train either. He started to look a little sour-faced and then he started to cry. And no matter how many people tried to please him, and there were plenty of them, he just wouldn't stop. But he was happy when we got back to street level. He liked the look of Hibiya Park, with its tall trees and tennis courts, and he liked the moat that ran around the Imperial Palace. If I'd had time I would have taken him to the toy section in one of the big department stores, but I didn't. And so I headed over to the

International Forum and cut through the convention centre.

It was a vast building with a glass roof shaped like the skeleton bones of a whale. The baby liked the roof and he shouted at it. Then he realized that his voice echoed and he shouted all the way to the end. And then, through the huge sheets of glass, I saw the Mitsubishi Building rising up between two other skyscrapers. I pushed the baby out into the sunshine and surveyed the area. The building stood on a broad street that ran down towards the Imperial Palace and up under a railway bridge. It was dark under the bridge, even in the daylight, and it wasn't until I headed towards it that I saw there were motorbikes underneath. And when I looked back I saw the Mitsubishi Building was no more than two hundred metres away. I could park the bike below the bridge and run back to it when the job was done. But this was going to be a difficult hit. This wasn't the docks or a backstreet in Shibuya. This was Ginza, a stone's throw from the Imperial Palace, and there were cops everywhere. Not only that, but there were hotels and expensive stores with security guards standing outside them. And there were cameras on every corner.

I pushed the buggy along the pedestrian path that ran between the stone wall of the bridge and the buildings. It was so narrow, and there were so many overhangs, it was like being in a tunnel. But it was my best chance of escape. It would take me over to the other side of Ginza, where I could merge with the heavy traffic. The only real problem was that there were bars and restaurants built into the arches of the bridge. I'd have to remember to ride slow in case anyone stepped out.

As I headed back towards the Mitsubishi Building the baby started to cry, for no reason, and so I bought him an ice cream. We pulled up outside Mitsubishi and I had a look around. There were square ponds and flower beds in front of the main entrance, and in the centre was a raised piece of ground with a garden on it. It looked like a small forest. There were half a dozen trees and plenty of bushes and smaller plants. If I climbed up on to the low wall I could hide in the foliage and shoot him from there. That way they couldn't even see where the shots were coming from. And it would be dark by then. Because he said he worked twelve hours a day, and when I was in the cafe it must have been about ten thirty. And so that was it. I sat by the ponds, in front of the building, and turned the baby towards me. He was still trying to take the wrapper off his ice-cream.

'Mikazuki!' he said, and gave me a dirty look. But when I took off the wrapper his face lit up. He held out both hands, and then he pushed it into his mouth. He was as happy as the Lump when he had something to eat.

I didn't like to think about the job then. It didn't seem right in front of the baby. But I have to admit that the thought of doing it excited me. But just then that clanging sound came back! I looked at the bridge but there was no train going by. It had to be in my head! I covered my ears and tried to get it to stop but it rang louder. I swear it was so upsetting it was driving me insane!

'Are you OK?'

I looked up to see a middle-aged woman looking down at me. She looked concerned.

'Just a headache,' I said, but I could feel my face cringing.

'You're very young to be having headaches.'

'It's gone now,' I said. And just as I said it, the ringing stopped.

'Well, as long as you're feeling better.'

She smiled and walked away and I sat there feeling bad. I'd heard about people who had ringing in their ears, but this was ridiculous. I turned to the baby to make sure he wasn't upset. But you've never seen a happier kid.

'You're very selfish, you know that?' But he didn't care. He just smiled as he ate his ice cream.

When the train stopped at Yoyogi I took the escalator to the top. I ran across the road, and cutting through the small park I pushed the buggy up the hill. When I entered the grounds of the shrine I saw Natsuko sitting in the shade of a tree. She even had the tea ready as though she was expecting me. But she was staring down at the ground like she was worried. And she was startled when she saw me.

'Yukio! You caught me daydreaming. Please, have a seat.'

I bowed before taking a seat and she poured me some tea. The worry lines left her forehead when she saw the baby and she smiled. 'Oh, he's such an angel!' She seemed to relax then and she sat back.

'Yoshe said you wanted to see me.'

'Yes, we're moving into the temple next week.

The work's almost finished. Can we call on you to help?'

'Of course. I'm not back at school for a few weeks.'

We were quiet then and I felt a little uncomfortable. It was like we couldn't think of anything to say. I mean, I'd known Natsuko for years, but every time we'd had tea together the twins were with us, and I was sure she was thinking about them. The worry lines returned to her forehead. She went to speak, but she hesitated and reached for her tea. Then she looked more determined and put the cup down. 'I really wanted to talk to you about the twins. Is that OK?'

'Of course,' I said.

'A Detective Maki came to see me a while back.'

Just to hear his name was like an unexpected body blow.

'I didn't mention it because I didn't want to upset you. He asked me if I knew why the twins did what they did, and I said no. Then he asked me about you. I said that you were a kind and decent young man.' She blushed a little. 'I even told him that I would trust you with my life. He seemed satisfied with that and he went away. I thought he was investigating the twins' death. But just the other day the head priest told me that he was a homicide detective investigating the Psycho Killer murders. Have you heard about them?'

'Yes, I've heard something.'

Natsuko frowned. 'I don't understand why he was asking me about you and the twins. I can't see any connection between their deaths and those murders. Not unless this Psycho Killer was in some way responsible. But the twins never mixed with any bad characters. They had few friends besides you. Yukio, is there anything you can tell me about their deaths?' Her face filled with pain. 'Because they were always the happiest of children!'

All of a sudden I felt bad. 'I don't know anything,' I said. But I looked away.

Natsuko sensed something and sat forward. And she had those large eyes that you couldn't get away from. 'I understand, Yukio,' she said in a delicate way, 'but I think something bad must have happened to the twins to make them do what they did. And somebody must be responsible. Maybe this Psycho Killer is to blame. And that's why the detective came to see me. Yukio . . . do you know who he is?'

Suddenly I had this urge to confess.

She came closer. 'Yukio, you're like a brother to me. If you know who he is, you can tell me!'

I almost broke, I really did. But then I felt a coldness towards her.

'I don't know anything, Natsuko. And I have to get the baby home.'

I stood up and taking the buggy I pushed him away. Then I realized what an idiot I'd been. I'd spoken to her in a harsh tone and I'd never done that before. I turned quickly and smiled. 'Just let me know when you're moving. I'll be glad to help.' But my voice sounded phoney even to me.

'I will,' she said, and raised her hand in farewell.

I was seething as I pushed the buggy back down the hill! What an idiot I was! All I'd had to do was stay calm and everything would have been fine. But I panicked and then I got angry. And what was that look on her face as she waved goodbye? She was hurt . . . Yes, that was it. She must have been hurt because of the way I spoke to her . . . But there was something else in that look. What it was I did not know.

All the way home I kept seeing her face as she waved goodbye. I replayed that image in my mind until I worked out what that look was. It was a look of horror. I understood then that I'd finally given myself away. Natsuko knew. And what would she do now? I imagined her calling the police. And my mind filled with hate. But I could never harm Natsuko. Not really.

16

I watched an ant crawl up the trunk of a tree. I don't ever remember seeing an ant at night before, but it wasn't quite night, not yet. Through the treetops I could see that the sky was still blue and that the moon was just starting to become visible. I brushed the ant off the tree and it fell to the ground where it really was dark. I didn't want to think about the ant. The ant reminded me of the Lump, and if I thought about the Lump I couldn't do what I had to do. And that was going to be hard enough. I didn't want to do it, I really didn't. But there I was standing in the shadows with the sword.

After a while a few stars appeared and the moon became bright. The sky was still pale but, because of the tall trees, the shrine grounds were almost dark.

Dark enough anyway. I made my way under the Shinto gate and walked as quietly as I could along the stone path. But I froze when I heard voices. They were coming from the street below, but I waited for them to fade away before moving on. I passed the temple and headed to the house where the nuns lived, but something caught my eye. Through the temple doors I saw candles burning and a silhouette kneeling at the altar. I looked around, to make sure that no one was there, and then kicking off my sneakers I slipped inside.

I moved silently towards a pillar and stood behind it. Then I peered around the side to see Natsuko. I couldn't see her face, because she had her back to me, but I could hear her quick, desperate whispers. What she was praying for I don't know, but she sounded confused, and she must have been. She was a Buddhist nun praying in a Shinto Temple. I couldn't help but feel sorry for her, but I didn't want to feel sorry for her! 'Be strong, Yukio! Kill her quick!' I took the sword in my right hand and stepped out from behind the pillar. If she turned around now she'd see me, but she didn't. And so moving in slow motion I put one foot in front of the other. But my foot creaked on a floorboard. Suddenly her head rose. 'Yukio, is that you?' she asked. But she never turned around.

How could she know? Part of me wanted to run, but I kept moving towards her. Then I saw the side of her face in the candlelight. She looked distraught.

'Have you come for me?' Her voice was quivering and her head went down. 'I don't understand . . . anything! The twins are dead and you have become what killed them!'

I took the sword in both hands and raised it like a dagger. But she turned and looked up at me. 'My beautiful Yukio!'

I froze with sorrow and shame. Then I stabbed her. I pushed the sword down into her good heart and then I pulled it out. She fell back on to the wooden floor and looked up at me. 'Yukio,' she whispered.

She wouldn't have felt much pain. I probably felt more pain killing her. And the shame was still to come. But I'd had to do it. It wasn't that I was scared of being caught or going to prison. But what I was doing was more important than what she did, whatever that was. Make tea, and be nice, and give off warmth. It was nothing really. I mean, I'm not saying I didn't enjoy her warmth; I did. But being nice never changed anything. It didn't save the twins. And it didn't punish the people who hurt them. Besides, I felt that there was a part of her that wanted me to do it. She was too delicate for this world.

I knelt beside her, and taking her hand I held it. I waited with her until she passed, and then closing her eyes I touched her beautiful face. I'd always wanted to touch it. I even thought about kissing her on the forehead, but that would have been disrespectful.

'You're with the twins now, Natsuko. They'll look after you.'

I went to the temple doors and checked the grounds. Then I turned and bowed to Natsuko's body before stepping outside. I put on my sneakers, retied the laces and walked down the slope to the bike.

I felt miserable as I rode to Ginza. But I thought about what I'd said and I hoped it was true. I hoped she was with the twins and I hoped she was happy. She always taught us that death was nothing to be afraid of because, as Buddhists, we're reborn again. And if that was the case then it makes no difference when we die. And so it makes no difference that I killed her. I wasn't just saying that because I felt bad.

I was saying it because I believed it was true. But I had to put Natsuko out of my mind now. Otherwise I'd end up dead myself.

It was dark by the time I reached the Imperial Palace. I followed the moat around and taking a right I rode along the broad road that passed the Mitsubishi Building. I headed under the railway bridge and parked the bike in the darkest spot. I took off my helmet and put on a flu mask. Flu masks look like surgeons' masks, but a lot of people wear them when they get a cold, even in the summertime. And so I could hide my face without drawing attention to myself.

As I put the helmet under the seat I saw the sword. I'd put it in the nylon bag and it was dark under bridge. I don't think anybody could see it, let alone steal it, and so I put the helmet next to it and left it at that. I put the gun in my belt and headed down to the Mitsubishi Building. I could see people talking outside the convention centre on the other side of the road, and there were a few strolling couples. But apart from them there were only the passing cars to worry about. But that part of Ginza was a business section and so it was usually quiet at night.

When I reached the building it looked deserted. The lights were on but I couldn't see a single soul at the windows, and there must have been about twenty floors. It crossed my mind that I might have missed him, but I had to carry on as though he was there. I scanned the raised garden to see where to hide. Then, making sure no cars were coming, I jumped up on to the low wall and crouched in the bushes. I looked around to see if I could be seen, but I couldn't. And so I stood up and headed through the foliage. I stopped at the edge of the garden and scanned the lobby. It was brightly lit and deserted except for an old security guard. He was wearing a blue cap and a blue uniform and he was standing to attention, even though no one was there. To my left was the path that ran around the ponds, which were lit up now by underwater lights. And to my right was another path, that led to the street. Either way he went, I could kill him. And he'd be close too – even I couldn't miss from that range. I dropped the girls' claws on the ground and taking out the gun I got ready.

Ten long minutes went by but no one came. I was just starting to think that everyone had gone home when I saw the security guard bow. My view was blocked by an interior wall and so I couldn't see who he'd bowed to. But then two middle-aged women came out from the main entrance. There were still people inside. Then more came. It was a group of younger men in suits. They were all laughing and joking and looked happy to be out of work. I watched them walk off down the street.

Suddenly I turned and saw people by the ponds! They must have come from the back of the building. There were three older businessmen and a girl in a green dress. One of the guys looked like the director. I scanned his face as he came closer. It was him! I took aim and pulled the trigger, but nothing happened. I cocked the gun and tried again. There was a loud bang and a bullet hit one of the men in the shoulder. He dropped to his knees. I fired again. The girl covered her head and started to scream. But I don't think I hit her. The director shielded his face with his briefcase and started to run. I took aim and fired three times. One of the bullets hit the briefcase dead centre. He dropped the case and fell face first into the pond. I'd got him.

I ran off the raised garden, but tripping on the foliage I fell off the wall. I hit the pavement hard, and it really hurt, but I got up straight away. But then someone grabbed me from behind and we both fell to the ground.

'You're not going nowhere!' said the old security guard, getting me in a bear hug.

'Let go, you old fool!'

'No!' he shouted, and pulled down my flu mask.

I beat him around the head with the butt of the gun, but he wouldn't let go. I got on top and smashed his nose until it broke and blood came out. Then I went to run. But once again he grabbed me around the legs and I fell down. And they can't have been paying him that much! I kicked him in the face until he let go and then I got up and ran. Boy did I run!

'Stop!'

I looked back to see two guys in suits chasing me. I sprinted across the street and under the bridge, and kick-starting the engine I rode away. I never even had time to put on my helmet. I pulled back hard on the throttle and shot down the pedestrian path that ran alongside the bridge. I whizzed past the bars and restaurants that were built into the arches, but it was OK. The path was deserted and the bars were empty. But suddenly a guy stepped out in front of me! I swerved to miss him and braked hard. But

I smashed into a wall and flew over the bike. My head cracked against the stone and I crashed on the pavement. Oh the pain! I felt like someone had hit me with a lump hammer. I held my head and got to my feet.

The guy staggered towards me. He looked a little drunk. 'Are you OK?' he asked.

The bullet hit him in the head and he collapsed like a puppet without strings. It happened so fast I didn't realize I'd done it. But there he was on the ground. It was quiet then and he lay so still. I watched him for a second, to see whether he'd get up, but he didn't. And so I put the gun away and picked up the bike. But as I did a sharp pain shot through my left leg! I bit down hard and kick-started the engine, but it wouldn't start. I tried again but nothing happened.

'Hey, you! Stop!'

I saw the two men in suits coming after me. I kick-started the engine again. It came to life and I looked back at them as I rode away. They came to a stop at the dead drunk's body.

As I pulled back on the throttle a loud noise came from the engine, and I saw that the handlebars were bent. I had to keep them at an angle in order to go straight. I came to the end of the pathway and stopped so I could put on my helmet. I saw that the engine was leaking and that the sword had gone. But I was in too much pain to care. My head was throbbing and my hair was matted with blood. It ran down the side of my neck as I put on the helmet. And the inner padding pushed against the swelling on my face. I almost passed out with the pain, but I fought to stay conscious. I had to get home.

I rode out on to the main road, and merging with the traffic I headed up towards the House of Representatives. But the bike was straining to make it up the hill, and no matter how much I pulled back on the throttle it crawled along. But when the road levelled out, it picked up speed. 'Please keep going!' When I looked down at my leg I saw a bone coming through my jeans. I swear I was in so much pain I wanted to scream. 'You're a samurai!' I said. 'Act like one!' But my voice was breaking up and the words seemed silly.

When I reached Omotesando the bike started to splutter and I saw smoke coming from the exhaust. Not much, but enough for a cop to pull me up. 'Come on, you can make it!' The bike crawled up Omotesando like a dying dog, but when I reached the lights at Harajuku station it cut out altogether.

And there were so many people around! But then something worse happened. I started to feel dizzy and my sight went blurry. Bitting down I got off the bike and kick-started the engine. I was sure it wouldn't start but it started straight away. I was so grateful I felt like crying, but I didn't. I rode through the lights and headed home.

And then I was passing Yoyogi Park. I'd never been so glad to see it! It was a beautiful park and it belonged to us. It was mine and the Lump's and the twins'. The Lump. I hadn't called her yet. She'll think I don't care and I do. And the Lump liked ice cream. I'll have to send her some. I'll have to send the twins some as well . . . No, I can't send the twins anything. They're dead. That's how all this began, Yukio, remember?

I took a left after the bend and headed towards the tracks. Hiroshi was on the tracks. He shouldn't be there. 'Hiroshi!' I shouted. 'There's a train coming!' But he just stood there and smiled. I pulled back on the throttle and rode towards him. But I never went anywhere. I realized that the bike had come to a stop and that the engine was dead.

I got off and went to push it across the tracks, but the sharp pain in my leg didn't like that, and so I left it at the side of the road. The helmet felt tight as I took it off, as though it had shrunk, and blood came down my face. I took the flu mask from around my neck and wiped my eyes, and then I went to limp away. But I stopped and looked back at the bike. I felt sad about leaving it. It had taken me away from danger so many times and now it was dead. I remembered the day I got it. I was so happy. And I remembered the Lump laughing on it. The Lump loved the bike as well. It wasn't just me.

'I won't leave you there. I'll come back for you, I promise.'

I limped through the small park where we used to play as kids. It was dark and empty and it made me feel miserable, but then something beautiful happened. It was daylight and the sun was shining and Miko was standing by the slide!

'I thought you were dead!'

She laughed a little. 'No, we've been on vacation.'

'We've been on vacation, Yukio,' shouted Hiroshi, running past.

But then the darkness came. 'Don't be afraid, twins. I'll protect you!' I said. But my voice sounded strange. I think my jaw was broken. Then the world spun and I had to sit down on a bench. When I looked up the park was empty and the sunshine had gone. But my head wouldn't stop spinning. 'I'll rest for a minute. Just a minute.'

'Up!' said the Lump. 'Up!'

I shuddered and woke up. There were no lights on in the apartment blocks and no cars on the road. And I was cold. I'd never been so cold. And my head was pounding. 'I have to get home.' I felt that sharp pain again as I got to my feet. But I gritted my teeth and limped through the park. And then with all the strength I could muster I forced myself up the hill. I was determined to get home, but then I collapsed on the pavement. It felt nice lying down, and if I stayed still my head didn't hurt. But then I was startled by a passing car.

'Get up! And don't stop until you're home!'

I got up, and ignoring the pain I forced myself on. I just kept going and going and then suddenly I was there. I couldn't believe it. I opened the front door and went inside. I'd made it!

I went to climb the stairs but I collapsed halfway up. I lay there and rested my head. 'Keep going,' I said. 'You're almost there.' But I couldn't get up and I felt so sleepy. 'A samurai would get up,' I whispered. I got up then and went to my bed. I rested my head on the fluffy pillows and pulled the white duvet over me. 'Yukio, it's us!' I could hear the twins calling me from the street below. 'I'm going to get up now, Miko. As soon as I can open my eyes.' Suddenly the pain jarred me awake. I'd been dreaming and I was still on the stairs. Very slowly I started to crawl upwards. I used my hands and my good leg, dragging my bad leg behind me. When I reached the top I crawled along the landing. And then I crawled into my room and collapsed.

It was almost light when I came round, and as soon as I did I felt pain. My knee was in agony and my head was throbbing. And my face felt like it had something growing on the side of it. But at least I'd stopped hallucinating. And I was glad. I'd seen some terrible things. But then, to add to my woes, the ringing started up in my ears. As if things weren't bad enough! I got up and staggered to the window in the hope that it was a train going by. And that's when I saw them. And there were so many of them. They came down the street in two columns, one on the right side and one on the left. They stayed close to the houses and they communicated in hand signals. They looked like ninja. Small men dressed in black body armour and wearing black helmets. But they weren't carrying swords. They were carrying long firearms, which they held in front of them. Following behind was a plainclothes policeman who I recognized as Maki. I saw more armed police climbing over the backs of the houses. And then, through my pain, I felt fear. Because I knew that this was it!

'Yukio.'

I turned slowly, like an old man, and going out on the landing I looked down. Grandmother was putting the bolts on the front door. 'They're here,' she said.

So she knew. She'd probably known all along. But when she saw my face she looked shocked. 'My brave grandson, what have they done to you?' Her eyes closed tight for a second and then she opened them. 'No matter. But now you have to do the right thing. Do you understand?'

'Yes, Grandmother,' I said. But my voice sounded like it was coming from far away.

'Good. I would not want you to dishonour the family name.' And then she did something she'd never done before. She bowed to me, and she bowed so low.

But I felt weak. 'I'm sorry, Grandmother, I do not think I can bow back.'

'That's OK, Yukio. Just remember this: I have always loved you, even though I never showed it.' Her face hardened but her eyes filled with tears. 'Go now. Do it before they come.'

I returned to my room and took the short sword from the wardrobe. Then I took off my shirt and tried to kneel down, but my knee wouldn't bend. Biting down I forced it to bend and then I knelt on the tatami floor. 'Do it quickly and the pain will end!' I faced the photograph of the twins and the statue of the Buddha and took the sword in both hands. But when I saw Hiroshi's face I realized something. I realized with absolute horror that he could never forgive me for killing his nun. And somehow it made what I had to do easier. I raised the sword and turned the blade towards me. Then, with all my remaining strength, I stabbed myself in the lower stomach. The agony! I pulled the blade up and across my stomach until it sliced open.

My eyes bulged and blood shot from my mouth. Blood and intestines splattered on the floor. Then everything went black and I fell.

17

I have to stand on a chair to look out the window, and when I do the cold wind blows in my eyes, but I'll do it for hours some days. There's not much to see, just the grounds and the high hospital walls, but if I pull up on the bars I can see Mount Shokanbetsu. Last night's sunset turned it a beautiful pink colour and today it's completely covered in snow. And it must have snowed down here last night because the ground looks a little frosted. The patients here are mostly women and they wave at me sometimes if they see me at the window. But I never get to meet them and there's no one out there today, it's way too cold. But it's February and we're seventy miles north of Sapporo, so cold weather is all you can expect.

I came so close to death. For the first few months

I wished I had died. I still do some days. It was worse when I was in the proper hospital. I woke up one time and my mother was standing over me. She blamed herself, of course, because she went off and left me, and that made me feel worse. But I never thought about her, not once, and I never thought about how much it would hurt her. And by the look on her face it hurt her a lot.

Her pilot boyfriend kept looking out the window like he couldn't wait to get back into the skies, and so after a few visits I told her she should go back to Vancouver. She cried then, but I think she was glad to be leaving. The media were hounding them everywhere; they even followed them to the airport. She wrote and told me that she'd come again next summer, when things had died down, and that she'd stand by me no matter what happened. She also told me that she'd bought a headstone for Grandmother's grave.

Grandmother put a steel pin through her heart before the cops could get through the door. She would have liked that. She would have found it fitting to die with honour like some old empress whose castle walls had been breached. And I know she was sick at the thought of getting any older. I think she might have done it anyway. Maybe I just gave her the excuse.

But I miss her now, a lot more than I thought I would.

The twins' grandad died soon after in a cheap flea-bitten room he'd rented in Yokohama. He was holding one of Miko's dolls and one of Hiroshi's paintings. It was five days before anyone found him. The coroner said that he'd sat by the window and waited for death. He was a good man and he didn't deserve to die alone. But my mother made sure he was buried with the twins. At least that was something.

Grandmother left everything to my mother, even though they never got along. Everything except the house, that is, which she left to Yoshe. Yoshe came to the prison hospital in Kobe, but I wouldn't see her; my mind was still bad then. Any time the detectives tried to question me I just sat there stone-faced and wouldn't speak. I was so defiant. And I couldn't believe how deranged I was. I told the psychiatrists that I was a samurai warrior reborn from a hundred battlefields, but they didn't seem impressed. They just scribbled in their files, and closing the cell door they walked away. And there was me shouting after them, 'I fought the Mongols at Hakata! I besieged Kumamoto Castle in the Satsuma Rebellion! And I fought on the side of the shogunate in the Boshin War!'

No wonder they thought I was insane.

My phoney lawyer, Mr Himura, who had a face like a skull, was the only person who was ever glad to see me, no matter what mood I was in. The case was getting big attention and he was always giving interviews on what, he said, was the reason for the killings. He blamed violent video games and he appealed to the government to have them banned. But the truth of the matter is that I never played video games, violent or otherwise, and I told him so. 'Leave your defence to me,' he said. And so I did.

Sometimes he brought his daughter with him, who also acted as his secretary. She looked like she'd been startled by a ghost and her face had frozen in fear. And whenever he answered his phone, which was about a dozen times a visit, she made a point of telling me how much fan mail had arrived, and what horrible things people had said. I couldn't stand her. I couldn't stand him either. They were more deranged than the patients. But it didn't matter in the end. The psychiatrist's report said that

I was mentally incompetent to stand trial. The judge at the court hearing said that I should be held in a secure unit for an indefinite period, and that's when they sent me up here. And it's not such a bad place. The food's OK and the staff are nice, and they let me walk in the grounds most days. It's just the cold and the smell of the disinfectant I can't stand. And they get you up so early. Why they get you up so early when all you do is sit around I don't know. But at least I'm away from Mr Himura and his creepy daughter.

As soon as my wound healed that clanging sound came back. It was so bad some days I'd lie there for hours with a pillow over my head. Eventually they got around to checking my hearing, but they couldn't find anything wrong. One of the psychiatrists said that it was brought on by something in my subconscious, but they're always saying things like that. If they can't say something clever they don't say anything at all. But one day it stopped and it never came back. And this is the reason why.

Towards the end of that summer, Yoshe came to see me. I wouldn't see her at first but I was glad that I did. Yoshe, who'd been a friend throughout my childhood, never said anything about the killings.

She never even mentioned Natsuko, and I knew it would have hurt her that I'd killed a nun. She just gave me a kiss and a big hug, like I'd done nothing wrong, and when she talked to me she held my hand. That's when she told me about the Lump.

When I was arrested the Lump's parents, not wanting to get involved, took Hatsu on holiday. They left the Lump with an old couple and told them they'd be back in a few weeks. Yoshe said that my name was never mentioned in the media, because I was too young, and so the Lump couldn't have known anything about it. And so she was distressed when she found out she wasn't going to Tokyo. She'd been looking forward to it so much. But the old couple were kind and they did their best to make her feel at home. And after a while she seemed fine. But the next day at school some of the girls stole a doll from her. The Lump became so distraught that the old couple were sent for. And seeing her condition they tried to contact her parents. But they were somewhere in Singapore and couldn't be located. That night the Lump was so upset she couldn't sleep. And so the next day the old man went back to the school to see if he could find the doll. But apparently the girls had put it in the incinerator. The Lump seemed more agitated the next day and she kept checking her cell. The last thing she said that they understood was, 'Yukio.' Everything she said after that wouldn't come out. She tried to speak. She tried to tell them what was wrong. But the words were frozen inside her.

But that night she went to bed and fell asleep. The old couple, having had little sleep themselves, went to bed as well. But the Lump's phoney parents had been so eager to get away they had forgotten to mention that she sleepwalked. The Lump got up in the middle of the night and headed down the road to the station. She was still in her pyjamas and she had her cell in her hand. The driver said she was looking at it as he came around the bend. He said he braked hard and tried to swerve but he still ran her over. All the neighbours rushed from their houses to free her body, which was trapped under the car. They talked to her and held her hand to let her know that she wasn't alone. And they put blankets over her to keep her warm. But my lovely cousin, Mikazuki, who I still lovingly call the Lump, died before the ambulance arrived. And so, in the end, the way of darkness did bring a great price. The greatest.

Yoshe held me before she left. And she promised

to visit me twice a year until the day she died. But I was so devastated I couldn't even say goodbye. I never spoke, or ate, or moved for more than two weeks, I just lay there. Because I knew that if I hadn't done what I did then the Lump would have been sent down to us. And me and Yoshe and Grandmother would have looked after her. Then the Om wouldn't have been taken away from her. And I know how much that severed head meant to her. And I know she'd have wanted to speak to me once it was stolen. When I close my eyes I can still see her distraught face checking her cell, frantic for me to call. But I never did call, even though I promised. And that, more than anything else, killed me.

When they couldn't get me to eat they sent for a Buddhist monk. But I didn't like the look of him. He was ugly and stern and his round glasses made his eyes look mean. But he told me that he was sorry for the Lump and he sounded like he meant it. And then he asked me was I sorry for the people I'd killed. I said I didn't know. And so he told me to think about them and we'd talk again.

Natsuko was the first one I thought of. She was one of the kindest people I'd ever known. It was a pointless, senseless killing and I couldn't believe that

I'd done it. And she probably didn't want to die; she probably just needed help. And then I realized that at some stage in that dark summer I must have gone insane. Because I'd never have harmed Natsuko if I was in my right mind. That's when I started to go through the files and the papers that Mr Himura had left. There was a report from Kako's social worker, who said that the thing he hated most was coming home to an empty house. Sometimes his mother would leave him alone for days. That's when he started hanging out with the Tanaka girls, but they weren't without their problems either.

They had had to be taken away from their mother at an early age because she was putting cigarette burns in them. They grew up in homes or with foster parents who didn't care for them because they were so badly behaved. The only family they ever had was Uncle Benni and Matsu – but she wasn't around for long. One social worker said that Louise was teaching herself to read because she never learned how. And a psychiatrist's report said that Riko had suffered from a mild form of schizophrenia all her life. And she had fought against it in order to get better, but she never did.

There were other things as well. The old guy who

had a daughter in a wheelchair had wanted to leave the yakuza for years. But there was nothing else he could do, and he needed the money to support her. His young apprentice, who only had his mother, was reported to be a loving son. Even one of the bodyguards I'd killed at the girls' apartment gave up his weekends to work with young offenders. No one had anything good to say about Yama, of course. Even some of the Tanaka clan were glad that he was dead. And his probation officer said that from the day he was born he was stone evil. But I don't see how that can be true. There must have been a time when he chased butterflies around a garden, just like Yoshe's baby boy. And when I thought about the Tanaka girls, they must have played with dolls and sung like Miko. And Kako must have laughed like the Lump when somebody chased him. The people I'd killed were just children grown up. And when I saw them that way I saw my true self. My earliest memory is of me on my mother's shoulders. I was reaching for the red autumn leaves and I was so happy. And yet I grew up to do what I did. That's when I realized that I wasn't a warrior or a samurai. I was just a murderer. And murder is a dirty thing.

And so I suppose the Lump saved me for the last

time. It was through her death that I thought about the people I'd killed. And it was only when I was sorry that the ringing stopped. I'll always miss her, but she was too beautiful a person for this world.

I heard a key in the door and I turned to see Nina looking through the glass panel. She's a blonde, blue-eyed Norwegian who speaks terrible Japanese. But she's always happy and so everyone likes her.

'How are you, Yukio?' she asked, handing me my medication.

I got down from the chair. 'Fine,' I said, and swallowed the tablets with a little water.

'Your visitor's here!'

She always makes everything seem exciting.

'You OK to see him?'

'Sure,' I said.

Lee, an orderly the size of a sumo, came in and put a pot of tea on the table. 'Any trouble out of him, Nina, and I'll use my latest karate technique.'

He gave me a dirty look and punched his fist into his hand. He reminded me of G.I. Joe, the way he was always fooling around, but he was a really nice guy. And he always gave me his manga when he'd finished reading them.

'I don't think there's any need for brutality, Lee,'

said Nina, joining in. 'Maybe we could just tie him up and tickle him to death.'

But when Detective Maki appeared in the doorway they straightened up.

'Would you like me to stay, Detective?' asked Lee.

'No! Couple of old Tokyoites like me and Yukio! We'll be fine. Right, kid?'

'Sure,' I said.

'I'll be just down the hall if you need me,' said Lee.

'Anything you need, Detective, just let me know,' said Nina, and leaving the door ajar she followed him.

Detective Maki raised his eyebrows. 'Who's that?'

'Nina. She's a psychiatrist from Norway.'

He took off his overcoat and put it on the back of the chair. 'Very nice!'

I hadn't seen him close up since that time he came to the house. But he was older than I remembered and as he sat down he sighed. 'You want to be mum?'

I poured the tea and he took out his notebook. Then he opened a file and looked at it. 'Did they tell you I was coming?'

'Yes.'

'It's just a formality before we close the case. You want to get it out the way?'

'Sure.'

He took a slurp of his tea. 'Hey, can I see the scar?'

I stood up and raised my T-shirt. He cringed and looked away. 'Sorry I asked!'

I sat down and he looked at me as though wondering what sort of kid I was. Then he picked up his notebook and got started. 'OK, here we go. Did you kill anyone else?'

'No.'

'Did you have an accomplice?'

'No.'

'Were you paid by anyone to do what you did?'

'No.'

'Did anyone put you up to it? Or incite you in any way to commit murder?'

'No.'

He made a note in his notepad and picked up his tea. 'No. I know they didn't.'

'So why did you come?'

'A final humiliation before I fade into retirement.'

'I don't understand. You were the one who found me, weren't you?'

'Yes, but I was also the one who had interviewed you. And in my report I stated that no further questioning would be required.' He shook his head. 'What was I supposed to think? I spoke to your grandmother, and I asked her: had you ever become violent, did you own a samurai sword, and would you know how to use one if you did? To all three questions she said no. She even said she stayed up late and would definitely have heard you if you went out. I mean, if it was just the Kako killing I would have suspected she was lying, because you were Miko's boyfriend. But like everyone else, my superiors included, I thought the Psycho Killer was a professional assassin.'

'But you followed me to the cemetery that day. And you spoke to Natsuko.'

'My wife's buried there! And it was Obon, don't forget. And I spoke to the nun because she knew the twins. And even she said you were a good kid. No, there's no way I could have known, but you try telling my superiors that! They must really believe that every detective has a sixth sense.' He looked angry then and he was quiet for a time. Then he looked at the door. 'Hey, kid, you mind if I smoke?'

'No.'

'They've got no-smoking signs all over the place. What do they expect you to do? Go outside and freeze.' He got up and looked through the gap in the door like a schoolkid. Then he lit up.

'So how did you know it was me?'

He chuckled as he sat down. 'We questioned over three hundred yakuza, but no one knew anything. I mean, gangsters always tell you they know nothing. But after a while it dawned on me that they didn't. The night after you hit Uncle Benni's I stayed late at the office. I just couldn't get it out of my head! And so I went back to the drawing board. Who was the first victim? Kako. Who had a motive to kill Kako? You. But that was a dead end because there was nothing connecting you to the rest of the murders. But I'd had a couple of drinks, and for some reason, I don't know why, I googled your name. A dojo came up, and searching the site I found a photograph of you. A picture can often reveal things that hide in real life. You were wearing your body armour and holding your headset. As soon as I saw it, I felt sure that you were the Psycho Killer. But when I enlarged that photograph I knew you were.' His eyes fixed on mine. 'There was just something of the killer about you!' He took a long drag on his cigarette and drank some tea. 'I got my boss out of bed and told him I needed an armed unit. I mean, I'd seen what you'd done at Uncle Benni's. There was no way I was going to arrest you by myself.'

'And so you were a hero.'

'Are you kidding? I was reprimanded. I never even got credit for the arrest! Ah, to hell with them. I'm retiring in three days and I can't wait. Heading down to Okinawa. Bought a nice little place by the beach. And it's so quiet down there, you know. For close to forty years I've been a cop in Tokyo. All those people! I can't tell you how much I'm looking forward to the peace and quiet.' Then he shivered. 'Boy it's cold in here!' He got up and put on his overcoat. 'You should see them about some heat.'

'I'm OK.'

'Anyway, where were we up to?' He sat down, and opening the file he read from it. '"Yukio claims that he was standing up for the Buraku, because they are persecuted in Japan." Do you still stand by that?'

'No. But I do think they are persecuted.'

'They're not persecuted, Yukio. They are discriminated against. It's a different thing. But times are changing and things are getting better for them.'

'But if you found out that Hiroshi threw the brick then—'

'Then he would have been arrested. And he would have faced the same justice as a regular Japanese. Look, if there was anyone attacking the Buraku in the street I'd be the first to arrest them. But that's just not the case.' He went back to reading the file. 'It says here: "Yukio had a mental breakdown after the death of his friends and came to believe he was a samurai reborn. He also believes he was consumed by chi energy, which gave him the power to strike down his enemies."' He looked up at me. 'You still believe that?'

'No.'

He made a note in his notebook. 'Good, because that wasn't chi energy you were consumed by, Yukio, that was hatred. And I'll tell you something about hatred.' He took a long drag on his cigarette and thought about the best way to put it. 'When my wife was alive I loved her. It was absolute and final. But hatred has no end. It's an abyss as vast as the universe. And no matter how many people you killed you never would have filled it. You're lucky we caught you when we did. You went from being an avenging angel, to a vigilante, to a cold-blooded killer. What would you have done next, Yukio? Joined the Red Brigade? Released nerve gas on the Tokyo subway?'

'I'm no terrorist!'

'No? I'm sorry to tell you this, kid, but that's exactly what you are!'

I felt some of that old hatred boil up. 'I was trying to stand up for the people!'

'Tell it to the family of the cop you killed! Or that guy outside the Mitsubishi Building who you thought was the director. Or the guy you gunned down in the street because he got in your way! You can't go around killing people, Yukio. And I see from the file that your heroes are the samurai swordsmen Musashi and Bokuden. Don't you know that their way is over? And let me tell you something else, kid – if they were alive today, they'd be in here with you. They were a pair of psychopaths.'

'I'm not a psychopath.'

'You're not evil either. But you don't have to be evil to commit an evil act. Good people do it every day.'

'The yakuza do evil things!'

'I've never known a yakuza to kill a Buddhist nun.'

I felt bad about that and he knew it.

'Look, Yukio, if the yakuza weren't there we'd have foreign gangs selling drugs outside schools.'

'You sound like you agree with them.'

He sucked on his cigarette and thought about it. 'It might sound strange, coming from a cop, but I do. You see, in every society there's crime. We have one of the lowest crime rates in the world for two reasons: one is because we're brought up with Shinto morals that teach us to put the community before ourselves; the other is because the yakuza keep crime under control.'

'But they mix with politicians.'

'And by the same degree, politics merges with their world. They know that certain things will be tolerated. But if they step out of line we'll have them!'

We were quiet then. All you could hear was the wind howling.

Then he smiled a little. 'I'll bow down to you in one way, kid. It took real guts going into Uncle Benni's like that. And facing that Yama. I wouldn't have liked to have met him at a police convention, let alone a dark night!'

I tried not to feel it, but some of the old pride came back.

'I saw the aftermath. What a battle that must have been! The only one you didn't kill was Uncle Benni, and now he's dead.'

'Dead?'

'Gunned down outside an Italian restaurant, of all places. And you know who killed him, don't you? . . . Matsu! Revenge for her brothers Tomi and that other one whose name I can never remember. She must have been sitting in her padded cell planning it for months.'

'I didn't know she was out.'

'She's not only out, she's running things! For the first time ever the yakuza have a woman boss. They should never have given them the vote, if you ask me. But she has all of the Yamamotos behind her, and the rest of the clans are falling in line just to avoid an all-out war.' Then he looked happy. 'But I tell you, kid, that's a fine-looking woman. She's forty and she's still got it. I interviewed her once. She has the darkest eyes I've ever seen, darkest heart too. She's cutting heads off all over the place – you're lucky you're in here. But boy what a good-looking woman. I wouldn't be frightened of going down to Okinawa if she'd come with me.'

He looked sorry as soon as he said it. And then he looked a little sad.

'I don't know. I went down there last week. It's so quiet. I sat outside my small house and watched the sea. And all of a sudden I felt frightened. You hear about it all the time. Men who've worked all their lives, and within a few years of retirement they're dead. Funny, isn't it? I've dealt in death for twenty years as a homicide detective. And now I have to go down to Okinawa and wait for it to come for me.' He looked tired then and he stared down at the table.

'You might meet someone,' I said.

He looked up at me and tried to smile. 'Thanks, kid. But chance would be a fine thing . . . Anyway, I'll have to get going if I'm gonna catch that sleeper back to Tokyo.'

He drank the last of his tea and collected his things. 'Well, I probably won't see you again, Yukio, but I hope things turn out for you, despite what you've done. Who knows – they might let you out one day.' But then he cringed because he knew that they wouldn't.

'It's OK,' I said. 'I hope things work out for you in Okinawa.'

'I hope so too. Goodbye, Yukio.' He turned to leave but then he saw my photographs on the wall. He looked at the one that Yoshe took of me, Mikazuki and Grandmother, the night we went to dinner. 'Hey, whatever happened to your little friend? Tummy Trouble?'

I felt sad when he asked me that, I really did. But then all of a sudden I felt uplifted. 'She's safe and well,' I said.

He looked relieved. 'I'm glad.'

I bowed to him as he left and surprisingly he bowed back.

Then Lee came. 'You OK?'

'Sure.'

'We'll play backgammon later,' he said, and locking the door he walked back down the corridor.

I returned to the window and watched Detective Maki make his way through the main gate. I hope things do turn out for him. I really do. I watched the setting sun turn Mount Shokanbetsu a glowing orange colour. It was as nice a sunset as you'd ever see – 'Beautiful!' as the Lump would say. Sometimes I dream of her. I see her running through a field of flowers that seems to be floating in butterflies. She comes to the side of a hill where the twins and Natsuko are having a picnic, and kneeling down she starts to eat. It's such a beautiful dream and it's so nice to see them all happy. But I am never in the dream. And I don't think I ever will be. I've built up too much bad karma to be with them.

But they're all long gone now in that summertime of the dead, and I am left alive, if alive is what you can call it. Because I know I will never run in Yoyogi Park. Or see the cherry blossoms bloom in my beautiful Tokyo. Never again will I ride my bike through the bright lights of Shinjuku, or compete in a kendo competition. That life is over for me, and rightly so. I know I deserve to be in here. But when the sun sinks and the darkness comes I can't help but be filled with sorrow. Because I view the world now through steel bars, wire mesh and reinforced glass. As though life is something I look at rather than live.

Also by Gregory Hughes

UNHOOKING THE MOON

SUMMERTIME OF THE DEAD

Gregory Hughes was born in Liverpool, the eighth child in a family of nine. Expelled from school, he spent several years in a home for wayward boys. He has travelled extensively around Japan and has a deep interest in its history and culture. His first novel, *Unhooking the Moon,* won the Booktrust Teenage Prize in 2010 and was shortlisted for the Guardian Children's Fiction Prize and the Branford Boase Award.

First published in Great Britain in 2012 by Quercus

55 Baker Street
7th Floor, South Block
London W1U 8EW

A CIP catalogue reference for this book is available
from the British Library

ISBN 978 1 78087 552 1

1 3 5 7 9 10 8 6 4 2

Printed and bound in Great Britain by Clays Ltd, St Ives plc.

SUMMERTIME

GREGORY HUGHES

Quercus